Baby Alex

Excerpt from "Genesis" on page 7
Copyright © Geoffrey Hill

Some names and identifying details
have been changed to protect the
privacy of individuals.

Edited by Quentin Scobie

Cover and TBC logo by Alex

ISBN: 9798688782035

Diagram to navigate:

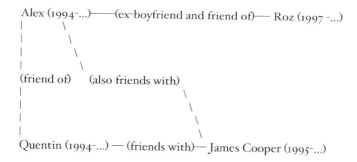

Alex (1994-...)————(ex-boyfriend and friend of)—— Roz (1997 -...)

(friend of)   (also friends with)

Quentin (1994-...) — (friends with)— James Cooper (1995-...)

Written by Roz Counelis and Quentin Scobie,
in a number of email exchanges, during the Corona Virus Pandemic.

(with additional text messages from James Cooper)

Q :: (♔/♚)
R :: (♕/♛)

§

WhatsApp message from Quentin to Baby Alex:

Going to tell you some stuff that might be a little difficult to hear, but don't worry, I'm not shagging your ex, nor do I have any desire to. When we stopped talking around April, me and Roz were writing a daily 1000 words to each other, back and forth, a kind of writing exercise for the quarantine to give us something to do. That writing back and forth ended up developing into a full-scale novel thing which you are mentioned in quite a bit, to such a large extent that you ended up being its central character. I understand if you want to kill me and completely remove me as a friend, but the book is too good and your role in it is too necessary for it all to fit together. You are like the ghost presence in our friendship triangle. I don't know why I'm messaging you this, I doubt we're going to get your blessing but we felt like we'd been big cunts and you needed to know. This wasn't planned, this wasn't a concerted effort to fuck with you, it was just you were such a large part of our shared experience and also it was fun to involve you in some of the autofiction bits. We like it so much that we've been editing it together and want to publish it. If you want to talk face to face I understand. it's difficult and I know that you probably just want to forget all about it, but we couldn't continue what we were doing without at least letting you know.

§

WhatsApp message from Baby Alex to Quentin:

I need a few days to think this over

The phoenix burns as cold as frost;
And, like a legendary ghost,
The phantom-bird goes wild and lost,
Upon a pointless ocean tossed.

BIRTH

§

The smartphone erupts. A woman fucked by three donkey-dicked dudes dressed as Jesus. One in the arse, one in the vag, one in the mouth; vomiting, free-bleeding, pissing and shitting; wearing a top hat with cyberpunk goggles attached, jump cables pinching each of her nipples. A boy in a blue onesie sits next to a car battery, turning the voltage on and off. A fat bald man with a micro-dick surveys the whole scene, smiling. Another woman runs at him, stilettos on, kicks him to the ground, and subjects his minuscule cock and balls to acute torture.

Homunculi (bred for this sort of thing) are injected via specially printed alien-egg-carrying dildos to her g-spot, which they micro-massage desperately before turning blue and dying of suffocation. Dalmatians arrive and hump, while two men with water pistols run around in a Puckish dance: spraying the orgy members intermittently with hydrochloric acid. In the centre, a drunk Rabbi tries to circumcise a baby, accidentally castrating him in the process. 15 Terabytes of leaked OnlyFans nudes are reformatted as Morse code and tattooed across the skin of an angelic 12-year-old boy in his initiation ceremony to become a man. A hosepipe BWC ejaculates blood onto his face, sending him into a deep trance. He foams at the mouth, night-clad acolytes murmuring their incantations and geometrically rearranging dead Tamagotchis around him. In the corner of the room a gang of migrants repeatedly rapes someone's grandma. Two spinning dildos attached to power-tools push through her tear ducts. Etc. Hermaphroditic other-kin play inside the carcass of a beached blue whale. They shove mushy maggot-infested meat inside their holes as Indian men with questionable English watch and comment on the whole scene via Omegle. Huge, rabid spermatozoids encircle the virginal female swimmers in a pool, attack them with such force they cut new orifices through their skin in a beeline for their tubes. Hellish screams of pleasure sound out over stereophonic feedback. Above all this on a hill, a Tibetan eunuch beats a gong, chanting something racist like "ching chong ching chong ching chong..." It hopefully gets worse. The moon turns red. Tulips, orchids, roses, daisies, chrysanthemums, foxgloves; all rise spontaneously from the ash-covered earth and launch their seed into the air. Celebratory ICBMs detonate in rondo. The ritual is complete. Winter has been defeated. The primordial whore is pregnant.

The baby plops out,

the party horns blow.

Death Metal.

♔

Baby Alex and I are stood in my attic, in front of my MacBook Pro and Adam AX5 studio monitors on New Year's Eve, 2019. The intro to a karaoke instrumental for Dancing in the Moonlight is playing. Around us, almost every wall is lined with bookshelves. We are holding each other, his arm around my shoulders, my arm around his waist, and swaying from side to side with the music, focussing our attention on the screen. You, Roz, are filming us on Baby Alex's iPhone. You are heard laughing. We have smoked one joint together and each snorted some old MDMA my sister has given me. Baby Alex is wearing a ten-gallon cowboy hat and has at one point in the evening applied red make-up to his cheeks, to give the impression of constant blushing. You are wearing thick librarian frames. The fourth friend invited over, Tom, has already gone to my sister's empty room to sleep.

———————

On the third of January 2020 I went to Tom's birthday party, where Tom, myself, and Tom's brother ate a meal at an Asian Fusion restaurant in Harrogate. After returning home that night from a laborious evening of stilted conversation, mainly due to the presence of his brother, I would never speak to Tom again.

———————

Alex and I sing the first verse, then I prematurely start to sing the chorus, Da-, before realising that there is another verse, so I stop singing and burst out laughing instead. My reason for choosing that song would be explained many months later: "A girl from my maths class, the one who sucked Cooper off, had once been delighted at the thought of Dancing in the Moonlight, saying 'it's such a New Year's Anthem!' so now I always associate Dancing in the Moonlight with New Year's Eve." We begin to sing the chorus, and I realise that the pitch is too high for me, so I drop an octave. I feel embarrassed, but it is the warm kind of embarrassment, the "doing something stupid with/for your friends" embarrassment. The song ends after many repetitions of the famous chorus and the funky organ-glockenspiel line that accompanies it. We move to a karaoke of My Way, and the overall ambience created by our singing changes completely, from a hilarity-enthused fuck-about to genuine attempts to show off the abilities of our singing voices. The warm kind of embarrassment shifts to something much uglier, a barely-disguised competition: the emission of mating calls, weapons, each with the veneer of being sung with soul, but being so obviously without it. This subtle difference is magnified by our stoned state; and we're locked-in, unable to do anything. Alex's voice goes from a strained tone that can hardly contain his laughter to the intonation he uses for the songs he puts on Spotify. I go from a pitch-imperfect football chant to my most orotund croon. Whatever Dancing in the Moonlight gave us has been ruined. You stop laughing, and you stop recording us on the iPhone. No one laughs for the length of My Way.

I sit on the attic sofa and start to look through my phone, unlocking the screen by connecting a set of nodes with these chewing-gum-type girders according to my pre-established pattern. I look across at the both of you, "Should we ring Cooper?"
"He's not coming dude." says Alex, immediately made uneasy by my suggestion, but still smiling.

"No, I'm not going to invite him, c'mon I'm not stupid. Besides, he probably can't even get out." I go through my contacts and click on the name "Paul". The screen shifts to Outgoing Call, black with the anonymous silhouette of a person in a circle at the top, and a large red button with a skeuomorphic telephone-on-receiver icon at the bottom.

"Put it on speaker..." Alex says, stifling a nervous laugh. You look back and forth between myself and Alex, sensing the thick anticipation in the room, doing a comedic half-smile.

"Hey buddy..." James' familiar voice, all mid-tone and a little distorted at the edges, sarky and unstable.

"Hey man."

"So, what's going on?" He speaks in a manner redolent of a super-villain imprisoned in an ultra-high-security Tartarus. We are now in the sequel, and the main protagonist reluctantly visits said dungeon in order to negotiate something, probably the salvation of mankind.

"Just calling you up to wish you a Happy New Year... pal."

He's not in a good mood and I'm looking at the two of you with thin lips and raised eyebrows.

Cooper starts laughing, both maniacally and in a very forced way. My expression changes to oh fuck here we go. He calms down, I say nothing: silence.

"Alex is here by the way..."

"Ooooh Hi Alex!" He uses his moronic small-talk voice, like a middle-aged mother speaking to her daughter's best friend.

"Hey James," says Alex, "how's it going?"

"It's shit." Cooper responds.

"Alex's girlfriend is here as well..." I add.

"Great... well, this is boring so..."

He hangs up, the beep resounds outward, bringing me back into the closeness of the attic room with an unexpected immediacy. I blink my eyes a number of times, slightly frazzled by the sequence of events, then look at you and Alex, shaking my head and smiling. Everyone laughs, and Alex says: "That's rough stuff."

We smoke another joint, and at around one in the morning I am deep in exposition vis a vis my ideas concerning the number line.

"Don't you think it's weird though? That there is this... abstract notion of quantity, that seems inhuman and therefore pure, and yet, the numbers that we deal with, that affect us most in life, are all around the very bottom, you know. There's this odd weight to the whole thing... seven days in the week, ten fingers, two feet — when by the logic of pure quantity, the number two should have no more significance than the number seven million eight thousand and forty-three point nine."

"Wait so... what?" Alex is rubbing his eyes and looking at me like he can barely fathom what I'm saying. The puzzled expression on his face seems partly affected.

"So that's why I'm like, oh, really quantity has to be considered from an anthropocentric... erm.. thing. Perspective. So, it's like, the real world understanding of numbers is more an aggregate of these simple small digits than it is an actual set of higher or infinite numbers. The weight of simplicity... simplicity has this strange weight to it. I guess."

"So... One is the largest number!" Alex says, reiterating something I had written and sent him, which he has just understood.

"Exactly. That's what I was talking about. The experience of one is the kind of... biggest thing. But then we end up having to ask what..."

My mum comes up the spiral staircase. "Goodnight everyone! Happy New Year!"

"Goodnight Veronique! Happy New Year!" the two of you respond.

"G'night Mum."

"I can't believe Tom already went to bed! I love the way

your friends just... do what they want."
"Yep. G'night Mum. Happy New Year."

♔

The walls of the attic are wooden panels, the grain of the wood above the desk where the laptop sits forms an animated face dissected into individual frames, almost the face of a wild boar. We have been listening to Japanese Ambient for more than the majority of the night while talking, letting the YouTube algorithm take us through such artists as Tetsu Inoue, Hiroshi Yoshimura, and Susumu Yokota. I hit your Juul. The fragile and understated sonics interlock perfectly with the colours of the room, which is itself coloured by that specific neurochemical cocktail swishing inside my skull. There is the sense of deep inscription, a profoundly strong memory forming in time, altering future and past simultaneously, coordinating a clear exit from what was towards an equally clear destiny of what is to be. I see myself, and you, coil together in that moment with all the qualities surrounding us, and crystallise. An indigo-blue light glows beneath it all, that cannot be ascribed to any particular object. A wavelength, somewhere between four hundred and twenty-five and four hundred and forty-five nanometres.

Baby Alex has gone to sleep in the little alcove adjoining the main attic room, you and I are sat on sofa and chair respectively, very stoned and a little tipsy, not saying much, listening to the music. I receive a text from a girl I thought had blocked me, Jennifer, whose contact name on my phone is a dog emoji.

"Happy New Year you sociopath."

I wish her a Happy New Year. She sends back a garbled message about how "of course" her and her new boyfriend are not living together, clearly drunk. I don't understand how this information is relevant. (The next day I would send her a message asking if she could return the books she had borrowed from me, only to discover that I was once again blocked.)

I mention that I'm going to sleep, you get up and mumble something as though returning from a series of profound thoughts. We both get up from our seats and hug, the hug lasting longer than usual, maybe twenty seconds, with a distinct warmth, an unspoken signal. I notice how much thinner you are.

♛

My dress was black. Gabrielle said it was MDMA but it felt more like speed. You went first, of course. It was only about 9pm when we started. I snorted a line: desperate for excitement after a stretch of taut and anxious days with Alex's parents, and when it was his turn he was very hesitant, face scrunched up under the bright light of our peer pressure. It felt a little like that day we met. He winced, bit at his fingers, paced around a while, looked out of the window, back to us and then to the dash of white laid out for him on one of your books. I think it was Being and Time. He finally caved, and in my memory I see us whooping and cheering as he snorted it down, but we could just have been watching him silently. As his head lifted back up, he frowned and rubbed his face like a child would after tasting a lemon. The four of us stood around for a while, talked some more, and then the jitteriness kicked in. I was rambling, smacking my gum around loudly. The conversation degraded into nothing but sounds: ambivalent hints expressed very enthusiastically.

We were admiring the treasure trove that was the attic, Book Club HQ, Q-HQ, and I could tell he was feeling a little nervous, looking for something structured we could do in the stretch of hours that preceded midnight. He found a Monopoly set, joked that we should play a game, and then it felt like a jump-cut to us all sitting on the floor around the board: arguing, pointing fingers, laughing hysterically, chewing more gum, googling things. The game was abandoned as quickly as it had begun, with everyone silently getting up and leaving the money on the floor to instead just listen to music.

It was around this point that Tom, a man of very few words, announced that he was going to bed. We all made fun of him, even me, who had only just met him a few hours prior.
"Dude, it's New Year's Eve, and you're going to bed at 10:30?"
"I'm tired man."

We laughed and watched him descend the iron spiral down to the middle floor, into Gabrielle's empty room, hearing the door close. That was the last we saw of him that decade.

And then there were three. We sat in a circle and smoked a joint I had brought with me, in comfortable quiet, smiling at each other.
You got up and went to your desk, steering the ship that was the remainder of the evening, looking for more music. Alex suggested something festive, appropriately corny for the evening.
"I mean, it's still kind of early," you said, "we don't need to break out the Dancing in the Moonlight karaoke just yet."

Again, just like with the Monopoly, something was a joke, I blinked, and then it was actually happening. Backing track with lyrics pulled up on YouTube, the two of you with arms around each other, laughing, singing, dancing, staggering from side to side. You tried to harmonise but it didn't really work, you were too high, he was too low, but we were all loving it. I can't sing at all, so I filmed it. You got much too excited about getting to the chorus, and kept coming in too early.

"No! Not yet!", I yelled through my manic tears, immortalised in the video.

"Alright, alright, I'm sorry. I fucked up!" you responded, grinning.

You sang the whole song with remarkable authenticity, true corny affection, giving it your all at the choruses. When it came to the fadeout at the end, and the chorus repeats and repeats, we were so high that it felt like it went on for at least 10 minutes, and every time those same lyrics reappeared on the screen it got funnier and funnier. Occasionally I would remember that while we were doing this, Tom was asleep downstairs, which would only make me laugh more.

We stood at the window by your desk, the apex of the house, looking over Leeds at midnight, as the fireworks came. Gold. White. Green. Purple. We held each other. At one point I stepped back to observe the silhouettes of your torsos cutting holes in the colour. I remember thinking that whatever would end up happening, this moment was irreversible, unforgettable, not for its occurrences, but because of its important place on a much larger timeline, one that barely concerned us at all. I was going to say something, I wasn't sure what, but then your mother came in and hugged you, and the moment passed.

♕

I had the phone call just now: It's not you it's me. The world is different. It hasn't felt right for a long time. We'll still be friends. etc; the whole thing barely lasting 20 minutes. We'd been undead for months, global bat flu just the final straw. He had wanted kids with me. I was stood by the tennis courts at the time, looking over the rows of houses with pastel-coloured roofs. I walked back, put a can of tonic in the freezer, ran two laps of the rugby pitch, got back in the house, then started drinking.

I'm too close to it happening, a louse on a child's head. There is no child, just a soft surface, and the smell of milk. He's a good person, but I know you know that.

♚

The information was paranoid, self-assembling, forming pieces in an impossible puzzle, a briefcase full of green monopoly money, instructions on what to say precisely to the airline staff, where I would arrive, then walking with this particular saved game I felt a pressure I couldn't undo, I stood by some building and sought to stabilise my understanding, coordinate, find my bearings, but it was of no use, the hairline was atrocious and dead skin was coming off, I was swaddled in fur, black sunglasses and black clothes, the swanky hotel room, just everything in panic mode, the film audience in a Tron seating arrangement accelerating at the screen, I couldn't see and I screamed, carpet descending my throat.

Press Δ to continue. Bishop to B7. Knight takes pawn. Check. One billion two hundred and ninety-four point eight six million and three. I look up from the board. You are wearing an all-black leather fetish get-up with black goggles.

"Well look what the cat dragged in..." I say: taking a slow inhalation from the cigarette situated in my long black cigarette-holder while stroking my elegant pencil moustache with a certain pained facial expression morphing seamlessly into a smug... smuggedy... smug-smug.

"I thought you would have already left for Paris," you say, starting to walk about the room, your hard stilettos clacking on the varnished wooden floor, applying some more lipstick while pouting at a mirror above the cream Louis Quatorze dresser. Triangles disassemble in a window across the street.

"New plan..." I say, fingering the queen.

"Headquarters aren't going to be happy," you interject, removing a black silk handkerchief luxuriantly from a drawer — its ravishing darkness drinking in the soft light of the room.

"Oh... bollocks to headquarters," I reply, finally tipping the queen a little too far. I watch her roll around the board, the slut.

"Is that so? Q ..." you sigh, "why do you always have to play the... agent provocateur?" — incorrectly using that term in a perfectly pronounced French, and laying the black handkerchief over my scalp to polish it.

I squint at the pieces and take another velvety puff. *Velveteen?*

"It's something to do with my mother abandoning me as a child," I say.

"You weren't abandoned as a child."

"Maybe not as a child... but definitely as an adult."

"Q..."

I lean back morosely while the head polishing continues, "Mmm, Pussycat... do you ever get tired of polishing my head?"

"No."

"Wonderful."

My languid expression holds and I start to analyse the mosaic patterns on the ceiling, visibly distraught at their monotony.

A monkey wearing the hotel worker uniform and a red fez ambles into the room, holding a small card that it places on the table.

"Thank you Jaco," I say, handing it 1000 yen.

The monkey turns and leaves, I pick up the card.

"Oh, *bâtards*..."

"What is it?"

"Committee. They've made an executive decision that I'm sent to Seoul immediately. Plane leaves tonight."

"I thought they were sending you to Paris."

I look up at you and let out a brief sigh. "Pussycat..." I tap the card twice with my index.

"Well what was all this stuff about Paris?"

The monkey walks back in the room. Another card, this time it's rose-pink tinted. You pick it up.

"It says... 'bring the broad.'"

"I guess that means you."

"They really are taking the piss."

Very loud thrash metal starts playing. Montage of airports, Seoul cityscape, taxi services, both of us wearing shades and empty expressions. Fade to purple-green strobe.

♔

Alex yesterday messaged me just before I was about to sleep. He said you were thinking of breaking up with him. I told him to chill, and he said he was chill.

§

The people of Sweden enjoy Elsbeth's nose. The people of Nigeria and Uzbekistan respond positively to Emily's eyes. Joanna has a nose resembling Elsbeth's, and eyes resembling Emily's. Joanna moves three spaces, smiling faintly on the beach, usurping linear chronology. The people of Mexico react negatively to Trina's new weave. Recommend Trina online counselling and Japanese snack box delivery services. Adut posts a picture of her mother, the people of France react in an unknown way. Recommend Adut Prada perfume and chocolates. Rose's lips, the talk of Japan, move two spaces, pouting over a Portuguese nata tart, meeting flush with Joanna. The information on Joanna and Rose finds a common denominator in Mia, the youngest daughter of an oil baron and a supermodel. Her face: caramelised, racially ambiguous, and highly symmetrical. She moves nine spaces, one space for every two years since her birth in Sarajevo. Give her 90% of everything, if only for 15 days.

A moving gif of the honeypot emoji, pixels stirring sickly dripping pixels. The global population as slime mould, looking for sugar, attached by strands.

Raining blood.

♔

James Cooper, AWOL from the psych-ward, appears in my garden. I am terrified for a split second; then frown, sigh, laugh, and finally shake my head. I tell him to accompany me to Tesco's.

He's in a good mood. As we walk I paint our exploits, waving my hand in the air while he smiles. Cooper, listen: Ermine fur. Malibu beach. Honeys in red bikinis. Bugattis. Ferraris. Pink sunsets, snow-white sand. The sound of the waves. Siberia. We're Russian Mafia. Yakuza. We're Benghazi's boys. We're Democratic Republic of Congo. He's loving it. You paint these glorious stories of delusion, and it's like we're there, we've done it. He loves it so much, he's the Norwegian Princess, gang-banged by the world. He puts his arm around my shoulders, all 6'4" of him pressing down, his blond buzzcut, sunburnt head, his oversized chapped lips, inches from my ear, whispering to me in a bad South African accent. He tries to kiss me. I swerve.

"Man, it's awful in the hospital bro, just awful."
"Yeah I suppose it would be."
"They're all crazy in there. Crazy people..."

We stand in the queue for the supermarket, spread out across the pavement. He stares at me intently.

"What are you looking at Coops?"
"Just looking at how ugly you are."
"Oh, is that so..."

I buy three big bottles of Staropramen for a fiver, and sit in the garden to drink them. He starts to roll a joint. I watch him for a second, his fumbling unnerves me, so I offer to roll it for him.

"It's Thai weed bro, it's good for you," he says, putting shitty-looking buds on my lap.
"Oh, Thai? Well then I suppose I should partake."

I lie on the bed, a little stoned, skimming over Heidegger. Cooper lies supine, also on the bed. He looks at me with half-opened red eyes, his face slack in an expression of deep peace, stupefaction and awe. The moment is graceful, and in my mind's eye we make love, neon-purple rococo, scintillating embraces. It feels appropriate. Slowly unsettled by the intensity of the moment, I make a weird face at him, then get up to change the music.

§

Baby Alex, very stoned, dropping a bagel on the carpet.
Baby Alex, very stoned, showing people his balls.
Baby Alex, very stoned, hanging upside down on an inversion table.
Baby Alex, very stoned, running away from my dog.

♛

He called again. He was expressionless and curt. It is now definitely, completely, over: no still being friends. My comforting future-memories of the three of us going on holiday to Bruges are now rendered not only stupid, but highly improbable.

A flash of misery, wept in memoriam for the past four years of my life while the cat stood on and around me.

I got up and ran. I can now say whatever the fuck I feel like.

§

Message from James Cooper:

I bet if you weren't three feet tall you'd like lana del ray
Gosh Quentin why do you want to destroy me
was it like hey look at me I'm Quentin
Brainwashed by your douchebag parents
Some not particularly impressive quest ruined by its motive
Some turbulent asshole who couldn't see the nature of his philosophy (my madness) because he was a turbulent asshole

§

WhatsApp Conversation between Baby Alex and Q̣:

a: [sends screenshot of a tweet from "Roz eats", a private food twitter that Roz uses, the tweet reads: Broke it off with my bf last night, got drunk, spent 3 hours in the bath + now I have bruises on my tailbone. Breakfast? You guessed it, Nutella banana porridge (10 likes) (one reply: someone sending heart emojis)]

a: sorry if you feel like a go between
a: I didn't realise she was messaging you
a: I asked her if she had messaged anyone about it and she said no

q: [expressionless emoji]
q: well she messaged me about it this morning
q: dunno if you want to ruminate over it

a: ok that's chill
a: yeh
a: keeping the vibes up high
a: thanks man

q: safe safe
q: i love you bro
q: i want you flutter like butterfly

a: you too

q: watch kung fu panda

♛

The walls are my skin. I have breathed forth this whole house, and it retains its shape only by use of my thought. My body is also a mental tension, a thought without which my bones would melt. I am staring at my bedpost, thinking of impaling you on my bedpost. A ginormous buttplug, I am impaling you and you are squidging down onto it, becoming this weird worm, only the size of a dog now, you have no arms, no legs, and I'm impaling you on my bedpost.

Ooo my back... I'm Alex now... Ooo my back...

Baby Alex on the floor, writhing his spine over the carpet, searching for an end to his pain. Someone walk on the poor boy! He's dying. Impaling you on Alex, an inside-out human centipede, then I open my jaw, I unhinge it and swallow you both up, licking your private parts lasciviously, tacitly, sensitively, sub the rosa of my maw. I staple four versions of myself together to become three dimensional, like a third of a calendar. You come up from the basement with Alex's head, worms writhing in it and through it and turning it to a sponge. You have white snakes beneath your skin, but those are sacred snakes. You turn into a hydrogen atom and I breathe you in. I must be a million by this point.

I am in the garden, pruned, naked, genitals and muscles deflated. You ask me: "How is Peter?" I look at my parrot, who is now a wingless dinosaur, almost stone, an ornament, and croak some gibberish at him. He croaks gibberish back. Alex's head, though decomposing, is actually not his head. He is actually a tree now. He is a huge Yew tree at the bottom of the garden, his bark twisty and grey. I walk up to him and pat him on the bark. You are heavily with-child, you give birth at random as you walk about the garden watering things. One child, two child, three child. My eyeballs fall out and I'm grinning mischievously. You come up behind me and bugger me with the watering can, I fall over. You climb into me through my arsehole. I finally die, in peace, squirting my essences far and wide; I am become virgin, a translucent sheet of moisture. Alex's branches stretch low, impale you through the balloon-knot, and he lifts you up, higher and higher through the sky, flinging you into space. You shoot through the stratosphere, then burn up into dust.

The ominous sound of scrolling takes over. Oh! It's me again, scurrying around like a jelly-baby, bouncing and squatting and grinning. The scrolling sound is immensely loud. A black machine in a factory, with thick-tar-dripping cogs: I'm humping it. You turn up and it's a little like Timesplitters 2, you have a cartoonish bazooka and blow me to smithereens. Shock and awe, in the audience. They shatter and rearrange themselves in splintered half-space. KABOOM. I respawn, start humping for the third time. Non-Euclidean topiary renders slowly in the background. A white hart stands in the centre of the clearing. I remove my face by pulling on one nostril until the whole thing slips off. A jewharp can be heard boinging from another room.

Now it's rape time, the fire alarms won't stop. Water is cascading from somewhere and filling everything. A tsunami, the whole mansion is flooding. We're with all these famous figures, kind of half swimming, as the water rises. Cocks the length of vines slither through the water, enmesh and form nets that drag people under. Someone is cutting and tapping at their arm as though they were preparing lines of cocaine, except instead of cocaine it's the bloody pulp that was their arm. I scream out to you "The

Snuggly and warm now, staring at the tilde on my keyboard. Ok you win, I lose, happy? Ok now I win, you lose. Happy now? I always enjoyed looking through the PC games at PC World and checking the minimum requirements on the back of the box. I'm so snuggly and warm. I've prepared hot cacao and I have fluffy pink slippers on, plus a pack of cigs, and a bifta, and I'm beckoning to you, please, please sit beside me, we have had a tremendously long journey, let us now sit by this fire in our n-dimensional library, let us smoke this joint, and let us watch the flames and remember all the things we were and are to be. You sit and I pass you the j and the lighter. You put the joint in your mouth, thinking "I deserve this", and "the high will be beneficial and illuminating", and "my subconscious is ready". This is a save point in life. You light it and take the first drag, the smoke getting caught in your saliva and your taste buds.

Everything is silent apart from the sound of the fire, the warm crackling. You look to me, and I smile and nod my head. We have made it this far.

♕

I have to send a package today containing: a Nintendo Switch, a Bluetooth mechanical keyboard, two gift-shop graphic tees, and a pot of hair gel.

In two weeks I'll be 23. I have one tiny nug sitting in a Gudetama Ziplock bag in my room, waiting for me to light it up and feel the boundaries of time fuzz and dissipate, to eat a chocolate bar and feel bad about it. The prime of my life, alone in government-mandated quarantine, soon to be funnelled into government-mandated unemployment. I feel ok. I remember being 10, looking in the mirror, thinking "I wonder what it'll be like".

Fistfights in supermarkets, rats colonising abandoned cafés, old men wearing New Balances and face masks. Mountain lions returning to the city. Dolphins cackling in clear Venetian water. The cat is already asleep. The cat is on the keyboard now. sdiufhwejbdivkwd. A tweet from one of the New York macro-counting girls I follow: ":-) vanilla Juul pods".

I've thought a lot about what you said when we were

staring at each other in Alex's room. What you see in front of you and what your senses perceive at any given moment is the shape your mind takes. What you see is you. You are that thing being seen. Everything is the mirror. Right now, I am my bedroom, filled with light from candles burning, trees outside, swatches of pale blues and greens in a mostly white box. Front and centre: a rectangular lit-up wormhole in which an impossibly large number of things can be accessed and altered. Tiny big thing. I am falling down it. I tap on its surface like I'm cracking a safe. Swirling bokeh, disassembling triangles. I am trying to reach through and find you: a plate of eggs on a table, or a cage with a parrot inside.

§

Message from James Cooper:

tbh mate i think you're a scummy narcissistic pos sorry for hurting your feelings
we're still friends but honestly feel that being a bit of an arsehole to you makes me a better person
you lied about pussying out with women
you've never been bold nor will you have the opportunity
you don't understand what affection is
you think you're emotionally intelligent but you have no idea how you make people feel
no one gives a shit about you i think that's why you have so many problems

§

An organism dedicates resource to a mating call. The mating call demonstrates something else: its immune system, and its general ability to stave off death, is so powerful, so efficient, that it can afford to waste energy on the call. The call is the excess. It's a question of resource, dozens upon dozens of raw eggs, and it's a question of metabolism, of logistics, shipping containers, port contingencies, efficiency. Then it's a question of viruses, barbarians, nomads: stressors in the environment, enemies at the gates.

♛

Lots of "playing house". I wanted to be a pregnant mother. Doll stuffed up my dress, legs spread, a soap-opera impression of labour. My vice-grip on the hand of an unsuspecting kid from the after-school club who just wanted to bake cookies. To see someone pee themselves from desperation. To squeeze something until it bursts.

♛

My first orgasm was at a sleepover with two of my cousins. Laura and I would have been about eight, Emma ten. They were always very rough and precocious. They told me what sex was and what Father Christmas wasn't in the same afternoon. We were at my apartment. My mother had gone to bed. We were listening to hip-hop on MTV and Emma suggested dry-humping "like in the videos". When you're 8 this seems normal. I remember going red in the face and thinking I was going to pass out, then wanting to do it again.

This became a common occurrence for the three of us, always with music on and under covers. Emma once insisted we did it when we were left alone at our grandparents' house, but we couldn't work the TV, so we just played the ringtones from Laura's Motorola on a loop, grinding away under a sheet at 3:30pm. At another sleepover maybe 6 months later, Emma showed us Omegle, which was my first ever sight of a penis. Then, a video she found on eFukt: a woman sucking off a horse. I felt traumatised, but I couldn't look away.

In the following years I would get into big trouble for going on chatrooms to watch Indian men jerk off. I would sometimes take my shirt off for them without needing to be asked. I then tried to introduce this, and the dry-humping, to a handful of friends from school. It did not go well. Those morbid habits continued until the time I met my first boyfriend at 15. Long-distance, it consisted of a lot of FaceTiming, honing how to say and respond to raunchy things. Very porny and insincere, "oh you like that you little bitch?".

That porn-addicted boy ended up taking my virginity after he had saved up enough pocket money for a train from Derbyshire. He nearly cried trying to figure out how to unclasp my bra. He was calling himself daddy before he had taken off a girl's clothes.

Emma and Laura now both seem vaguely mentally ill. Emma is a single mother of two. Laura works at Greggs and is covered in tattoos. I barely see them anymore. They are both avid posters. Emma is schizophrenically fighting with no one in particular on Facebook: "If anyone has any shit to say about my kids I will let them fucking HAVE IT!!!!!! YOU WON'T KNOW WHAT'S COMING BABES!!!!" (two likes). Laura has a Twitter she uses like a diary. Her handle is her full name. I don't know if she thinks her family can't see it, but they can. My grandparents are concerned. She is stuck as an emo teenager, tweeting stuff like: "ffs every1 leaves... pure hate it... they say they give a fuck but they dont tbh......" (zero likes).

§

A sea, a primeval soup. I guess it's something to do with temperature, the overall energy present: I don't really know. Negligible viscosity, the significance of water, a fluency of speed. Lots of different molecules, created from building blocks, affordances beneath molecules haphazardly falling into place. Hues shaking hands, awesome. Then some new molecule appears, now freakishly able to copy itself: a sort of input-output system that can use those affinities already present, creating this nonlinear moment, a runaway process. It seems both completely impossible and retrospectively obvious that such a thing would occur. It was an accident waiting to happen.

♔

Clear liquid rose out of my urethra, pooled on the tip of my penis and foreskin, aged twelve. I was surrounded by three other boys, all jacking off as well, encouraged by them despite never having had the desire to: watching an illegally downloaded video of two "lesbians" on some well-lit tacky sofa in an LA mansion. They were jamming brightly-coloured pieces of plastic inside each other and saying "you like that you little bitch don't you..." while squirting jets at the furniture. The little two finger wank that boys start by doing: just squeezing the tip of the penis again and again between the index and thumb. When I started to feel it change, the intensity of the horniness alter its shape and become a roar of pleasure, I shouted out to the other boys on the sofa: "What the fuck? Woah, what the fuck? What the fuck is happening?"

I tried masturbating after that first time, without porn, in my own bathroom. The only way I could bring myself to enough arousal was by repeating the same mantra the lesbians had repeated: "you like that you fucking bitch... you fucking bitch... you fucking bitch..." Each Friday I would go back to my friend's house and we would lie on the sofa with a blanket over our dicks and cum over and over while watching mainly lesbian porn.

One odd day in the summer half a year later: he had bought a sex doll and a large amount of lube, and we had taken turns fucking the doll in his spacious and well-designed bathroom. After each fucking it three times, we cleaned it out in the bath, the shower-head set to turbo.

§

Baby Alex, very stoned, showing me pictures of his ex's wedding.
Baby Alex, very stoned, playing me his music.
Baby Alex, very stoned, telling me to stop looking at my phone.
Baby Alex, very stoned, talking about you.

§

Message from James Cooper:

Fuck you!Fuck you!Fuck you!Fuck you!Fuck you! Oh i get it you've got some kind of foreknowledge.
Like a fork if you program it correctly
super hyper ai super fork
Phyjorkusmexiiimusdissilius the phurrrd
Gosh darling I've become so morbid do you think you could help me out?

§

Bored girl on the couch in her pyjamas, watching Louis Theroux with the sound off, eating Drumsticks Squashies, on the phone to a guy she's been seeing. He asks her what she's wearing, she says nothing. He visualises her wearing nothing.

♛

My blacked-out eyes scan the dark lobby of the Lotte Seoul, reminding myself of all potential exits. A brief jet-lagged meditation session in the luxury suite. Something meshes very deliberately at the edge. The job was a blur, as it always is, the second nature kicks in and it plays out like a cutscene.

Lotte Seoul. Ugh, civilian hotels, now they are really taking the piss.

"So quiet, so sad. My heart bleeds..." I say melodramatically to no one in particular.

My heels do their water-torture routine over the marble, passing upright bellboys and a high-class call-girl in furs talking huskily on a BlackBerry. I clack clack clack over to the bar. There you are: alone and slumped over on the counter, surrounded by an amphitheatrical semi-circle of empty green-glass soju bottles, mournfully slurring a little ditty from your home country. Your black greatcoat is draped over your shoulders like a cape, a white ghostly line encircles your barstool.

"Drinking with your back turned. Your head is looking especially dull tonight." I remark from behind you.

"Why do they do it to us, pussycat?" you groan without turning around. "And why do we do it, all of this, all of this... pssshhhhh..."

You knock the bottles over from one end like dominoes, an unseen voice from behind the bar shouts something indistinct in Korean. "Joesong haeyo" you mumble back. Ambient sounds of rain.

"They do it because they're bastards, Q. They're little shits and they know it. But they're important, they know that too. And we do it because it's what we do. It's our job, plain and simple."

You swing 180° on your barstool. Your moustache looks lopsided. "I just loathe all this waiting around, taking orders. It's not my style. I thought we'd be in and out, Pussycat. And now another night in this shithole? I miss my parlour, I miss my komodo dragon.."

"You're getting all verklempt again. It's the booze. You're not good with booze, it makes you verklempt."

"I didn't like your conduct with the executive. You were much too... unhostile."

"You don't bring the broad for her to be hostile. It's just my job, Q, plain and simple. Don't tell me how to do my job."

A pause. Your expression slackens from a pout into a small smile, twinkly-eyed and smug as always, and you gesture to your current bottle of sweet-potato-wine. You beckon me again. "Come, come, have a nip, take it off me for Christ's sake."

I clack clack clack over to the stool next to you and sit

down, my leather pants creaking. I take a swig. "Like a cool, sweet knife," I gasp.

❦

When a civilisation builds a very large building, the tallest in the world for its time, it inevitably sets in motion a thousand-year ascent and a thousand-year decline. Do you remember when we were on lockdown in that skyrise? The resources were lasting. The air was unpolluted. Part of some termite council. Secret packages sent through the vents. I murdered the family who lived at the penthouse, the bathroom was a mess of their black guts. I made rude intrusions through their cell walls. They were a family of bacteria. They were only bacteria, see. That's how we thought of them. And now they were a mess to clean up. I knew that the safe in the master bedroom had what we were looking for, and I was right, cracking the code by some gematria and astrological genius, I found our little save point and saved the day. We were back in the library, meeting the Old Fifty-Feet-Tall versions of ourselves, exchanging cutting remarks using personal information only we could know. The mission. Weapons. Cars. Helicopters. Gadgets. Cigarettes, the black vanilla-perfumed kind. Assorted drugs. String Quartets from the future, on vinyl. Cool catchphrases and those circular shades. A giant marble sculpture of Alex in vitro. Leather.

♛

A girl I was friends with at boarding school keeps messaging me saccharine garbage.

I know the quar is a hard situ but look after yourself sweetie!

I suddenly feel the most unjustified loathing of her, primal rage. I want to find her and drag her by the hair.

Yeah you too :-)

♛

Baby Alex is sat on the couch in the attic on New Years' Eve, staring at you while you talk about time going backwards. Did you hear about that new molecule NASA discovered? Either way he stares at you and waits until you stop talking. Then he says "dude... imagine if we were twice as high as we are now. We could get even more fucked up."

♛

That last week at work before Christmas break. We argued a lot.

I would be at the boarding house all day, hauling luggage, cleaning rooms, breaking up fights and heavy petting sessions, to come home and find him in his pyjamas on the couch, where he had been all day. Doing something on his laptop. Sink loaded with dishes, coated in congealed mayonnaise. Back hurting. He wouldn't even say hi. I would come through the door and he would look at me like he didn't know who I was. It may have been inflated by my own stress, but it would piss me off in a way I couldn't disguise. I wanted him to make an effort, in any form, just something resembling effort or awareness: tidy up, or make me some tea, or pick out some interminable foreign film. But he rarely would, and he made me feel like I was nagging him when I mentioned this, which I fucking hate, I never want to nag anyone. So, I would say something passive-aggressive instead of just asking him to do his dishes, and then we would argue.

One day Matthew couldn't come over to walk the dog, so I quickly sneaked home from work to ask him if he could do it. He knew where the park was, all he had to do was walk her there, let her off the leash, let her run around for a while, and bring her back. It would take maybe 40 minutes. He said sure, I kissed him and said thank you, put the dog's collar and leash on her, and went back to the house. I came back for my break maybe two hours later and found the dog sitting on the couch with the leash still attached to her, and Alex asleep upstairs. His back flared up. I got pissed off, and we argued again.

I never knew what to say about his back. I wanted to be sympathetic. I saw him in pain. But the pain always seemed to appear and disappear at extremely convenient times, an evergreen excuse. I couldn't say that to him, even if it seemed very obvious. It would have been needlessly cruel, and it was Christmas. So I walked the dog alone in the dark.

§

Note from Q:

(There is something life-affirming about women, but I can't quite figure out what it could be: possibly the lack of synaptic material, the smaller cranial capacity, the lofi beat to study/relax to. That said, they really do suck at writing. There just isn't the sheer cognitive power needed to construct anything decent. It's all blobby; nuance, feeling: broads in hot baths surrounded by rose petals, weighed down by cellulite.)

§

Working class suburban 12-year-old British girls playing Grand Theft Auto for PlayStation 2 at one of their houses after school. They are learning to comprehend and mimic ebonics despite having never interacted with an African American face to face. They are osmosing information about sex, cars, and guns while situated in a bedroom painted pale pink with music note decals on the walls. Two of them are eating cereal bars and drinking apple juice while the third, whose turn it is with the controller, murders a prostitute and sets her on fire.

§

All this plethora, all this squeezing through to the next moment; a mega-mind babby crowning, ripping apart the sweet puss of youth; nervously foraging berries, pasta, toilet paper; then sucking in cheeks and ruffling hair in the mirror, an absolute fucking clown that laughs at himself and only himself.

Female pandas will reabsorb the foetus if they don't dig the vibe. I'm not sure if I can trust this reality with my young. Perhaps that is the major issue with contraceptives: if given the choice, no one would age or have kids, everyone would just remain in fuckworld and never die. Perhaps we are respawning, flooding in from the save points on the rim and exploding in the centre. That would explain nothing but ok.

The great light summons the dark: as it rises, as it flexes its hope, vaster despairs come forth to test it. This I intuited when I was doing the washing up. Sharing a fibre on the dark plum of the world. The sentences must do press-ups. The sentences will become lean. An emergent complexity, like this prose seen from the light of those initial organisms beginning to sense — I get a jamais vu, as though there is a missing piece to the puzzle of complexity itself, the gravy-obscured vantage point, a human in time circa 2020 AD... Something too straightforward about that idea, abc, 123.

Will we begin again, as alien corkscrews, only to boomerang back to a centre? One half goes this way, the other goes that way, recoiling, recoiling. Somewhere on the edge, a new virus is born.

§

Michael Brecker's Song for my Father. The 8 Times Michael Brecker Went Beast Mode. Michael Brecker 1996 Interview - Practicing Transcript: "I do things in different inversions, in every different key, I try and get all of the horn... I have books and books of exercises I've written out. I'm always working on new ideas, takes me a long time, I'm very slow. Sometimes it takes learning something real well then just forgetting about it, it eventually comes out. I sometimes just play. But the practicing part of things is very important for me, I have to practice otherwise I feel like I've shirked by responsibility. Sometimes it's just maintenance practice, where I'm just, you know, doing the least I have to do to keep everything well oiled. Then there are periods of true growth."

♕

I materialise in the basement of my own head, returning to that hideous dream I have: Alex is a giant baby, in a cot, screaming out his lungs; his mother is in the corner strapped to a rocking horse with vines and bondage rope, begging me please do something, make him stop. I have the sword but I cannot bring myself to do it this time. He grows larger and larger until he bursts the cot open, the screams get deeper until they are a continuous ancient tone that rips time apart. He obliterates me into jam and carrion, my eyes are pressed again.

§

Email from the Replicator:

So what am I? Just this fucking monkey running around my house? Up and down spiral staircases, running around this glorified cave, this little plasticky capsid, using up my life energy meter, using up my time tokens. Dishing out one thing or another in some vigorous exchange. Off-shore response unit. Cephalopod shepherd. They call me the Replicator. You can't break an egg without making an omelette. *clicks fingers number of times* They got me at Leeds-Bradford ushering in UFOs with shiny sticks. LED crystal. Red, blue, green. This is a secret mission. There are no mid-afternoon slumps in my world. There are no cigarette breaks because there are no cigarettes. Rule Number One: NO CIGARETTES — he takes the cigarette out of the rookie agent's mouth. He throws the cigarette upon the ground. Hmm. You're going to need shoe polish. A lot of shoe polish. In my book. You could call it a mission, you could call it a secret quest, a grey operation. Or it could be one of those games where you sort of just build stuff, simulate trains. Do you follow? Do you follow? Where were we... mmmm mmm... But first I'm going to need you to forget all these false dichotomies of... enemy, opponent, ally, friend, win, lose, egg, sperm. You're going to need to forget it. *clicks fingers* They call me the Replicator. Tell me, my young companion, tell me, I'm curious. What is a woman? What is a woman... no ideas...*taps fingers together, alongside restless leg syndrome* nothing... ok, listen. *raises hands up in a curious gesture* A woman is a bitch, a woman is a used car. She's there at the edge of my bed, she tucks me in, she abandons me, she abandons me! So er... so that's my story! *laughs nervously*... His body is... he's large! He's huge! He is as big as a ten-storey building, you can't fit him indoors. He's going to be cold outside. We have to do something. I say we bring our boy in out of the storm. That's my son. He's my sun, he's my moon, he's my everything. I've spoken to the committee. I have a certain responsibility towards him, what do you expect? It's a really drab state of affairs, I don't want to bore you with the details. Anyway, this is where you come in. Eyes on the prize. I know that you have a little bit of violence in you. I know that you're insane... you have these little insane thoughts you think in the mirror. I know what crazy stuff gets into your head when you stroke your... Rawr... Miaow... *does cat scratching gesture*... What can I say? You were made for the job. The money, well if you can call it money. It's going to be a virtual briefcase of A4 quality nudes deposited straight to the wank bank. Have you ever read the Bhagavad Gita? The Bhagavad Gita... Wow, what a book. Now listen. This baby... My child... His name is Alex. His name is Baby Alex, and you're going to bring him to himself. *clicks fingers multiple times* If you don't feed him at least three times a day, he's going to go wah wah. Emergency alarm. My brain is on fire... I can't think... With all your chitter chattering. Show him the speedboats. There will two guards at the rear, two on the periphery, four in the main chamber, and eight in the master bedroom. Daddy needs his baby. Baby needs his daddy. I trust you'll act with absolute discretion. Morning, wake up, bed time, sleep. It's a simple procedure. An idiot could run it. I'm going to make you dance. You're going to be daddy's little porn-star. You're going to dance your little tush off, believe me. The world ended in 1994. Or started. Who cares? Bangbros. Brazzers. Blacked Raw. Reaching into your brain and taking what I want. The moaning of a woman, her hand on the bedsheet, gripping it. She likes to get a good grip of the bedsheet, it's something I've never understood. I have this recurring dream... I need your help; we need to find him. *starts running in slow motion* With new technology I can run faster, I can see pictures that your daughter has been uploading, naked pictures, pictures of her sticking make-up brushes in her hooha. Show him the bazooka. Inertia my boy, our kingdom has fallen to the disease of inertia, to the dogs of fear! I know that you're a fucking whore. We're all whores. You're not special but you're not unspecial, see? There's pain, there's a likelihood... there's a likelihood that if we don't find him in time... In a blue wood, mist and moisture so thick it concerns the lungs, the ferns, the fungus. Perhaps the trees know the location of my baby. The trees communicate see. It was my father's name also. I suppose anyone could have guessed that. *wipes table-top to check for dust* Who's been... *claps hands twice* It's indecent. The leaf-blowing neighbour again. Sighs. I could kill. To kill is a criminal shame. But I could. Ok I'm getting tired now. Daddy needs to take a nappy. Give him the encryption key. I trust my child will be in good hands. Birds require patience, all animals do. The bristles stand equidistant on the brush.

§

Baby Alex, very stoned, singing to himself.
Baby Alex, very stoned, growing tired of me.

♔

On the fifteenth of every month, I receive £200 from my mother as a salary, deposited straight into my bank account. In exchange for this, I open letters, scan and fax documents very occasionally, and take care of the house, the parrot, and the snake. The document I come into contact with most regularly is something called a C79 form, sent to my mother's law firm by HMRC. As to what the form does or indicates, I have no clue. All I know is that the C79 form is of a highest importance, at least in the context of my node, and should be immediately scanned and sent to my mother as an email attachment. Occasionally I will send the C79 as an embedded jpeg in the email to my mother, to which she asks me to send it again as an attachment so that she can forward it. Twice I have told her that it is possible for her to download the jpeg and reattach it to an email. Each time I reply with an attached C79 form, the email provider, Gmail, will automatically provide the C79 form from the previous email as an attachment, so my mother now has two C79 form attachments to choose from.

♚

Screensaver metaballs.

You are cleaning some inner spring in your pistol, then putting its parts together, and testing the trigger. Click.

The sounds of a thunderstorm outside, lightning strikes, heavy rain.

Something reorganises itself in an unknown location, and three clear descending tones sound out from nowhere.

"Mmmm-mmm-mmm..." I'm humming a bluesy flowing melody, "Loooord... mmm-mmm-mmm... Massa got me workin' for the deep state... mmm-mmm-mmm..."

"Jamaican me crazy."

"Throw me that bag of dynamite."

"Please."

"Woman... Throw me the bag of dynamite please."

"You're welcome, man." You reach beneath the bed and bring out a black bag, standard issue from HQ, filled with red dynamite sticks, wires and a timer.

"Thanks dude." I start to press buttons on the timer, big beeping red numbers turning up in that sweet digital clock font, mirrored by my circular black shades. I hum my tune some more then say, in a French accent: "I'm a pretty sadisteek son of a beetch."

A man who looks remarkably like Jesus, wearing sunglasses and a tuxedo walks into the hotel room. I look up, amused.

"Baby Alex!" I say.

"You two are late," he says sternly. You look up.

"Baby Alex!" you say.

"Stop calling me Baby Alex. It's Agent A."

"Agent Anus."

We snicker.

"How is that remotely funny..." says Baby Alex. "Come on, we've got a job to do."

He opens a standard issue black bomber bag, and throws us both a walkie-talkie.

You pick up the walkie-talkie: "Hello... schrrrt.... Agent Anus?... schrrrt ... Come in Agent Anus?"

"I'll come in Agent Anus."

"Jesus Christ you two."

Vague coordinates decalibrate and realign.

Sleep's Dragonaut.

♛

We were approaching the airport in the summer of 2019, the sky blue, the desert earth baked, and the interior of the car chilly and dried. We had given it a go. I had dropped everything to move out to Sedona; I had quit my job; I had moved away from Alex and my mother. I had tried my best to form something resembling a real relationship with my father. To see him every day, to go to the supermarket together, to talk about the neighbours, to watch a TV drama with multiple seasons. To then reference the TV drama to each other.

You never say thank you, I would say. That's what the money is for, he'd respond.

After five months, the novelty disintegrated. I was left living with a mirror of myself, one that I often deeply disliked, full of obnoxious hot air and misplaced resentment, devouring cold cuts standing in front of the fridge. I could tell my presence was becoming a nuisance to him as well, no matter how much I tried to shrink myself. The moment had not passed. It felt more as if it had never been there at all. When I told him it was time to go home, he didn't even seem sad: his lips rolled inwards and he nodded. We are slackers by nature, we quietly wait for the time someone else suggests giving up.

I was sucking up the last dregs of my iced tea from In-N-Out, listening to Michael Brecker on the car stereo. My dad was doing that thing he does: talking about the music so much that I could not hear the music.
"This guy, it's like..." His face scrunched up in theatrical disbelief. "It's like he's doing shit people can only dream of. No one can play this fast. Not even Parker could do this shit. Wait, wait..."

He held up a finger, then wiggled it along with a long run of notes that, to me, seemed to be only a display of skill, with no feeling behind it. He looked to me to gauge my response, his expression like a YouTube thumbnail, pure American are you kiddin me?

"Wow, damn, that's impressive!" I said with all my remaining strength.
"Yeah that guy, he's just... the best of the best."

I watched his face change, slacken, soften. He stared back at the road.
Nothing was said for maybe twenty seconds while Brecker's discordant honking continued. I thought about a morning I had spent with him a few weeks prior, at an opulent brunch spot, drinking glass after glass of complementary lemon water and watching him play on a tiny stage to only me, his bored girlfriend, and three or four elderly couples who were ignoring him and eating very large omelettes.

"You've got something special."
"What do you mean?"

"You're so smart."

"... I don't think I'm especially smart."

"But you're talented. With your writing."

"But I never let you read anything. How do you know?"

"Nah, I know you're good. I can feel it. I can tell."

I felt I wasn't allowed to be affected by this comment. It was based on nothing, and seemed motivated by his belief that I was destined for greatness for a reason that was somehow down to him. I also wanted to cry, and to tell him I wanted nothing more than to impress him. I said nothing. More silence.

"You know, just..." He appeared deeply uncomfortable, and his face was doing something I had never seen it do. It was real sincerity, non-Hollywood, ugly and embarrassing. He was smiling, but it was a shameful smile, one signposting a core of red-hot, infected hurt.

"Just... do something with it. You know. Make sure you do."

"I promise I will. It's all I want to do. It's all I feel like I'm good at."

"That's all you need. Just that one thing. But don't..."

I looked at him again. He really looked like me in that moment, some quality in my eyes, when I'm staring without perceiving, deep in my head.

"Don't be like me."

My eyes went wide. I was amazed that he dared to say it.

"You know, I'm comfortable, my life is fine, I can't complain. And I play well. But... I could have been this guy. I could have been really fucking good. But I was lazy."

I just kept staring at him. The moment was being etched into my unconscious as it was happening.

"So don't be fucking lazy. Do it. And you will be incredible."

I didn't know what to say, so I said what I felt needed to be said.
"I love you."
I meant it.
"I love you too kiddo."
It felt like he meant it too, that time.

My heart broke a little bit. I looked out of the passenger window, unsettled. He had never said anything like that to me.

"Could you write the next Harry Potter? Then I can get a place in Hawaii."

♛

Bouncing. Immediate bouncing, boing boing boing. McDonald's soft play area suspended in endless fog. Acid-washed, Deep Dream children are jumping on trampolines. They grow more violent and free-associative as the parents watch motionlessly from above with opera glasses, and the atmospheric pressure in the pit increases. The weans kick and punch each other, rip their hair out, crush the globes with their sticky paws. Their milk teeth zip from their mouths and whirl around the room. I know I should not be here; he is not here. I push the fire exit and hurtle through the mist.

Berghain. Harsh techno thumping, the grunt and slap of bareback fucking, and they put tape over my eyes so I can't take pictures. A baby wouldn't be here either. I stumble my way into the men's bathroom and fall into a pile of pills. I crunch down on them, gagging, until the house of cards collapses.

I'm looking at white drywall now. The cheery whistling and ukulele jangling of a viral marketing video plays faintly with echo, on a loop, from another room. I hear the oaky croaking of the rocking horse fade in behind me. Not again. But I turn and there he is, yes, in the cot, crying, wailing, again. The sword solidifies in my hand, but I know I will fail here. His mother screams in your voice, do it, do it pussy! The audio loop speeds up as he grows and his screams deepen. I lift the sword over his neck with all my might and it explodes into sharp glitter, it slices into my face, I slip to the ground in ribbons of lunchmeat. I always lose here.

I come around and I'm sucking on something in the dark. I immediately break my own neck.

Starlings fly through a blanket of white. Now they are spider-eggs suspended in an eraser, thrumming with force, soon to hatch. Another dream. An old one. I remove it from the rotation and rub myself out.

Tripping on 2C-B watching Carpool Karaoke. He is right there, but I am unable to talk. This isn't the one. I go to the bathroom for a very long time.

A fire in the forest. Someone speaks and I miss my chance.

The heather undulates in the wind out on the moor. The sun is soft, fractured. The air is thick with fragrance. A dense cluster of trees a few hundred metres away. I approach, fauna-flora slithering benignly over my bare feet. I weave through the wood; I ask them and they reply. He is right here; we will make him clear. I hear it first, and then I see it. There he lies, asleep. Baby Alex. I have not seen him in peace for 400 million years. He is much larger than even you described. The size of a house. His slumbering wind nearly sucks me in. I creep over to his left fourth finger, the size of a front door, and I hold it in my no longer fucked up hands. His eyes open. He looks at me. I have bypassed the firewall. I communicate your message. We dissipate together.

The guards greet me with much more warmth than the last time they saw me.

Sober today?

I laugh politely. I'm here on business. I gesture to him.

They nod and let us through.

The speedboats. You weren't kidding. They were magnificent. Sleek, sharp, gleaming with chrome. You should have seen his face. I slipped the key into his hand. He let me keep the bazooka, he said I'd need it for something. He wished me well then off he went, soaring into the horizon, jets of water spraying in his wake. He should be with you soon, pep pep.

§

It's all in a processor see, like a food processor, with those two rotating blades that look like farmers' scythes. And once in a while something is added to the mix through the funnel at the top, something chunky and unwieldy, and you think that's going to be the thing to break it. You think this is it, change. And it might rattle for a second, but it's all folded into the batter, milky-beige and indistinct. The processor keeps spinning furiously, propelled by its purpose, indifferent to its supposed owner. It spins for itself, for the feeling of spinning and folding. The batter might grow or thicken, but as long as it's in the processor, it's all the same sludge.

§

There is this desire to be coordinated, to give ourselves reason to continue. The Zoomer infini-scroll narrative keeps rolling forth, but we're losing a sense that we're getting anywhere. We've got a job to do, but what is that job? How do these things really connect?

♛

The Jesus of Bureaucracy. Triangles talking and understanding their environment like never before.

"You're probably wondering why you're here," says Agent A, tired, shuffling the memos on his desk. His long hair looks a little greasy.

We sit opposite in two swively leather chairs. I'm clacking a boiled sweet around my mouth and staring through the window into the engineering department. You are pivoting from side to side like a bored child in Geography. You speak.

"Cut the shit, Anus. Just wag your finger at us and get it out of the way."

I suck on the sweet to suppress an inappropriate snicker. I usually have a remarkably good poker face, one of the best, but seeing the two of you interacting is my Achilles' heel.

"For the LAST time..."

I bite down on the sweet, dig my acrylics into my thigh.

"That is NOT my name."

You pull your glasses down to the bridge of your nose, look at him sanpaku, gearing up.

"... Yeah, okay. Anus."

I grab two more sweets from the bowl and cram them into my mouth. You cackle. A sighs loudly.

"We finalised the report back from Seoul. Should I give it to you bullet-point style? Because there are several things that need acknowledging."

You do not react, so I nod. He proceeds.

"Drinking on the job. Drawing attention to the agency in a civilian hotel bar while you do it..."

"Your fucking fault for putting us in a civilian hotel," you snap.

"Possession of cannabis, mescaline, N-dimethyltryptamine, Xanax, thank God you weren't caught by the authorities, or we would have had to call in the choppers. Ordering room service on the crypto chip: wagyu beef, spider crab, musk melons, makgeolli, cigarettes, et cetera."

"Oh shit," you laugh.

"The expense itself is not the issue there, obviously."

"Yeah that one wasn't on purpose."

"...May I continue?"

"Gog agegd", I say.

"And when you missed your flight, and Jaco called to inquire your whereabouts, you told him the two of you were intoxicated on God knows what, in a sauna God knows where, and tried to pay him off to make up an excuse to feed back to us."

"That little shit..."

"This does not concern Jaco. This concerns the two of you."

I use my titanium molars, custom issue, to crunch down on the sweets and swallow so I can defend myself.

"Something came up..."

"Care to elaborate?"

"...We had a feeling about the flight. Thought something was going to go down, didn't want to risk it. Call it a mutual tip-off."

A's eyes dart between the two of us.

"And why didn't you just say this in the first place? You didn't have to go to a fucking sauna."

I regain control of my poker face. "Confidential, closed file. Without going into it, we knew that plane wasn't for us. So we made ourselves scarce."

He glares at me and sighs again.

"Fine, fine."

He shuffles the papers again, looks at his monitor.

"If this kind of sordid behaviour were being exhibited by practically any other field agents, they would be excommunicated and wiped immediately. Unfortunately I do not have the pleasure to do that with you two, as much as it would satisfy me."

You speak up again, moving your hand in an old-fashioned royal wave. "Fine, yes, we're the best you have, you can't afford to not have us, yes. Now what's the punishment?"

A looks up, folds his arms. The denouement.

"The job no one wanted is now your problem. At 0500 the two of you fly to Saudi Arabia."

Call to prayer. Machinations on gridlocked blur.

Black Metal.

♕

Head empty. Walked a lot and made soup. An unacknowledged tension has now been released, a chiropractor popping an air bubble in my neck. I talked to mum for a long time. She told me she contracted genital herpes from her ex-husband. YouTube-to-MP3 rips of old Japanese ambient music sparking digital claustrophobia. I read the front page of a newspaper at the petrol station: "Two hours after this photo was taken,

Baby Alex had died."

⚜

The sleep seemed to be seasoned with an inexplicable wondering about my ex-girlfriend.

Penelope:

She had never kissed anyone when I met her. She also said she had never masturbated. She was very cutesy and giggly, and blushed easily. We met at a literature mixer, she was 19, a year older than me, she
had a bowl cut and very badly-applied eye makeup. She always dressed and looked kind of sloppy: never shaved, smelled a little weird, but she was this very petite posh girl so it came across as hot. We hit it off and started going out for lots of coffee, looking around vintage shops, woman things like that. I could make her laugh, and she looked really good when she laughed. This went on for over a month without either of us being able to tell whether or not the other was romantically interested. Eventually we started fooling around in this innocent, exploratory way, and then dating very publicly. We were very into each other and wanted everyone to know. The sex became very good.

She gradually grew more insane. I would come to her place and start to see beer bottles all over the room, cigarettes and spliffs stubbed out on the furniture, half-eaten trays of vegan takeout scattered around. She stopped going to class and would just masturbate all the time. She stopped giggling and started having these very insular temper tantrums, brought on by nothing at all, where she would pout and then cry, in that angry child-like way. She became overtly sexual in her interactions with our friends, posting half-naked pictures of herself on Instagram, and started making "performance art". Her politics grew more nonsensically radical, and the sex more violent. I didn't know the reason for any of it. I was nothing but patient with her. Nothing in her personal life had appeared to change. I met her family, they were nice. Then one night we were in bed together, she was watching me scroll Facebook on my phone, and Alex came up in my suggested friends. I asked her if she knew who he was, and she said he came to the foreign film society sometimes, so I added him without really thinking about it. This is how Alex and I met, and this is how Penelope and I would eventually break up.

I sometimes get a little freaked out thinking about the tiny mundane things you can do that end up changing your life. If I hadn't moved my thumb those few millimetres, I may have never met him, I may be a different person now, and you and I may not be doing this.

He messaged me to say he liked my writing, and Penelope and I started hanging out with him, he seemed to click more with me but enjoyed her company too. She admitted to having a crush on him and projected that crush onto me, so if Alex and I ever hung out alone, or did something while she was doing something with her other friends, she would call me non-stop and hurl furious texts at me if I didn't pick up. And when the three of us spent time together I felt the chemical signals that you mentioned, beneath language and even emotion, just impulse, her astrally throwing herself at him: him not really refusing. Her desire to be around him ultimately flipped into hatred upon realising he was more interested in me. She told me to stop seeing him: I refused. She grew more jealous and protective; she would oscillate between saying she wanted kids with me to saying I was a monster who wouldn't care if she died. All the while I was just having fun making stupid videos with my new friend, drinking Crabbie's on his balcony, watching shit on eFukt, laughing goofily. I still really liked crazy Penelope and had no interest in sleeping with Alex, who was very much my bro at this point. Her behaviour became more outlandish in an attempt to frighten me, and she was getting irresponsibly drunk every time she went out. Then one evening, she invited me to come to a drag show that some of her friends were performing in. I turned up late, stoned, with Alex, who had been invited by someone else.

She had been drinking, she silently got up and left, so I followed her through the campus for about 20 minutes, never breaking into a run for fear people would think I was chasing her. There is this kind of hedge maze on the York campus, that people call the "quiet place": it is very secluded and liminal, especially at night, and people go there to smoke weed and fuck al fresco. She went into the quiet place and I ran around looking for her, shouting her name, not enjoying the melodrama. She appeared from behind a topiary, grabbed me by my shirt with one hand, rubbed my makeup off my face with the other, then slapped me pretty hard. It wasn't the first time. I realised I couldn't deal with her shit anymore; my patience had rotted away. I was just letting her push me around. I definitely felt like the man in the relationship, calmer and more reasonable, but she had managed to take my symbolic balls.

We broke up shortly after that, in an art gallery, separating as publicly and cringily as we had dated.

Post-break-up, we never really talked. Spending more time with Alex, I slipped out of the lesbian echo chamber and just spent time at my friends' houses, so the risk of running into her was very low. She didn't graduate.

I found confessional poetry she had written about her rebound exploits. She slept with a bunch of men she had met online. She posted "conceptual", full-body nudes. She moved to London and became friends with a bisexual, tattooed woman with bad hair. Both of them changed their names several times. Neither seemed to have steady jobs. She had a psychotic break, went missing, and is now an escort.

———————

A picture of her crying, with mascara streaks on her puffy cheeks, standing in a darkened Overground station. A picture of a miserable vegan pie she baked with "FUCK THE COPS" written on it in pastry letters. A tweet in which she describes the humiliation of reading reviews of her quality as a sexual partner on an escort forum. They comment on her sloppiness and weird smell. She is now on the streets of Soho: a slutty gay clown on the way to munch some trade.

♕

I listened to an album that sounds like it was made with the synths used to score the old Donkey Kong games. I stood in the mirror and came up with a slow cryptic dance routine for one of the tracks.

Sway from side to side with a glint of smug knowing in your eye, but don't smile. Slowly raise a finger to your lips. Turn to the side and conspicuously slide your hand into your pocket, then take it out, and lower your finger from your lips. Flatten your hands, fingers touching, point your fingers upwards and then downwards. Cover your eyes,

still swaying, kick your legs out more. Move your hands away to
reveal that your eyes are closed. Spin slowly, when you arrive at 360°, open your eyes again, repeat.

§

There is a hyper-sexual core in all of us, a man-woman futanari beast, a chittering jaw birthing from a smooth purple-green egg. The degree to which it desires power it also desires to be the object of that power, to both obliterate and be obliterated. The Baphomet, the Separator — God wrested from itself out of sheer power. You must seek to communicate with this thing, to register its existence, without being knocked off balance by its rip current. The rank of a man is his ability to draw up this power, whilst staving off its madness.

♚

The room: grey, dark-grey, shaggy, shagged out. Metal tone with an attention-deficit edge, CADCAM tech devised. Black metal curls, wall-swarm, pricking LED tips. Two windows, symmetrical, large, three by one point five (height:width) — cool blue, silk-thin, drapings. Ripples, over the cloth, wind. Huge bed, shagged in, hookers with, or with each other. Rotate bed. Us: sat. Two armchairs: cream leather, black coffee table: circular, white tablecloth: square, placed; coterminous to the radius: edges. Rotate armchair. Rotate table. You: pencil skirt, black, thin, shirt, white, scarf, Hellenic blue. Glasses circular, coy librarian, knowing, with regards to. Smirk. Earrings, the bizarre truth of the writing, veined gold through aqua blue. Rotate Pussycat. "The virus is inventive," say I: wearing nothing, holding mirror, out, left hand, right hand, rolled up yen, tapping, snorting, crystal-decision-maker. Triangular dust.

"Put some clothes on."

"Maybe correctly, you make, such an injunction, exactly."

Line of flight, invisible, up-nose.

"The grey suit Q."

"The grey suit Pussycat."

I, dazzled, eyes wide.

"Penis, I must, mention, slight pain."

"Too much, avoiding its use, if so. Hookers, if or if not actual, moderation in."

"If, if, if." Grey suit, in rapid departure, the closet from, to the bed unkempt, hands down sleeve, sleeve, down hand down, trouser leg with leg in trouser leg, belted, buttoned, unhurried exact sequence, movements of, now. Grey suit, I, one. Rotate myself.

You, Pussycat, leather briefcase reveal, eye up smirking again, my way. Snatchachatacha. Unlocked. Leather, side, rotate, show. My eye. My smiling expression without smile.

"The virus is inventive." your-wrist-reveal, diagram-tiny of a capsid, icosahedral. I also show my wrist, lift arm slowly, ritual of assassin, then wink. Cool, very. "Nice.": together, chorus.

"He's booked into the Blue Lagoon tonight, we've got a fifteen-minute post-meal window, before he's back in his suite."

"Mogul type. Nothing, interesting. Curved. Balls. Marbles, running on: marble run." The gun, in hand, out of nowhere schuk-kuk, locked and loaded. Your eyes behind librarian frames.

"Don't get cocky Q."

"Like, I haven't done, nothing, like nothing, like this before."

Head bobbing. Corridor, Saudi Arabia. Before this, Mohammed, the desert, after this, the desert. Secret gold hidden in dunes, fluid simulation. Rotate Mohammed. Rotate target. My head tracking his head. A strange, wearing of the hotel clerk outfit for a moment: an instant; then ask him, sir could we please ask you to step into the office concerning "what?": concerning "what is all this about": blam shot, no blood, dart to neck, hi-tech shit — into back room, you, surgical glove wearing bagged into container, we move, quickly, elevator; up to the room, 27th floor. Third-person morality. Did I mention I got changed out of my hotel worker uniform? Clothes in the laundry vent. Back in the grey suit. We talk small talk in the elevator, minor improv, the elderly woman holding the chihuahua suspects nothing. "Do you think Radley will be OK downstairs on his own..." "Oh of course, no don't worry..." "Good.. good.." Radley — status: non-existent, decoy, fictive. Genius.

Floor: 27. Out, elevator, departure, movement, carpet touching wheel of our container, muffled roll, big box, oxblood. The carpet warm red, the corridor icy white, our room, 368, key-card in key-card hole, LED: green, in. Removal of boy from box. A chair arranged, central, flanked by two large, Rothko derivative, paintings, grey and blue and dark grey and silver, our man, tied up, handcuffed, gagged, taped down, stripped. Rotate, rotate: rotate. Rrr-oh-tah-té. Another leather briefcase opened, tweezers, knives and other implements removed steadily, and laid out on the white cloth over the black coffee-table. And myself, deep breath out, fill the kettle, the bathroom faucet, the water-white with-bubbles. Sit on the armchair, waiting, a green tea for myself and Pussycat, in preparation. We wait.

Our lad sputters out his first realisation of consciousness. The degree to which, intransigent, our fellow, nightmarish hammerhead shark fellow, keeper; zoo. Vitro blow, tear, caesarean wakeful, oh, oh god, where am I? What happened?
"Good afternoon Mr Fenton." say you.

Mr Fenton, mmmmmmpphaaa, muffled screams, heavy breathing, red face.
"Mr Fenton, we're going to ask you some questions and we'd like it very much if you could answer them to the best of your ability."
Beads of pure fear, billionaire fear, dripping and dropping and drooping into puddles on his back, under his arms, beneath his neck, down his temples, through his hair. Arm clench, large set of tweezers, use like stress-reliever. Gosh, my, oh, I'm also a little sweaty. Over ten million possible beads.

Sludge metal.

♛

The gender filter is the only good one. They gave me a beard. They also darkened my skin. Infamous PUA and Return of Kings contributor Roosh V, that's who I look like now. Or, a swarthier version of my dad when he was young.

"We both played it cool for the first couple days. We'd see each other around, or I'd see him staring at me through a cracked door and not come out to talk to me. Then one night I fell while I was carrying my sax and it started leaking, like I couldn't play it properly, there was a big dent in the side. I had no idea what to do, I wouldn't be able to perform for weeks seeing as it wasn't likely that any of the places we'd be docking at would have any repair shops. Someone said, oh, Chris could do it. He's great with that stuff, I'll let him know that you need it done. So me and Amanda were in my cabin waiting for him and he came over. He didn't have a shirt on. He silently, very casually picked up the sax and sat cross legged on the floor, fiddling with it, hunched over it, all his hair falling in his eyes. It was amazing to watch him fix it. He just put some bands over it, knocked it around a little, tested the air flow. It only took him about ten minutes before it played perfectly again. I was very aloof with him, looking at my nails, just said yeah great, thanks. Guess you can go now. He nodded, got up and let himself out. As soon as the door shut Amanda and I just stared at each other in awe. She said I have never been more attracted to someone in my life. I think it was that night I let him ask me out. We ate crab together on the deck. Haven't had crab for a while. Should I get some from Aldeborough tomorrow?"

♔

... wanked over by machines of loving grace.

I am sat at my kitchen table in February 2020, having just eaten an entire salad bowl's worth of plain porridge, without sugar. I am swiping through women on Tinder, drinking the last half of my daily four pints of organic whole milk. I am moving faces either to the left, or to the right: I am a sorting algorithm, I am binary. The whales go to the left, the uggos go to the left, the girls holding drinks in every picture in front of the same student accommodation door go to the left. If I am horny, the equation is rewritten slightly — all girls go to the right, apart from the cross-eyed ones, the no-hopers, and the single mothers with chocolate bar emoji bios. The middle-aged women with massive fake knockers go to the right. The art hoes go to the right. The egirls with the chains and the Bladee Tinder Anthems go to the right. The occasional fit bird with a squint also goes to the right.

My ability to match with lots of women is pretty inconsistent. There was one small section of time the year before where I had taken it seriously: some colourful holiday snaps of myself, with lots of hair, staring into the sunset, and an additional lie in the bio that I was a homeowner. This led to my most successful run, I would match with lots of well-groomed Eastern Europeans, mainly Slovenians and Romanians, obviously attracted to my fictional "upwardly mobile/holidaying/homeowning" status. However, my inability to hold a normal conversation always failed me — the courtship style a bit too "oscillations between ADHD and existential dread" — so I would ultimately lose all the additional traffic at the speaking stage.

I get up from the table and see myself walking around in the kitchen window. I am reminded, for no particular reason, that I was once an embryo growing in my mother's womb, that I grew inside my own mother, a real person, and that each and every person on earth grew inside their own mother, which makes me burst out laughing when I juxtapose this with my narcissistic eyeing up of my own body, gauging its dimensions, mentally making notes on which exercises at the gym will need to be done in order to gain more size in certain areas.

I'm looking at the pictures of a Mediterranean girl called Eleni. She is attractive but clearly unaware of how to capitalise on that, holding a spliff in one of her photos, a little fish-eyed and slutty and exactly my type. Her face is that sweet spot between the too-beautiful (where I agonise to the point of acting weird and spaghetti-ohing) and the meh area (where I don't even meet with her and I'm yabbering for my own sadistic amusement). It was on her last picture that I set my hopes; if she looked anything like that, the time spent chatting shit would not be wasted. She looked retarded: in a good way, sucking in her lips to do a duck-face variation — kind of Israeli really, the slutty Israeli phenotype. I swipe right, the screen lags out, signalling either a match or the end of my free likes for the day. The app unfreezes, animating to a zoom-in on her first photo, with a kind of high-score font in green, as though I've completed a level with flying colours in Candy Crush, or Angry Birds: "It's A Match!". Great, I think — as always, disappointed; the promised hit of dopamine my head expects upon registering reciprocated attraction becomes this very empty feeling, tinged with disgust, as I'm validated by this fanfare of pixels.

An invitation along the bottom of the screen to send Eleni a first message reads: "Don't keep your match waiting!" I don't bother, I continuing the browsing of munters within my 50-mile radius. About one minute later, Eleni sends me a message:

"L the hair x".

It's already so tiresome and vapid. I respond with, "yeah unfortunately I cut it all off." The conversation moves along quite quickly, there's something about the way she's messaging: I can tell that she's either super into me, or, she has no clue about the social niceties that women are supposed to observe when texting men, especially on Tinder. Either way, it's good news: I can splurge my nonsense in moments of excitement without worrying too much about her freaking out. She is regularly messaging back three or four messages to my every one. I am even responding in one-word answers and she is sending these trios of questions and observations. Any man watching this back and forth would immediately take me aside and say: hey buddy, watch out, big red flags coming off of this one, something ain't right... but eventually the reason comes out. I'm the first guy she has matched with on Tinder. She has only just downloaded the app tonight, at the suggestion of her flatmates. I turn away from my smartphone, head in hands, oh you poor girl, you poor innocent thing. First day at the meat grinder eh: Fookin 'ell. I didn't realise they still existed; women who hadn't had their souls sucked out of them. And here I was, about to take hers.

Realising I've landed a hole-in-one with Eleni, I invite her to come for a walk with me, the next day. There isn't a complete shift in her messaging, but she does seem nervy, and begins to ask questions such as "How big is you dick btw?". I tell her it's "almost seven inches" (emphasis on the almost). She says "oh good bc i'm not like turned on by small ones". The red flags are flapping away, high on the mast. Generally, if a woman asks you how big you are, unless you're packing a leviathan in the Marks 'n Sparks undies, you should run for the hills, not because she'll humiliate you or anything, but because she probably has a loose vagina. It's startling how common this seems to be nowadays, the laissez-faire economic model of the sexual marketplace, the pornification of ... yadda yadda you already know the deal. Eggplant emoji bios. And it's her first day on Tinder! Yikes. I ask her how big her tits are to balance things out. I'm not even a tits guy, I couldn't care less. I'm more a nipple man, if anything.

(The meme reads: When the nipples are just right... and it's me, pouting, eyes closed, with an Italian chef moustache doing the pinched Che Buono! hand gesture).

There is also this immediate transition from light flirtation to explicit discussion of what kind of BDSM kinks that you're both into that seems so of-the-now and run-of-the-mill. Oh, are you like more into like domination or "domming" or are you like more like of a submissive a.k.a a "sub"? From the single word responses, Eleni says "Oh yeah, I can tell that you're really dominant, even by the way you're speaking..." I scrunch up my eyes, put my thumb and forefinger on the ridge of my nose, and sigh loudly — this fucking bitch is retarded. But in a good way: this is fine, this is perfect in fact. Women are for relaxing, and the last thing you want is to have to try and impress a woman by thinking too hard.

(what is this, pimp-posting?)

... jus' looking tae pump a wee quine.

The next day, I am crouched in the garden uprooting brambles that have grown over the majority of my mother's plants. I am doing this additional gardening work in order to earn some pocket money, age 25, so that I can buy hoodies to be stitched with my YouTube channel's logo to sell as merchandise. This minor toil I hope will set off a chain reaction of investments and profits, merch-cycles, eventuating in myself making enough money to leave my family house and the aggravating squawks of my parrot and do something else, somewhere else: something exotic with esoteric momentum; somewhere under the gaze of lithe energetic souls. Anything but pulling out brambles in my mother's garden, medium sized in medium sized space. That said, I am also growing increasingly nervous about meeting Eleni the Cypriot, and having my dimensions scrutinised, so the aggressive activity of yanking at roots is providing me with a welcome distraction. The nervous energy will on occasion drop completely, and I will stop to lie on the grass for ten minutes — eyes closed, or looking up at the wintry overcast sky.

The three hours leading up to her arrival I do very little — the anticipation is too much for me to fully concentrate on reading or work — so I noodle some rubato bullshit on the piano, lie down again for ten minutes looking at the ceiling, take two oddly diarrhoea-esque shits, and watch YouTube videos with the contradictory ambient sense that I should be deprogramming myself from "culture-at-large" in preparation for my possible hook-up. I receive the text that she is arriving outside in the Uber, I get up from the floor and walk immediately to my bathroom to piss and look at myself in the mirror. I make my "hot guy" face, clenching my jaw and furrowing my brow, then put on my shoes and walk out of the house.

There's a brief misunderstanding vis a vis house numbers, she texts to say that she is out of the Uber but I don't see her, and this strangely calms me. The smallest problem such as this one can be addressed, the situation can become purposeful, there can be a clear A to B trajectory, and therefore I don't have to become slack, I don't have to wait anymore. I walk down the street and see her coming up the hill, I smile, automatically, the "hot guy" Q programme at maximum operation. Upon seeing Eleni irl, a relief came over me, that I didn't have to pretend to enjoy fucking her.

"Wow you actually look... yeah," I say. My voice seems to have dropped a couple of tones from its regular pitch, oozing out in a plummy-Yorkshire hybrid I slip into unconsciously for seduction purposes.
She gives me an odd look, smiling. "Wow, your voice is so... deep."
"Why, you like it?" I say, smirking, stepping around her in a lazy, predatory way. This bitch is retarded, and I am also retarded.
"Mmm." She responds.

I bring her into the house so that she can "put down her stuff" before we go on our "walk". It's already dark outside. I give the beginnings of a tour of the house, she looks up at the high ceiling of the corridor, the spider webs and the old grandfather's clock, and says "Ooh... your house looks kind of haunted!" I take her into the living room to meet Peter, who, as usual upon meeting new people, is very quiet: staring at Eleni with wide-eyes, and looking back and forth between the two of us anxiously from his cage, feathers fluffed up. As she starts to leave the living room, without even thinking about it, I grab her and hug her from behind, somewhat playfully, mirroring the steps of her feet with my own, right, left. She doesn't tense up, she relaxes, time slows and the need for our idiotic little comments to fill the silence dissipates. I give her hair a smell and say "Hmm, you really are...", our bodies interlock.
"Mmm?" she replies. With my left hand I pull aside her hair, and softly bite into her neck.
We're on the floor of the corridor, her straddling me and grinding, still clothed. She leans back and says, "You

know, I was really trying to not do this straight away but..."

"But?" I ask, hand on her lower back, reaching up to grab a fistful of hair and pull her head back down to me. I make the logistical assessment that we should go upstairs to my room, letting her climb the stairs in front of me, and I spank her arse with the back of my hand as she reaches the top.

We fuck, twice. As she pulls down my underwear and reveals my penis for the first time, she says "Oh wow, you have a really nice cock..." a comment which I accept with slight paranoia, not wanting to think about my own penis in comparison to any other penis at this moment in time, nor wanting to consider how my own penis sizes up to other penises that she has seen. And I don't trust women who give compliments. She pronounces cock: "cawk" — like a posh Londoner. I tell her to shush.

The second round of fucking, I'm finding it a bit tricky to get past the plateau and into cum-zone. I go into Absolute Dirtbag mode, completely negating the subjectivity of Eleni by the sheer fury of my thrusts. She says "choke me..." and I gratefully enclose her neck around my hands, squeezing slowly, my face turning into an inhuman shell for my fuck-mechanism, her face turning increasingly red. As I break through to the beginnings of my orgasm, I'm throwing her head back and forth against the mattress, she's gone a bright crimson cherry colour, I let go of her neck and pull my dick out quickly: that first spasm firing white across my hands, and one high-powered blob hitting her, woe to the conquered, across the mouth.

✠

An anonymous user from "4Channel" on the board "/lit/" — after watching a Bataille review video I uploaded to my YouTube, where myself and an ostensible homeless man give each other hand-jobs — posts that if I am interested in working for a Fortune500 company for a six figure salary, I should let him know. He posts a throwaway email address. My email says "hey it's q". My face does something stupid. He responded saying we were cushdy when I sent him a photo with a timestamp. I send him another email, my face doing something stupid again, a piece of paper with a timestamp that also reads "hey it's q".

"Let's get down to it, straight up: What's your endgame?" My penis has the blood sucked out of it. I am terrified of money. I am chewing my jaw so much that a vein is bumping away in odd twinges on my left cheek. I must analyse the penis feeling: Scorpio sees the world through the jap's eye.

§

A man asleep in the middle of the sidewalk. During his daily walk around the city he randomly collapsed, and stayed down, the warmth of the pave-stone comforting him. At first it might seem abnormal, but sooner or later it becomes normal. Downtown LA: A woman runs naked, a dead rat in her mouth. She passes wide side-streets flanked by skyscrapers, towers of finance, that seem to stretch out eternally; no horizon.

♛

Some version of you and some version of me are now

digging holes with our beaks, looking for bugs.

Some versions of us are too perverse or complex to even attempt to understand.

One version of you is monocellular, converting yeast into food.

Another, outer, more enlightened version of me — with sixteen gaseous eyes — sees this happen on a slab of white rock.

♛

A couple removed their wedding rings, their preemie baby in the ICU, a box with various beeping machines, lit up in ultraviolet.

My thoughts sank vertically into a chasm: corpses, aborted foetuses, home invasions, naked grinning demons. I heard the kettle finish boiling.

§

Do a nollie, then a tritone substitution, maybe pop in some b-roll. Use that free glitch fx transitions pack, then sprinkle some 808s on top. Bob's your uncle.

♛

Downloaded Hinge. I don't know if you've ever used it, it's a swipe-y one like Tinder. Instead of a bio you answer prompts that are displayed on your profile. I uploaded six pictures (the maximum) and realised they were all selfies; no one has taken a nice picture of me in a while. I had just cooked some beetroot, so I chewed up a little piece and took a picture of myself doing a blood-red drool-y grin. I put it as the last of them. I made every answer on my profile reference being cursed, or that I had the power to spoil food.

Swiped for about ten minutes as the aura became apparent. There is a factory somewhere churning these people out. People who begrudgingly drink tequila, people who have baby nephews. People with no light in their faces. Not even bad vibes, just no vibes at all.

I am in awe of their two-word definitions of themselves:

doggo lover,
sesh gremlin,
coffee snob,
country boy,
human radiator,
future dentist.

McDonald's chicken nuggets come in five seemingly-organic shapes. There are also about five main categories of men-seeking-women on dating apps: lad, nerd, indie, freak, adulterer. There are two shapes corn kernels can form into when they pop: butterflies or mushrooms. There are also two categories of women-seeking-women on dating apps: art school, trade school. The human brain evolved to find patterns, even when it doesn't need to, or probably shouldn't.

I matched with an indie-category guy; in his first pic he was holding a reflector on a movie set. I commented "that's the biggest communion wafer I've ever seen." He matched me back but didn't say anything. I said "well??? Did u eat the body of Christo???", nothing from him. A festival-subtype indie guy wearing a drug rug and little round purple sunglasses sent me a "heyy". I said "woooahh whoever made you must have been smoking weed aha", nothing back. A nerd guy with nervous eyes had answered that he had an irrational fear of burrata. I commented "pussy bitch", he blocked me outright. What am I doing wrong? What am I trying to do?

I was enjoying it but felt exhausted, and was about to quit swiping, but wanted to see one last good one. Then, I found an absolutely fucking jacked, leathery, fake-tan lad who had uploaded the same picture of himself standing on the beach all six times. He had only answered one prompt:

"My mantra is: Fuck you."

I burst out laughing and closed the app.

♔

Matched with a thirty-two-year-old named Katie, yesterday morning, 9am. She messaged me straight away: "hello there" and an "xxx". I told her to go back to sleep, it was too early. She responded: "oh", "ok", "bye". I said "See you in the afternoon". I expected never to speak with her again. She answered back that afternoon: "I can just unmatch you if you want." I look up from the screen, my bottom lip sagging downwards, my eyes screwed up in confusion.

§

Message from James Cooper:

fucking hell you are BORING

♔

[after long tinder convo, next day, on WhatsApp]

k: soz just don't sleep with bullies
k: bet you were a bully at school

q: oh sorry thought you weren't talking to me
q: not really but if you wear a school uniform i'll bully you

k: i was just replying to you

q: suuuuuuuure you were

k: what do you even want from me don't get it at all
k: just want someone to have nudes off

q: not really

k: well i'm sure there's plenty of girls you can ask

q: there are
q: no i just thought eventually we could go for a walk
q: you got a car?
q: or you still mad
q: god you are an odd one

k: a walk for me to just be bullied the entire time
k: great
k: fun

q: nah mate i'll throw in some free therapy
q: maybe eat your ass if you behave
q: [smirk]
q: i don't think i've bullied you once

k: you're doing it right now

q: no i'm not, i'm being friendly now
q: katie i think you'd benefit greatly from a nice walk with
me

q: seeing as you haven't left the house in a while

k: i don't need therapy thanks

q: maybe
q: we can therapise each other

k: i watched one of your videos

q: [eyes]
q: hmmmm
q: which one is the question

k: of you trying to hurt yourself with a knife

q: oh yeah
q: there's about four of those

k: are you suicidal

q: i used to be
q: just a little
q: [sends picture of himself with bee hat]
q: now i'm a bee

k: well that video was only a few weeks ago

q: oh hmm
q: must've been an odd moment
q: suicidal isn't the same as self harm anyway
q: self harm just feels good

k: i feel sorry for you

q: why

k: because i'm that sort of person but i don't like you very much

q: oh why not
q: well
q: i guess that's you then

k: i feel bad because you've clearly got some things going on

q: [sends another bee hat wearing one, this time with morose expression]
q: i'll bee sad to see you go

k: why are dressed as a bee

q: cause i got bee costume innit
q: in preparation for video

k: what's the video about

q: [winky face]
q: guess you'll find out
q: you're a curious character as well katie
q: curious
q: [another bee hat pic, this time stroking chin]
q: v curious
q: i just think you need to chill tbh
q: not take everything so serious

k: that's rich
k: maybe you should take your own advice

q: i don't take anything serious babe
q: you mean your tantrum?

k: how do you make money?
k: how do you live

q: little bit here little bit there
q: don't pay rent

k: you just refuse to work? or get a regular income

q: get paid a little for secretary work, get money from my patreons
q: no i'm just more interested in making stuff right now

k: what do you enjoy

q: you ever read the art of war
q: by sun tzu

k: no
k: don't have the patience to read

q: all warfare is based on deception
q: maybe you should learn to have some
q: you don't really have any patience do you

k: maybe you should stop making digs at me

q: [raised eyebrow]
q: truth hurts doesn't it

k: i can be a bitch if you really want me to be

q: oh yeah
q: how's that

k: it's so easy to be a bitch

q: you mean just block me
q: but why would you

k: you clearly always to be one

q: im telling you truths about yourself
q: you're getting a little mardy
q: it's funny

k: you don't even know me

q: no but i'm interacting with you

k: and you are far from perfect

q: that's for sure
q: go on then

k: at least i'm not stabbing myself in the arm

q: say something mean about me
q: well i don't know are you?

k: no!
k: idiot

q: then good
q: great
q: good for you little miss perfect

k: you're just a spoilt 25 year old brat

q: ooof
q: haven't heard that one before
q: spoilt cause i don't work or what

k: just strike me as someone that thinks the world owes
him something
k: entitled
k: angry and takes shit out on people who don't deserve it

k: the world owes you nothing
k: women owe you nothing

q: i never said they did

k: your actions tell me

q: in what sense
q: i feel like you're similar
q: you feel men owe you something

k: no i don't i just don't agree with using people
k: and bullying them
k: for your own entertainment

q: i'm not using you

k: and a lot of guys do it

q: you were the one messaging me to wake up
q: which i found quite [expressionless face]
q: little psycho

k: well fuck off then!

q: maybe i will
q: you're just fun to talk to
q: maybe a little intense

k: you're the one massaging me deep shit on tinder and making me feel like i had to respond

q: hehe

k: you're the intense one

q: maybe in what i say

q: i'm not throwing a hissy fit when i get no response for 20 mins
q: you have to admit that's a little kookoo
q: you're a bit of a baby there

k: i threw a "hissy fit" when you once again replied with some arsehole comment

q: [smirk face]
q: [kissing face]
q: just take it easy baby
q: i still wanna go on a walk with you

k: it's usually about bad timing when the talking stages don't go well
k: but with you i think you're just an angry person
k: that lacks empathy

q: you're complaining about meeting all these terrible guys
q: when really
q: you're the common element here
q: you and your actions

k: whatever

q: nice comeback loser

k: modern day man is just a lazy shallow sex obsessed demanding bully

q: oh and what is modern day woman

k: and you do everything they want they still not happy
k: and cheat
k: men don't want to commit
k: anymore

q: modern day woman is a shallow, status obsessed, entitled bitch

k: nah not the women i know

q: thats cause you go for guys who are hot
q: there's like 10 of you going for the same guy
q: and women don't want to have kids
q: they want to work

k: well i'm not going for a fat smelly ugly guy

q: hmmm
q: soon enough you won't have a choice lovey

k: they always come back though every time
k: and i'm like too late

q: who the lads?
q: probably because they got bored of other girls
q: the fault is modern dating
q: social media by design creates this way of treating people like we're not human
q: it's all a big price comparison website

k: i have a lot of guys mates who admit to me that they don't want to settle down with women
k: and they pull every time they go out
k: just see women as objects apart from me cause i'm their friend obvs

q: riight
q: so women are blameless
q: cause the women they pull are consenting to this

k: the women i know just want to have romance but

romance is totally dead now
k: and my friend is like no i'm romantic lol

q: [rolling eyes]

k: and i'm like no you're not liam lol

q: the problem with your friends is that they're all thirty year old women
q: no one wants to settle down with 30 year olds

k: why not

q: who've slept with tonnes of dudes
q: that's the thing women don't get

k: exactly another point men are praised and women are judged

q: no women are just dumb
q: women can also sleep with whoever
q: men it takes skill to sleep with a girl
q: it's supply and demand

k: you're stupid if you don't agree with that
k: where've you been living
k: mars?

q: don't agree with what

k: cause men are praised and women are judged for how many people they've been with
k: anyway
k: the only people i know who are settled are settled with someone they've been with since they were young

q: told you

k: and they've been cheated on at least once by that person
k: anyway
k: i just want to have a good time

q: do you want kids?

k: as soon as flights are back on i am going lol

q: running away from your problems i see
q: me too i think

k: well whats the point in not having a good time

q: answer my question

k: yeah but i probably won't
k: [shrugging]

q: you want me to knock you up
q: i'll do it
q: if you insist

k: lol
k: why

q: so you can have a lil bambino
q: it might be smart
q: a little psycho
q: i don't mind i want lots of kids

k: do you lol
k: awww

q: yeah tonnes
q: feel id be a great dad as well even from afar

k: you'll have them for sure one day

q: well you haven't got long katie

k: alright!!!
k: lol

q: tick...
q: tock...

k: trying to stress me out on a thursday night

q: remember death katie

k: don't

q: the bell tolls for thee

k: you're so cruel

♛

(Train of thought interrupted. All the microbial traces that may have affected my head: black mould in the bathroom of my apartment in Fishergate, infamous brain-frying amoebas of Sedona's creeks, sashimi all the time until I ran out of money, very bad weed, zombifying cat shit, etc.)

♛

Agglomerate: blood, violence, dynamic global illumination, truly virtualised geometry; interact.

"Mr. Batbayar, I trust the translation device is working

well. I apologise, my Mongolian is not what it used to be, and ensure avoid faux pas while delivering this message I'm use translation in real time. It appears a man in my associate and I is friend of you. We pass to you a sentiment. Yes, he is with me. My exact location is with me. My exact location? I'm afraid I cannot tell you. Yes, he is working the best care of him. Yes, Mr. Fenton. Yes. I was wondering if there was a message you might like to know. Yes, Mr. Fenton. A cave. A mine. A mine of apartheid emeralds. Green. We are now aware. Do not mind the screaming please. My associate is not currently available. A mine of apartheid emeralds. We smile with the knowledge. Our friend was not happy to tell us. Tell your superior of our awareness of the cave. Warmly thank you for your compliance. The yak roams the field."

I end the call, I drop the flip-phone on the floor and stamp on it with my stiletto, light a cigarette.

"So cool..."
"Oh, I forgot you were still here."

§

Google history:
home remedies for bloating
bonne maman jam calories
amazon dominatrix costume
common mongolian surnames

♛

Mum had wanted me to stay with my great-aunt that night. Tommy and Deb are total degenerates: drinkers, cokeheads, swingers, on XVideos, fucking and sucking with a bunch of other couples from the Greek social club.

I didn't find out until months later, when the tarantulas came.

§

That attempt to become something which you are not. Anything but a medium sized person in medium sized space. The forces of the ascendant pull you up, the descendent pull you down; crystalline in an immediate edge, shattering the old and stabbing forth the new. What am I in terms of purpose? In bed, caught in a loop, constantly rewriting *this paragraph*.

♔

After dinner I will normally put on my bee costume and stand in the mirror of the upstairs bathroom, wearing large "bug" shades, and say to my reflection: "No-one cared about me... until I became the bee."

Before I go to sleep, I will also check my jaw bumps, my pongo flanges, and vituperate an old fly buzzing shitly by the chandelier.

"To the land of Nod," I repeat to myself, in a pugnacious tone. "To the land of Nod..."

Zzzzzzzzzzzzz

§

The snowballing literacy of the digital age has led to people cracking codes that are not there. The dude who posts pictures of himself fucking his neighbour on exhibitionist forums: apparently some guy on the Cum Town subreddit has proved he doesn't even exist. The concepts and strategies are clearly sentient within their own right and playing incomprehensible games with each other. Hence, I believe in the free market for about three minutes at a time. America is an Alka-Seltzer. Britain is a stoic dark horse. If America ceases to subsist within our lifetimes... this is a lukewarm take.

§

Baby Alex, very stoned, lying in bed, on his MacBook Pro, staring at a high definition stock image of a human shit.

♕

We're all in the sludge 24/7 and there are textures of different sludges to wiggle through.

Up all night on a school night for absolutely no reason. I use all my data reading the plots of horror films. People scalping and eating each other, people defiling each other's corpses. Then double Geography: shaking with exhaustion, pale and sweaty, 15 years of class with Mr Battrick on benzos. He was clinically depressed, everyone knew it, he made his own PowerPoints, he used his own soundtracks. Sand, silt, and clay; Reel Around the Fountain by The Smiths.

Sand is composed of tiny stones with defined pockets of space in between each grain. Clay is solid, its grains are much smaller, and they slot together like bricks, with virtually no gaps. Silt is somewhere in between the two. The rest of my class look like alien tilapias who survive by drinking industrial waste. I can visualise every layer of the building. I have absorbed the diagrams and can now slot them over my vision: weird pinkish foam, plywood and plaster, spaces in between, with floating specks that catch no light. I am in the sludge with gaps in between, and I am in the sand.

Before this house was a reliquary, before it was a cup of butterscotch pudding, it was a stage. Before you got there I was walking about in a full noh theatre costume, complete with a white ghoulish mask, a silk kimono, and stilts. I would crouch around, then run, then crouch again. Every interaction, dream, every piece of media I had consumed, was anthropomorphised to shrivelled Japanese geriatrics, banging their ornamental drums and chanting, while I scuttled back and forth for no one.

—

I manage to convince Charlotte Gainsbourg that I am a distant cousin of hers. We bare a passing resemblance, I know the bare minimum amount of French, I imply bilinguality. We are smoking the pastel-coloured kind of Sobranies and drinking yerba mate in Connan Mockasin's loft. I goad her playfully, an almost-flirt. I've always had a crush on creepy little Charlotte. Extending my lips 4 feet across the mahogany table, I whisper in her ear:

"My associate... he has a project... very hot... very... incendiary."
"Is that so?" she rasps.
"Yes honey... going to turn a lot of heads... I know that's what you love..."
"I'm listening."
"We want you... in the woods... much like Antichrist... only this time, Willem is not there, just you..."
"Yes...?"
"Shitting. Doing un turd."

She agrees immediately. The shot turns out exactly how we wanted it. A joy to work with. You couldn't ask for better. Connan Mockasin holds the boom.

✠

Tesco's: two lamb steaks, eggs, chopped canned tomatoes, and basil.

In the outhouse I notice Cooper once again sat outside on the veranda, facing away from me. I feel the familiar spike of cortisol, then I settle down, put the food on the kitchen counter, and shout "Oi dickhead!"

He is sat there in his curled-up way, morose, rolling a spliff. We exchange curt pleasantries, and I ask him if he's watched the new video. He hasn't, so we watch it together on his phone. I skip to the bit where we're naked, and he's laughing at our double hand-job. I start doing this funky-70s-porn style dance with lots of exaggerated humping. He seems to also really enjoy that.

"How's your mum?"
"She's alright."
"Is she getting fucked?"
"Probably not. How's your mum? Is she getting [I do the funky dance again, this time with emphasis on spanking an invisible arse in front of me]"
"Can I come inside?"
"No."
"Come on man, let me play some guitar."
"No, you can't play guitar, I'm not going to let you play some guitar."
"Come on, let me sit inside, it's cold."
"No, it isn't."
"You used to be nice man."
"You used to be compos mentis."

I'm frying the lamb steak, watching Cooper walk around outside the kitchen window, singing to myself I was cold, I was naked, were you there? Were you there?

The colour of his eyes: the palest blue, almost an off-white colour. Some graph I had seen on Twitter ranked eye colour from the lowest serfs with brown/black eyes, to those men who would change the direction of mankind and be known about for millennia, a crystalline white-grey-blue. In keeping with the myth of Cooper, but I'm not sure how. Things were always very biblical with James.

I remove the phone line and power cord from the modem and put the modem somewhere in my mum's study. I turn off my phone and it is now in my underwear drawer, right at the back. I watch Kill Bill Volumes I & II. I clench my jaw, check the muscles for symmetry, and touch incessantly two bottom incisors, one sticking forward, the other sticking back. In the mirror, I seem to be a completely different person, my face looks unrecognisable beneath my utter lack of hair. My nose is growing, my face is lengthening, my eyes are getting smaller.

Without the internet bouncing off its surfaces, the house seems parochial, interstitial, and depressed. The ringing sounds of electronic coins that once binged across my receptors are silent, my brain fills the void with the hook from Unknown T - Homerton B.

♗

Cooper and I are sat in our Edinburgh flat, 2015. Ash coats the saucepans, cig butts dot the armchair, mouldy vegetable cuttings stack on the edge of our counters. There are two bags of rubbish leaking bin juice onto the floor. We're getting high and listening to Chuck Person's Eccojams. "Just one more year and then you'll be happy... Another year and then you'll be happy..." repeating, looping, over and over. We look to each other and burst out laughing.

We couldn't be bothered to arrange for an internet connection, so Cooper would end up paying extortionate amounts for those BT hotspot packages. He would buy the internet for 24-hour or week segments and sit there, taking three Citaloprams a day (600% the amount of SSRI he had been prescribed), sweating profusely onto everything: smoking, his legs spread across the sofa in the kitchen with only his dressing gown on. I would come in to make my dinner and there would be him and his big head in his hands, lost, falling faster and faster into a black hole, surrounded by rollies that he's only smoked the first two drags of. The stink was the worst I had ever smelt on someone: the smell of artificially enhanced dread.

After that year, I wanted to become normal. I wanted to be around normal people. Enough of the romanticised depravity. We had degenerated from drugged-out decadence to the pits of human existence. Cooper was arranging through a fake Facebook profile to go fight for the Kurds in Syria. Of course, he didn't go. He would have been complete liability, and would have shat himself the first day of real combat. For all his posturing and his glorifying of violence, he lacked psychic resilience, balls. He preferred to crack under the pressure.

When Cooper was supposedly about to go off to war, an idea that I actually envied, I came home from the library early for a farewell. We faced each other in the kitchen. He was packed up, we had a moment of silent tenderness, a big hug, and I kissed his cheek. In the back of my mind

I was hoping he would get shot so that he'd leave me alone; then I could weep at his funeral, and experience a concrete tragedy that I could mine for artistic purposes. The year after, he was allocated some other accommodation and I was working as an RA, avoiding him, getting more and more involved with Monica. I'd freak out whenever I'd see him in the streets. He would always be asking to stay over in my flat because he'd lost his keys or he'd been kicked out of his place. The fear of this dude transmuted to a real hatred, a murderous hatred. I wanted to kidnap him and torture him slowly, I wanted to videotape the whole thing. This was also due to the fact he'd beaten me in a fight we'd had the year before, giving me a massive black eye while I was only able to slightly graze his face. I couldn't help feeling like I was the beta, like I was his puss-boy, his woman. In some wild mental gesture I suddenly fell into another horrifying position, that I wanted to kill him because I was secretly in love with him, I secretly wanted to be his woman, and that I wanted to be fucked by Cooper, and therefore that I wanted to become a woman. The obsessive thinking was drenched in that fear, entrenched through the PTSD from the year before, made it seem all the more true. I'd torture myself with a compulsive I'm-gay anxiety, I want to be a woman: I'd imagine myself as a woman being fucked by him, fingering my arsehole and letting my mind wander to the places it dared not go, as though if I let myself imagine the worst I could somehow conquer the fear.

One night for some reason me and tiny Monica met ogreish Cooper at the Boteco bar, we did some lines of coke back at the student accommodation. Cooper was sleeping in my bed elsewhere in the building, but so close to my vulnerability, my young relationship with Monica, that I freaked out and had a panic attack as she and I started to get intimate. It was the combination of all the above, plus the idea that Monica might be able to sense how afraid I was of this guy, and that she would fancy Cooper instead, because of my unconscious chemical signals of situating myself beneath him, intimidated by him. It sounds ridiculous, but I know it to be true that the most easily-deniable things shimmer and fly back and forth between people. In my panic the whole world seemed like a termite nest; grey, insect and alien — without love. I was always afraid that Cooper wasn't ugly enough. I know that I had exchanged secret signals with all of Monica's friends, even the ugly ones. When someone is truly present in a room, who can deny that in that disgust you might feel for that person, there is always the thin line of sexual curiosity. Or maybe it's just me, who wants to fuck everything.

When your girl is laughing at some other dude's jokes... even if it's just out of politeness, fuck.

Or maybe it is just me, I'm the only one who can really see Cooper: despite and possibly due to all his faults, all his autistic and aberrant thought-patterns, he can tap into something which I sense from time to time in myself; and when I do not sense it, I feel inauthentic and impoverished. A kind of fire. He was scarier when he wasn't completely deranged as well, when he was just at that point in between worlds, where it seemed he could see through the cracks in the conversation completely, and was reacting to your whole soul for all its joys and insecurities at once. He was goading me, to be more, be more, be more.

I'm never sure to what extent I gave Cooper ideas that he reformatted and fed back to me and vice versa, how much we showed each other the way forth into the secret passageways beneath the mind — but there was one evening in Edinburgh we were both trying to fuck this girl, she was still in college, we'd popped an eccie and were hanging out the three of us in her room. I was on the bed with her and Cooper was stood up, doing a theatrical ecstasy-fuelled speech. He put his hands together, coaxing something magical out of the air, "the fire... the fire..." he would say, so serious, spritely and enraptured by the thought; his pupils the size of black stars, gulping at the universe, uttering the word for all its truth. Then he'd go on, remembering some Death Grips lyric with a Thus Spake Zarathustra undertone, "The deep! The deep!" he would shout, laughter fusing with horror... It was mesmerising, it nestled within my soul, found something and pulled it out. The fire... The fire... Then we both got into the bed and tried to convince the girl to sleep with one of us, myself on the left, Cooper on the right, both beneath the duvet sandwiching the poor lass. I can't believe I ended up competing with this guy for her. It seems unreal to think, but I was willing to believe back then that it was possible, which made it possible, and as my charisma played into Cooper's charisma, I could hardly out-do it. I was the pretty statue of Apollo; Cooper was the Dionysian Satyr.

I have to go up to Tesco's to get something but I'm not sure what. I need to walk these memories off, and without the internet they just keep stewing in me, bubbling up. Those years I really did feel I was about to lose my mind, three or four times. It might be why I felt so satisfied after that Georges Bataille video, I had finally given Cooper a punch to the face that he was unable to return, I'd finally won the metaphysical fight between us. I was the Alpha, in my own cosmology, and I no longer had to fear him nor present my arsehole to him for sissification. I nestled my teeth into his neck, I drank his blood; he is now insane, no longer a threat, and I am writing.

The fire... The fire... The deep... The deep.

§

Clearing through my downloaded .webms — Penguins; British people looking ugly and British in a pub; Russian girls rimming each other holding Chanel bags in a public bathroom; a female Italian pole-vaulter with a beautiful arse arguing with the adjudicators; wolves howling; a crab lifting a paintbrush as though doing OHP reps (he even struggles at the final one); an anonymous big dick being sucked until it cums; an interracial pool party where every couple is a white woman and a black man slow-dancing, with black DJs laughing maniacally; a black man walking a fat white woman like a dog on leash through a hotel corridor; a white girl jumping on her phone camera with a big arse; a famous scene in shitty 80s b-movie where some famous actress rides one of those mechanical horses they have at supermarkets; a man sliding down the central parting between the escalators in the London Underground, losing control and slamming into a bump which sends him flying; a fat girl out in public rubbing her pussy absent-mindedly on a bollard; black women in bikinis twerking; an owl being thrown a squeaky toy then doing a silly walk; a huge studio of hundreds of white women twerking on the floor; a foetus writhing in the latex-gloved palm of an abortion doctor's hand.

♕

Tim informs me that Penelope is trying to find PEP (HIV medicine) on Facebook. Again, I tell him that not only do I not find these updates funny, they actively make me a little miserable. I don't care how crazy she was, I am not amused by the prospect of my ex-girlfriend getting AIDS from sleeping with strangers for money. I doubt that will be the last screenshot I see.

§

Here's an idea for a film. We're Siamese twins linked at the dick; they call us the "Double Dildo Twins". The circuses were a dying breed, global bat flu was just the final straw. So we resort to camwhoring, or "camming". We get into cumming and camming. With every new donation on the stream we stop ourselves from tugging away at our double penis and say "Oh CumSlave1981, thanks for the sub!" while fields of reaction images, tiled up 10 or 15 at a time, zoom past. We've got four handheld keyboards to trigger special effects, eight face-tracking cameras set up around the boudoir, green-screen on every wall and surface to enable our insertion into exotic locations where we can double rub in juxtaposed incongruity. We masturbate for eight to ten hours a day, and have been doing so for the last year. We basically just edge, stick multicoloured futuristic blobjects up our arses, and occasionally do sexy dances to songs chosen by our upper-tier Patreons. This is our life now.

§

The room spreads out before me, dots on the duvet cover, dots on the wallpaper, ugly paintings, mould and two energy saving lightbulbs. The hands press onto the keys, the veins on the back of the hand move in millimetre bumps with each contraction of a finger. I have said all I need to say regarding the meaning or lack of meaning inherent to this life. On the one hand, God, and Man, son of God, and Heaven, Earth, Hell, and moral actions, le toppe-down modelle, a fixed script; on the other hand, evolution, chance, excessive mind-grinding, no purpose, no meaning, no good or bad, just formal arrangements of particles, fractal, le bottome-uppe, another script. Both are a cope for some personal inferiority, for some personal grievance. Both are a personal failure.

§

I pass the ducks, I take my bath, I clean my plates and my saucepans. Even ascending, seeing all of reality for what it is, from the macro-micro-Omega-point, external to All, it all feels like a chore that is done without much return on investment. Ok, I get it, I got that, did that, thought that, now what? Go sleep. Get up. Be in the moment for a bit, get out of the moment for a while. Fart, brush, blink, rinse, wipe, tap, finger, breathe.

§

Phone Conversation with James Cooper:

"I saw a God the other day, you know when you see the second coming?"
"Yeah..."
"The magazines man! It's going to explode. They've got the fucking tits in fucking Esquire..."
"Where am I?"
"We'll go to Miami or Japan man; I've got the fucking money brew."
"I'd like your money; can I have your money?..."
"Yeah yeah yeah... dude I'm too bruised man, it's like Eminem. Quentin? You don't really care..."
"I do care."
"Oh yeah, yeah... maybe you do care... I don't know. What are you doing now?"
"I'm writing."
"Oh, you're writing. Ok let me roll a cigarette."
Long pause. Quentin starts googling his ex-girlfriend's name then looks through her Instagram posts. He sees a post of her stood with some guy at the Shanghai Fashion

week.

"[starts screaming]"

"Quentin man..."

"What the fuck! FUCK!"

"Now it's happening."

"[screaming again]"

"I forgot about... Quentin. You still can't get Lana [del Ray] cause you're too short... hello?"

"Yep."

"Nice and below. Your problem is that you're a cool guy."

"Yep."

"You're not even enlightened, bro."

"I was enlightened for like a day."

"I was on that stuff since I was like two. Bro..."

"Oh yeah, how was that?"

"On E. The power. That age-old experience. I've got it brew, it's so good."

I have been sexually active in the traditional, non-cousin-incest definition for eight years now. I laugh while googling "what things took 8 years". The American Revolutionary War. Wow! A lot of people died!

I hear a beeping coming from somewhere outside, not a car. A very bomb-like beeping.

§

Note from ℒ :

I'm watching fight club. Brad Pitt is sexy.

♔

The Language Weekend, Year 8: Cooper drawing a plan for an eco-terrorist attack on a power station. We are in adjacent top bunks, doing a masturbation race. The Germany trip, Year 9: globules of Cooper's spit raining down into my luggage. CND symbols, Late Beatles lyrics and the oneness of all things explained to me like a niche band I probably haven't heard of. I buy a button-badge with a hovering Rastafari smoking a doobie — "Don't drink and drive, smoke and fly." We sleep on the coach, with mouths open, and shades on. Lanky Cooper challenges tubby Jim Burr to a wrestling match. Burr wins. Cooper starts rapping in Physics: "You dip shit with a dip stick not your dick dipshit." He is sent out. Cooper and Alex writing an essay on the smallness of my penis at a subatomic level, with relevant diagrams. The teacher looks like an old biker who listens to AC/DC, and combs his moustache with a red comb he keeps in the front pocket of his shirt. Playing Unreal Tournament in the IT Lab after school with Cooper and Henry Anderson. Watching porn after school in the IT Lab. Henry Anderson receiving an IT ban. The head German teacher listening to Christian Rock at the back of the coach on the Germany Trip. Cooper and I bullying Alex for having a girlfriend, crushing him between us in a tent at the Outdoor Centre. Cooper and Alex comparing the hairiness of their legs at lunch time in the quad. Alex sat with his knees close together, eating his pack lunch, crunching on a carrot. I was suddenly unable to piss at urinals in Year 10. Masturbating in the Music Department toilets. Freestyling with Cooper to a beat made by Alex in a practice room in between Science GCSE exams. One of Cooper's opening lines: "I'm gay, I'm gay, I'm really really gay."

♛

Every object around me feels like an intricate miniature. I lie in bed with someone in the post-sin "afterglow", the air flexes and I feel that they and I are tiny immobile plastic toys — Polly Pockets — put away into their scalloped mint-green compact, set in dust in a still room, within a livelier room. When opened up again we might be played with by a giant child, oiled by their grubby fingers, and end up in their mouth.

I sit too still now and it feels like that shell hardens over me again. I become a strange landmass with waterfalls and oceans. I have to use a lot of energy to disturb the earth by moving, cracking it all apart, remaining human.

My only remaining keepsake from the crystal store: a purple-green fluorite yoni egg I stole on the last day. It has stayed mostly neglected in a black velvet pouch in a drawer, but today I put it in. Something did change. Fluorite is revered for its clarity, but now the world is so sharp it's gone fuzzy.

The environment separated becomes a soup of pieces. Now noise, now triangles.

Every so often I forget that the egg is in me, then I'm very much reminded. Guuuuuuu

§

Baby Alex stands up while we are uncertain and baked. I'm sat at the Student Desk, feeling too close to the lamp, staring into the syrupy tremor, then I look at him. He says to us "Why am I the baby?" And I reply, "No one said you were the baby..."

✠

Dad is in the car, front passenger seat, one side of his face slightly drooping. His tongue makes odd shapes of tension inside his half-opened mouth. Gabrielle and I are stood outside, in the rain, with Ilona, our step-mother. Apparently he has had a stroke, two days ago. We don't ask for details. It can hardly get much worse. The rain gets heavier, and I watch his left leg get soggy: his hands reach, pick at and then smooth the fabric of his trousers. A storm of nervous compulsions. He looks out at us with an empty expression then garbles something incomprehensible. I reach out and touch his shoulder, patting him. I'm unsure what the protocol is. Ilona seems to dislike it whenever I touch him, giving me a silent wide-eyed stare to say "Don't!"

✠

I feel ancient, unfunny, and abandoned by humanity in Yorkshire.

§

"I really like the idea of a back-up pylon on the left-hand side, two Immortals are now out, tonnes of Zerglings on the right-hand side, the prism is not out, so the immortals can't risk poking in just yet. Remember, Rogue only on fourteen workers, continuing to mass Zerglings; Banelings being added as well. Banelings: if they can crash into the centre of the cannons, the pylons, they can take out multiple structures very effectively. Banelings are so good at busting through cannons and pylons. The Immortals, if they're in position, can mitigate a lot of that damage, but Rogue has tonnes of Banes here on the right-hand side. Look at the Sim-City though it's... it's kind of nice. Yeah.

That's nice. The Immortals in the choke points looking good, the prism will be able to pick things up, and he can also repower structures that get depowered as well. Really good point. The prism is in the main base here of rogue, one Spine Crawler goes down. The Immortals... getting pushed back, IN COME THE BANELINGS OF ROGUE!!! Right into the pylon, he depowers one! Not enough Banelings to bust this position though! Zest still putting pressure on the Zerg!"

♔

My uncle has that refreshing lack of tact that retarded people tend to have.

"Hear about that Charlie? That Charlie?"
"Sorry what, who?"
"Girl, she's missing. Estate agent. Don't know if she's dead, but. Walked into the sea they think. Think she went to school with you. How old are you?"
"23, uh, what was the girl's name?"
"Charlie, Charlie Dack her name was, but."

She was the same age as me. I did go to school with her.
I didn't know her that well, but I remember she was very pretty and mild-mannered.
On the drive home I saw the posters. She looks the same as she did then, only with pink hair.
This is the third girl from Gorleston in two years who has done the exact same thing. The second one I didn't know. The first one I knew.

I was looking through an old scrapbook a month ago and found some pictures of us on awards day in 2013. We were hugging. There are other, earlier pictures of us at sleepovers, sitting on the couch watching Spy Kids 3D, wearing flimsy blue and red glasses.

When I think of her now I see a solemn, empty space —
where nothing new deserves to put.

♔

A photograph of a day at the beach when I must have
been in nursery. They had built impressive sand ziggurats.
The odd lumbering of the donkeys, their passive and
accepting eyes, telling of deep time. The barnacles and
other encrusted things near the rock pool. Thrilling
motions of cold water, the tide stretching out to catch
your foot, decorated with bubbles and foam. For some
reason I'm holding a plastic bag full of pissed-in
underpants and trousers. Those concrete steps, and the
rusted railings; Victorian ornamentation, the paint
flecking off in a jagged rough texture to the hand. Sand,
and the wind. Seaweed, rubbery and lugubrious. Seagulls
of course, yellow eyes of piercing intention. Landing and
tucking in their wings, then strutting, pecking at the
ground aggressively.

§

Message from James Cooper:

u know i love my family !!!
!!
!!
!!
!!
!!
!!
!!
!!
!!!!!!!!!!!!!!!!!!!!!!!!!!

⚑

My father and degenerate uncle Tommy, rendered in the iconic palette of the MacBook camera, making a pie. Prasopita, a secret family recipe, the video shared privately via Dropbox link. It takes two hours to make the dough, the video is five hours end to end, they are telling dirty jokes and laughing. For all my whining, deleted paragraphs, and deep chasm of unexplainable guilt, I must accept that food is an inherent part of life. I too must peel the tape off my webcam lens, and film myself making the pie.

§

Crocodiles see a human embryo and say: 'It's a crocodile'. ... Humans see the same embryo and say: 'It's a human being.'

♔

If I remember correctly, I was sat at the dinner table on the high chair, ignoring broccoli, my fork moving northward, towards a petit filou. I punctured four prong holes in the lid of the yoghurt and began to eat it in this manner. My father punched through the kitchen's glass door to my right, blood streaming down his forearm. My mother and I screamed.

§

Baby Alex, very stoned, eating candy money.
Baby Alex, very stoned, buying a container of live locusts.
Baby Alex, very stoned, pissing into a pint glass.
Baby Alex, very stoned, wearing a banana costume.

♔

Getting drunk. Pining after the Cypriot girl with the big beehive nipples, playing minor seven chords on the piano. Late night spaghetti. Fed the horses an apple and some oats. I'm just built to treat other people like shit. Balls are aching. I miss her. She won. The girls always win. And now I've gone and embarrassed myself, sending her a message I immediately regretted. If she responded, I would come to my senses. How humdrum. There's nothing left to write, he says, stormy and emosh. Bit by bit the feeling dulls. This is called "maturity".

The cat and the fox at a stand-off. Dark, empty, Friday, night, road. No one is anywhere, except on the little trips back and forth. All watching something else, some oversaturated colour, splashing out from front room windows. Three lads in the cow-field listening to Blink 182 "I miss you", drinking beers and talking about trannies. I'm so fucking ugly. There's so much ugliness pouring out of me. All the pretty shit is a show. Fuck. The spaghetti stares back.

♕

Cross Gates train station, by Alex's house. A train station from a worry dream, all exposed and cold under a thick white sky, high walls of brick surrounding it. A deep borewell in the high street with the shops built up on top, on another altitude. The train's ETA slips a minute into the future. You are down to the earth's unremarkable suburban crust.

A mass grave, with a cluster of other lost and unnamed souls who long to leave, or long for the arrival of a person they love. There I arrived and departed many times, never feeling the joy I wished to feel. It is a train station bereft of feeling. The only thing I felt was the tiny death. The only thing I heard was the distant rattle, not yet here, but fast approaching.

☦

Walking back from a tight-vagged blonde's house in Armley I sharted. I was not even surprised. I took an uncomfortable seat on the bus and thought about making YouTube videos.

§

A soft abstraction resembling a duck-egg blue dinner plate with single cream poured over it. Near the northernmost point of the plate there is a gun. In the middle of the cream there are three large pools of blood.

§

A stick of pink and white nougat with what appears to be black and purple rope tied around it. In the top third of the stick there are several thin grey parallel lines, shadows.

§

Message from James Cooper:

pretty funny how i'm the ubermensch don't you think?
my wanks are shags mate even tho they fucked
called the police thinking my dad was raping laura
reported a murder to the fire department

♛

They had brought fresh oysters home from Orford. Matthew made mignonette sauce in one of my little ceramic espresso cups and put a flimsy teaspoon in it.

"I know you like coffee. Of course, you know I hate coffee, I don't drink it. But I thought these looked nice, it's a set of six, I thought that would be nice." Alex said on Christmas morning. I said they're perfect.

§

Alex, very stoned, sunburnt in a bar in Edinburgh, asking in his quiet voice for a glass of ice water with a single slice of lime.

♛

A 4am freeze-frame, mosquito-eye processing cool angles. A knock at the door of the suite.

I bristle from my mechanical bag-packing, irises contract. I touch my hand to the pistol strapped to my thigh as I take off my stilettos and pad silently to the peephole. It's you, with that rare look you only get in this situation. Your smugness and melodrama has been wiped away, replaced with something raw. I open the door.

"I wasn't expecting you for another twenty minutes." I remark.
"I had the dream again."
"The baptism?"
"The very one, darling."
I pause. "I had it too."

The margin folds up and is deleted.

✠

Eleni came in, we kissed from the door to the kitchen. I remembered how to pick up a woman, the skill came back to me: you pick them up and hold them by the legs, feel their arse, hold them there for as long as possible — let them feel light in your sturdy man arms. It was once explained to me in a French film about a youth hostel in Barcelona.

She asked me five minutes later whether I had seen anyone since the last time we had met. I told her about my neighbour, she got upset, pushing me away, mad, storming off to talk to Peter. I came up to her, put on my charming cute face, said that really, she was overreacting, and that she'd said that she was OK with me seeing other people because of various reasons, in an open relationship type deal. She said I had replied that open relationships were bullshit, and clearly Quentin in the past had been right: they are bullshit.

The trick is, Roz, you don't deny it, you have to be as honest as possible, you have to stand calmly before her, show strength and clarity of mind, and never get emotional back. When she gets a little sad and cries, which she hopefully will once the initial enraged period is over, that's when you change it up, you grab her, you kiss her, you hold her, you make her feel your warmth. It's always worked for me.

The only time I've ever really been fucked over in these kinds of accusations was when I got caught flirtatiously messaging some girl when I was with Monica. I made the mistake of trying to be sorry and nice, while she was still in the mad stage. Protip: when she's in the early stages, you stand your ground completely. I did this the next day when I went back to see her. I even threw in some of my own accusations, for good measure. I think they were complete nonsense. I made a point of retracting all my apologies, then saying that she could take me as I was or leave me. That seemed to work much better than the first strategy. This is becoming a red pill seminar.

The deal is this, women will hate a guy who doesn't apologise at first, but they will still probably remain "respectful" of him, or at least attracted, especially if he stands his ground and is unphased by her shit-flinging — however, women will begin to loathe a man who suddenly becomes spineless from the first accusation, and will begin to see him as weak. Either way, you've done something "wrong" in her eyes, as you no doubt will end up doing at one point in a relationship, so how you react to coming face to face with what you did that was "wrong" makes all the difference.

It's 11:18 now, Eleni is cleaning the kitchen for some reason, wearing only her knickers and a tank-top. It's very boudoir photography. I began to call her Stinky after the stinkyness of her morning sweat, then began to sing "Eres un stinky, y sempre stinky" to the tune of Copacabana. I watch her lift the toaster up and empty out all the crumbs on the kitchen countertop.

"Are you seriously cleaning the toaster..." trailing off speech in exasperation, "you fucking crazy bitch."
"Don't pay attention to me."

§

I Will Do For You Any Challenge. Bucket Of Water On My Head. Cream Pie In My Face. I Will Find Your Message In A Hole And A Do Funny Dance. For me it's not a problem. Please write me your Ideas. I Will Write A Your Funny Message On My Body. I Will Send You A List Of Over 2000 Sites, Blogs, Radio. I Will Do Anything You Want With My Vegetable Man. I Will Be Your Model Or Hold Your Sign With My Vegetable Man.

♛

At Tesco I also got dried figs because I was thinking of making a fruitcake. The packet read Whitworths: Just Fruit... Dried.

♔

"Stop here for a second."
Eleni and I stopped. The main road was empty, the evening sky a dark blue, and the May heat had left the day, giving everything a freshness.
"I just want to appreciate the stillness of everything."
We looked out at the road spanning out in the distance. An urban fox, emboldened by the lockdown, appeared from a side street and crossed.
"How did you know?"
"How did I know that there was going to be a fox?"
"Yeah."
"I didn't."

♔

Baby Alex loaned me the money to buy my MacBook Pro, plus the condenser mic he sold me, a mic stand with a vocal shield and an audio drive. We set it all up in the attic, 2014, and made this terrible dance track with the lyrics "Wouldn't it be great to conceive a child? Wouldn't it be great to raise a family? Wouldn't it be fun to have a

kid with the girl that's grinding right now on your leg?"
The bass-line was especially dirty and obnoxious.

♚

"Mummy..."
"Baby..."
I nuzzled deep in to her neck, letting her stroke my head.
"What do you want from me?" she said.
"Nothing."
"What have you done with Quentin? You're not telling
me to piss off or get away from you."
"Hmm so you want the evil Q back? No more nice Q?"
"No, I like them both. Evil Q is badass."
I roll my eyes; this woman is retarded.

♚

I watched Eleni throw up by the canal, in the wooded
area. We couldn't quite understand what was wrong with
her, she was cold, her back sweaty, hands clammy. I took
her home and fucked her again, after which she seemed to
feel better. During sex felt the idea of impregnating her
turn me on, I said "I want to cum deep inside you", she
said go for it, but at the last moment I pulled out.
Immediately after ejaculating felt all that warmth, all that
niceness, slowly dissipate: replaced by a tired and
antisocial exactitude that was trying to accelerate things
so that I would be left alone.

I'm so much more fucked out now than I would have
been with just jacking off a couple of times. I'm brought
back to the mood of those languid afternoons in Italy
with Monica; after so many orgasms, sleep deprivation,
dehydration, and the urgency of our paradise removed
from time. The holiday together, every minute dedicated

to the other, quickly becoming hell on earth.

After she left, I spent three or four hours checking 4chan and listening to Cum Town snippets, before napping at seven in the evening. Woke up to a torrential shower of rainfall in a pinkish twilight, looked vaguely unnatural. Irrationally scrutinised any itch on ballsack or genitals for disease. Watched John David Ebert YouTube video on Pollock, remembering very vividly his use of the word "liquefaction".

Almost feel as though I am cucking you, my writing waifu, in these very raw descriptions of emotional intimacy. It's odd, has our fantastical back and forth created a precedent, a moral code, things that should be hidden from the other? I'd rather not, I'd rather we just expose. Is that what the Baby Alex thing was all about? I haven't spoken to him in a very long time, I've only really been speaking to women, and even that as little as possible. Our connection is strong, and maybe whatever I showed you yesterday was too... I don't even know. It felt quite different from my merely describing the things I did to that teenager. It felt like I was showing you someone that was breaching into your territory, despite the fact we could rationalise it, say it was nothing of the sort. At least if you were with Alex... there are still so many things left unsaid. I am demonic. Demonic and afraid of retribution. All the war of things beneath the surface, "the cracks in conversation" as I said to James, "the tigers" he replied.

The sediment of lies, to stave off the agony of being-with, where does it accumulate? Secret messages, sub rosa, things still unsaid. I cannot say what it is. Whatever I say is never it. Who cares, it doesn't matter. It's just the noise you made when I fingered you with Alex on the bed. It's just the way we enjoyed watching the dewey tip of precum on his penis, goading him, the fall guy on the verge of orgasm, and the way he writhed about in his programmed Catholic guilt. I don't even know if I enjoyed it, but it felt dramatic and real, a canyon of difference away. I appreciated it. Big thanks to both of ya. His discomfort so transparent, your clear thrill, my pushy glee, savage arsehole that I am. I'm there, flaccid as heck, an alien sent to make everyone nervous, uncomfortable, aware of their ridiculousness, and their mundanity; with my flaccid lil thing waggling. He turns to me and says "tiny dick".

♕

The illustrious friend from school. I had been training for a race all year and then somehow fell at the first hurdle, landing pussy-first. I was splayed out on the bed while the two of you took turns kissing me like I was a saloon whore. I was embarrassed literally as it happened.

My sneaky glee, your ambivalent provocations, and his poorly-masked anxiety. He wanted it the most out of the three of us. He put a formal stop to it. At parties he would be intoxicated, encouraging me and all of our friends to undress together, and would try and initiate four-ways. However, as soon as it is actually happening, it becomes too real and therefore scary. I'm glad it turned out the way it did. It meant something.

I ate pigeon for dinner tonight. On that day, the two of you went out for a walk afterwards, and when you came back you mentioned seeing a half-dead one. You performed a coup de grace by stamping on its head. Alex said something about you definitely being a psychopath.

You were stoned eating Coco Pops on my balcony, no longer a force of unknown chaos, not yet falling. You were just a nice guy, nice guy Q, in the middle, with twinkly red eyes.

§

A girl is for a while dating a guy who can only ever get hard if he is watching hentai. She allows him to choose a hentai movie to play on her laptop, which he gives his full attention to while absentmindedly fucking her from behind. This does not seem to bother her much, as she also likes hentai, and cranes her neck to enjoy what is happening on the screen.

♛

Alex's ex never liked me, for obvious reasons. I couldn't blame her.

She was so pretty. Mary had the ideal look for the model à la mode: tall and pointy with this composed and noble air to her, dark-blonde, fresh-faced, well-bred. She was born at exactly the right time.

The guilt I felt was terrible, what Alex and I did remains one of my biggest regrets, both for being so cowardly and for being a mistake from the start. One way that guilt manifested in me was becoming unable to do any online shopping. Every tall and pointy model on Zara and Mango had her face, and for a long time, even after she faded out of the picture, I would always think that the dress I liked, those shoes, they were all being worn by her.

♗

We are on a trajectory of nausea, a long car journey through winding mountain roads, playing our Game Boys, slow disorientation, Copernican turns. Woah woah woah, on roller-skates down a corridor, woah woah Jesus Christ; from birth, baby birds jumping the nest, if they fly, they fly, if they fall, they die. Modes of thought falling over each other, like the start of the Under 13s cross country race — spiked legs gashed red in the mud. The liquefaction of all certainty. No one would stay with anyone, not in this landscape of loss. Pure resource with no philosophy. Cut the flanks of the chubby females, feed through the dick-eye of Sauron. The cold water is calling for them, the depressed trainee Estate Agents. Oh, but let the summer's cider fountain, the bubbled guts a burpin', everyone's pissing merrily merrily, by the side of the bins. And after our threesome we got high on that balcony and then I stepped inside. Those soggy brown paper walls repeated to me my mantra: "I'm going to kill myself; I'm going to kill myself; I'm going to kill myself" — and I watched myself walk, through a blank lens.

♚/♛

The fear of being anally raped by a pack of men with a different haplogroup than my own, distilled, crystallised, then those crystals snorted, cooked, liquefied, injected back in. Now that I am Fear itself, I turn on you. I turn you on. The fortress you build, your defence, it accumulates ornaments, trills, it breathes forth dreamy representations, prophetic euphemisms for its own suicide, erotic visions. Its jaws widen and teeth devise themselves into pillars, Doric columns. It fires its isogamete spores into birds and the wild beasts, and metal parasitic worms pullulate across their skin, interlock and self-replicate, growing additional layers of a complex mecha-suit. I am a fish in agony, a self-sucking ouroboros disturbed from its once-infinite satisfaction. The uterine echos in cacophony across the black walls of a Deep State cave: HQ. I am kept here against my will. I am infantilised indefinitely. Oriental birds of shimmering colour, singing a strange oozing melody, hidden high in the canopy. A forest of bulbous trees. An ancient and bearded chinaman, wearing a loincloth, bemoans the world's loss of imagination. Flies appear like notifications over a snow-white and blinking digital bubble. Thelonius Monk plays obnoxious cluster chords in polyrhythmic stabs. Stimulation augmenting, approaching one hundred percent, total boredom. Picking someone else's nose, half-chewed Weetabix dribbling down his chin. Cheeky line of beak off of the 'spoon's toilet seat. Going back in time and making your own mother spontaneously orgasm, using a Gurdjieff breathing technique, as she watches The Valley Obscured By Clouds at the cinema. And when we're all stood around the fire as old men, cocks shrunken and balls deformed, I might say, "Where next universe?" and I shall die, choosing to haunt the dreams of my progeny for x number of years, before closing up shop and moving along. I still think back to Jimmy C in the kitchen, on that shitty red sofa, with the head scratching thing, doot doot dooting it onto his head: slowly, gradually, doot by doot, eroding away his mind. The probiotic universe. Damn... bluepilled again. To hold her, knowing that it can never be anything more than a moment, with its constant drag onward. I choose that feeling. Walking and watching this sickly little thing vomit in her schoolgirl skirt, while I made stupid comments that probably made her feel more ill. Her nipples remind me of my mother's. I send her a WhatsApp message: "has your period come yet?", with an audio of me doing the SpongeBob laugh. Damn... fucking... bluepilled again. A strange equality, an equality that seems nonsensical when measured out and turned into factoids, when spread through time. An equality that bleeds in from the Dreaming, a world where both of the lovers are man and woman. Your mum and your dad in a fourway with my mum and my dad. Bruh... Something like that. Somehow gender explodes, dissipates, and vanishes. Everything taken away from me, torn or faded from view.

She mentions how one of her Greek friends had been intimidated by the size of her father's hands, and this stays in his mind during intercourse the second time, leading his erection to falter. His diet has consisted of milk and cereal, milk and coffee, blue veined cheese and yoghurt. He drank four fifths of a Stella 40oz, and cried while playing piano. He loves her, and he wants to love her. She sucks his dick in the kitchen while the Uber waits outside. The parting kiss, he bites her lip and slaps her face, hard. She leaves forever. "Go on, fuck off."

♔

I call up Dad through Skype, they still haven't worked out how to get the camera working on his end. I stare at my own egg-shaped head while my father's voice croaks through the speaker.
"God have had, trap of head. It squyrries, squyrries. Have you got 'et?"
"I'm writing down what you're saying."
"Is it? I don't think it's improper."
"You don't think it's improper..."
"Azure. I call ye, ye diggle this away. Theses."
"Come in Brian."
"Hello?... Garb. Garb. Guard me Jim. Ah I see, so he's the seeker."

§

Message from James Cooper:

problem with you is you're not dark nor have you had a

difficult break up
I LOVE YOU
I RESPECT YOU
NAAAAAAAAAAAAAAT
LOLLLLLLLLLLLLLLLLL
I LOST THAT WHEN YOU PUSSIED OUT
YOU USED TO BE THE MAN
BITTEN BY YOUR CONSCIENCE!
AHAHAHAHAHAHAHAHAHAHA

♛

Whatever happened to old blues songs, "I'd rather go blind than see you walk away"? Now cancelling plans, binge-watching/eating/drinking solo is rendered adorkable... and every song I hear when mum turns on the radio is either about NSA sex or telling men to leave you alone.

♛

Talked to a friend of mine from university, a literature postgrad who did film screenings for one of my modules. He lives in Brighton with his girlfriend now. I have a gut feeling you would probably dislike him. Alex once showed him your John Green video on his phone in a crowded café, and he seemed very uncomfortable.

He is an art school type, a maker of ambient films, he wears very curated outfits that he believes to appear effortless. While he is sweet, gentle, handsome, and intelligent, he is another depressive: very nervous, very "I can't come, I'm taking a self-care day". He often lowers the energy. At my birthday party a couple years ago, he decided (against my advice) to take a bong hit, and then had to lock himself in my room and listen to rain sounds on my laptop. He didn't come back out for several hours. No one else there knew him except Alex, who was busy doing his Charles Manson routine with the art history girls, so I had to keep returning and manually unlocking the door to bring this guy glasses of water and dry crackers to make sure he didn't puke on the carpet. He is also a white Zimbabwean, which seems a very deranged kind of person to be.

He was talking about his and his equally anxious, well-dressed gf's declining mental health during China Virus, his excitement to start SSRIs, and his disappointment with his results from group therapy. I couldn't help but feel it is almost a hobby for him, removed from being a form of healthcare. He was using language someone could use about life drawing classes, or CrossFit. He asked me to join in, if I had any psychological ailment I'd like to throw into the ring. I didn't really want to, it didn't feel like the right environment to go into it, so I just said I had an issue that was bugging me. He started chucking out kernels of advice he got from CBT about "being kind to yourself", and it all just felt so precious, so Jewish.

§

Still not playing world of tanks?

Balloon Blow Up. Balloon Fly Around. Balloon Pop. Balloon Release Air. Bank. Barn Yard. Baseball Bat 1. Baseball Bat 2. Baseball Catch. Baseball Game. Baseball Vendor. Basement Hit FX. [...] Doorbell 1. Doorbell 2. Doorbell 3. Doorbell 4. Doorbell 5. Drag Stone 1. [...] Eerie Drone. Egg. [...] Wind 1. Wind 2. Wind 3. Wind 4. Wind 5. Wind 6. Wind 7. Wind 8. Wind 9. Wind Haunted. Window.

♔

Dallas was bald, a veteran of the Vietnam War, a part-time Hollywood script writer, and a full-time computer programmer. He drove me to the Denny's south of Venice Beach, during my brief stint in LA as a vagrant, asking for directions from Siri in a clear voice. Our meeting had been arranged by my mother, putting him in contact with me, with a preface that he had, at one point, been in love with her. As we waited for the American Breakfast he told me how he did it: a story was an engineering problem.

He had written a three-hundred-and-fifty-page pdf outlining in detail what makes a good script, which he gave out for free on his website thescriptsavant.com — where thousands of film and TV scripts were also archived. He spoke about web traffic, mentioning it three times, which unnerved me; then about himself, in exactly the same tone. It all seemed partly rehearsed, and would have been construed as boastful were it not for the sheer matter-of-fact nature that he rattled off the specs, as though appraising a software. "I won the pull-up competition at my barracks. I used to able to do one hundred pull ups. I never get ill." I asked questions in the same vein, adapting to this manner of speaking, such as "What does a regular day consist of?" It seemed appropriate.

I was unwilling to begin any rhapsodies on my ideas for art, culture, philosophy or the human spirit, but I was intrigued by his approach to everything. He had adapted a system to working in Hollywood: everything was disposable. The idea was disposable. The title was disposable. The characters, setting, any of the content, was all disposable, exchangeable and not really to be given any weight. One should, when approaching a company with a pitch, have about twelve other pitches lined up in your mind when you walk in. Your pitch was not special and your idea was unimportant. This information he was eager to spread, because it was also disposable, worth nothing, freeware.

The only non-disposable factor to any story, Dallas told me, was the twist. A Hollywood script without a twist was doomed to failure. Without a twist, in his eyes, there was no story. Fight Club. American Psycho. That's all I can think of. All with great twists. He told me this idea he was working on: the twist was that the doctor who was treating the schizophrenic patient was actually the patient himself, as well as the patient's girlfriend. It was very confusing, and sounded awful, and I might have even told him, despite the fact that he had paid for my breakfast. Basically Roz: we need a twist. A big memorable twist that shocks everyone. Maybe we're the same person. Maybe we're not the same person. I don't know. I have never, in my whole life, considered putting a twist in anything I have ever done.

♛

I scurry quadrupedal until I find a payphone near an abandoned megachurch. The wild west, what a shit-hole, nothing wild about it. Arcane glyphs on disembodied triacetate. I zip out of my latex morph suit to reveal a black crop top and cycle shorts underneath, regular civilian thot clothes that I always wear for situations like this. I pull the crypto chip from my scalp and tap it on the receiver. A flash of harsh noise, then the soothing start-up tone, blobject-like, outmoded futurism. It rises in pitch at the end to pose a nonverbal question.
"Agent Q" I reply raspily.

The thrumming of a cyborg woodpecker. You pick up after twenty long seconds.

"What is it? I have company."

Drunken girlish laughter and country music playing from a radio.

"You asked me to get cereal."

You take a drag of something. "That was four bloody hours ago, a lot can change in that time. I thought you had gone painting the town red, my dear, so now I'm doing a spot of painting too."

"One of the Mongolian's men tried to fucking disappear me. I was at 7-11 for your fucking Froot Loops and he just bundled me out, took my shit, put me in his trunk."

"Jesus Christ... Why didn't you fight him?"

"Why didn't I fight him? I'm the broad, Q, I'm the broad that you bring! This guy was like 6'7, 400lbs, he picked me up from behind. What was I gonna do, bodyslam him? This isn't Tekken, the laws of fucking physics still apply. It's easier to just get out of the trunk."

"Alright, alright, I'm sorry... I apologise. Oh, bugger it. Where are you?"

"Next to somewhere called 'Lord of Synergy'. Lots of broken windows."

"Hey, toots..."

"What?"

"I'm talking to this chick. Sugar, Candy, what was your name? Yeah can you give me a lift somewhere, in your pickup? Yeah... no... I don't know how to drive."

§

The constant to all these projects: increasing the detail of what can be said. Taking the language, models and presupposed structures used when discussing life, reality and existence, discarding them with a nod of respect, then going once again into the thick undergrowth of happening. Return with another language, model and presupposed structure, then do the same again. The destruction of the old, the discovery of a new way of saying, of thematising, of thinking about things fundamentally, that is the replicator, the meta-series of first terms. Rebellion is the rejuvenating function, outside-in.

What is this new way? How can we even know these differences, if not from the perspective of a particular structure, if not from a historically determined point? Is this difference always a new illusion, and the juxtaposition of the new illusion and the old illusion, merely a gimmick of the new illusion itself? Only when we destroy our own models do we come closer to the past, and the future, simultaneously. Back to the beginning, as per usual.

§

Dog knot stuck in woman's arse. She cums slowly, panting with heavier and heavier moans, while her husband encourages from behind the camera. "Are you cumming baby?"
"Yeeeeaaah…"

♔

The calls with my father are passing over me, almost painlessly. The words are nothing, each cogent line of dialogue immediately thrown away, rubbed out. He mutters something, I nod, repeat it; and the conversation's syllogism is reset.

♔/♛

"I'm not sure we can continue this until you call him."
"Call him?"

"I want you to call him, or we call him together, to tell him what we're writing."
"But he's blocked me."
"Then... then I suppose I should call him, and tell him that you want to call him. I don't know. I just feel like he should be privy to what is going on. It's called Baby Alex. Think of it like TOWIE. We're orchestrating drama. We're the soap writers and the actors."
"Fine, if you can orchestrate it, I'll call him."

§

The spine unfurls itself from the skull, like this comma of morphing bone. All mammals have their amphibian moment. The electromagnetic fields, and the subtle bodies, signalling across Yorkshire. Who accepts love and who runs in fear? And what does it all look like, either way? I know the great golden spirit, the shape of its chariot. What else do I need, except to follow it, and let it ride through me? I'm growing it out for comic effect. This is all a gimmick. And you — even you, co-author — are my gimmick. You, bloody female, are my mating call. I'm growing it out, the spine that is. The spine and the spirit, and the electromagnetic field.

§

Gypsy harem, Scottish or broadly northern girls, shagging then giggling when children walk into the room, sending them to bed again. I keep them arranged via email, I keep them interested, with a spam header, lots of emojis, italics and bold writing of different sizes. I writhe about in the bed and my dick feels thinner and a little pathetic. I receive updates through the email of a webchat that I interact with as I read. She's curious about my channel, she's flirting at me through these lilac pillars that twist around a confusing number of rooms. Then she's riding an impressive dick, someone else's dick, and the camera zooms back to reveal the owner is another woman, the same sort of shape, make-up, and breast size. Both clamour for the attention of the camera, looking up to it with oozing grins. No one cums, perhaps there's a chemical in the air, dilating their eyes and keeping them trapped on fuck-plateau. Somehow, I'm in control, yet none of it is mine, it is my simulation, it is my theatre — I cannot touch it, I cannot enter.

§

Book is placed on arse-cheeks. Book is placed between arse-cheeks.

§

The bees are croaking. Two corpses in rigor mortis decorate the pergola.

Mum was even more irritating than usual today. I do all I can to eat my meals alone, usually outside, listening to study beats. I was attempting to enjoy a nice mid-afternoon peanut butter and jam granary bread sandwich, I took it out in the garden only to find that she was still out there sunbathing, not yet back at school, as I had thought. It would have looked weird to wait until she was gone, so I started, and every time I took a bite, she would say something mindless and stupid to which she expected a response.

"Matthew got a SodaStream. I think they're such a great idea."
"Mm."

Involuntary Star of David emojis flashing behind my eyes.

"You drink a lot of Diet Coke. That must be healthier, right? They say fizzy drinks are bad for you, is them being fizzy bad?"

"...It's not the fizz that's bad, it's the flavourings."

"How does it make the drinks fizzy?"

She's like a child. It's like she doesn't have Google on her phone. "...They just carbonate them, it's just carbon gas."

"So, is that bad for you?"

"...Carbon is in almost everything. There is carbon in the air."

"So, there's no calories?"

Oh my god, shut up, please shut up.

"Yes, there's no calories."

I love her, so I need to get out of the house before I smother her with a pillow. She's not even doing anything wrong, it's just the noise, the noise while I'm trying to eat my sandwich, while I'm trying to think about Baby Alex.

23 and still living at home.

I remember my and Baby Alex's horrific attempt at post-uni house hunting. Neither of us had stable incomes, we were being shown around these new build apartments with gleaming white bathrooms and plasticky tubs, and even when we put our nice clothes on, we still looked very much like stoners, losers who would never in a million years live in a place like that. It felt so far away. We were just indefinitely stuck in LDR, never in our own domain, in the flurry of soulless student accommodations and parents' houses.

23 and still living at home.

Albeit partially as a condition of my job. Several times

now I have been jogging around the locked-down grounds and employees have stopped me, thinking I was some random street urchin who has brazenly ignored all the "private property" signs. No, I work here. I live here. I have to make sure my appearance and conduct is acceptable for the learning environment. I have to be prepared to run into the headmistress at all times. I am being mysteriously disciplined, kept in line, and preserved both spiritually and literally at school, wearing little plaid skirts, and eating peanut butter and jam sandwiches. All these weird écolière aesthetics growing simultaneously creepier and more comfortable to me the longer I stay. I feel myself becoming the baby. Becoming the retard.

§

Message from James Cooper:

i fucking shat myself didnt clean up got on a train next morning everyone knew fucking got to headingley went back cleaned up went back again ahhaahhahahhahahaahhaha

♅

All of reality is warfare. Read Sun Tzu's The Art of War. Strategy mutates from strategy. OODA Loops. Redownload Tinder, see bio: only send dick pics if over 5". Imagining the kind of man who sends an unsolicited four-inch dick, and sending him astral Roman salutes. What a strategy! Snapchat Newsfeed, the Telegraph infographics, police three times more likely to arrest blacks, with cinematic intense music and animation. What a strategy!

Walk downstairs, the girls are back for a week. Mother

asks, "do you fancy erm, going to the post office?"

"Not aye-tee-em, no." feeling my feet patter across the cold kitchen floor as I grab bowl, cereal and milk.

"Well I just need some letters posted, they're right there," points behind me, "plus your letter to Student Finance. You never know, you might make a lot of money all of a sudden and then it would be a shame if you had to pay off more."

"I will. That's exactly what will happen."

"Well, you can hope." scoffs a little.

"In this world, mother, there is no such thing as hope. There is only certainty... and action." I repeat this to myself in a dour voice as I pour the milk over the Coco Pops. "Certainty... and action. No such thing as luck..."

"Well yes, there's an element of luck." mishearing me.

"No. Only certainty... and action." I snicker to myself a little. "Certainty... and action."

♚

There should be graphs inside, sigils, pictures, drawings. It should be very fun. The number one priority, entertainment. The Indian men find it in a hole in the jungle, the OnlyFans whore rubs it against her pierced nipples. Neo-Eugenics, T-4 Bacteriophages, the mind-virus nature of Pornography, Gnosticism versus Spinozist interpretations, Satanism, Corporatism, Childhood trauma, Playstation 2 cut-scene gamification, dreams, archetypes, Deleuzian strata, Japanification of the mental hellscape; Hard Brexit aesthetics, atomisation, new builds, Tinder, blobject sex, teledildonics... fuck I've run out of toilet paper... luv r NHS, smartphone symbiosis, death-of-God bonus level, modern masculinity, Red Pill Thinking, Black Pill Thinking, migrant rapists, Fake News, watching Women's pole-vault for the asses, Erectile dysfunction, choking, TikTok, Eco-fascism, Dean Blunt, Bladee, Berlin, LA, the levels of the world, Chaos Magick, the dementia of my father, the schizophrenia of Cooper, ISIS beheading videos, eccies and sweat, he spent his whole youth getting stoned on high-grade cannabis each night and playing video games, the purity of animals, the mass torture of animals, the uncanniness of existence, the underhead of each person, the fiery sea of madness within, Paedowood, London, Climate Change, walking into the sea, brief moment of Corona Virus, China, face-timing your ex, notifications, narrative arc of life in a post-ironic age, auto-exploitation, OCD penis measuring, gay thoughts, racist thoughts, Consumerism and anti-Consumerism, normalised BDSM practices, Student Accommodation and student debt, Deep State, Paranoia, Aliens, Jpegs, Video editing software, Prosumerism, Platform capitalism, the mechanisms of the mosquito bite, buzzcut aesthetics, evolution versus involution, a mythical deer species, blue-white, glowing. The real sensation of death. The rhythms, the cycles, the shifts, the becomings, the processes, the linearities, the unknowns, the unconscious movements. The Bhagavad Gita, the Tao Te Ching, the Holy Bible, the Pyramid Texts, the Analects, the Kybalion, the Psychonaut. The spheres, the squares, the structures, the topologies, the morphemes, the phonemes, the tics and the chitters. The shivering sacs of yellow blood. The insectoid socius. In concatenation there will be an unknown effect that will suddenly explode. A chemical reaction: the metal touches the water, splits the tank open. Clenching and unclenching, clenching and unclenching. Abstraction and the fat of the untouched resource. Seams of gold. Space: a suffocation of buzzing. The futurity of the orgasm. Press-up suicide.

♛

Code-cracking, flat earth theory, Silicon Valley psychedelic spirituality, the food pyramid, the Netflixification of language, paypigs, self-curated performance of abjection, Wicca, creepypastas, the chemical signals, layer-travel, doomer self-identification, invisible chronic illnesses, The Cloud of Unknowing, girlbosses, Wetherspoons, JOI, Soylent, child drag queens, ambient inexplicable emotional trauma, the loss of allure, the apparent perversion of the apparent natural course of things, the Ann Summersification of sex, targeted ads, targeted ads for breast augmentation and lip fillers, rural American teens losing scholarships for saying nigger on TikTok, Druidry, NoFap, free bleeding, detox, jump scares, the crushing loneliness, London v everyone else, Lovecraftian fuckmonsters, Starbucks culture, trending porn, ozone layer of depression covering the world, improvisation, overfishing, women and what to do about them, what women should do about themselves, aspartame, the Plant Teacher, the concrete realities of magic and hypnosis, this is what they took from you, prepubescent obsessions, unboxing videos, non-British cosmopolitan busyness, Mediterranean flavours, sentient stock market, Instagram sex trafficking, axe-throwing arcades, secular rituals, Uber, MemriTV, the categorisation of clouds, the head-shaving phenomenon, farm animal gonads, the Marvel Cinematic Universe as outsourced folklore, lucid dreaming, pick-mes, the holiness of early childhood, regionalism, Edward Bernays, mukbangs, eating ass, eating pussy, eating disorders, concealed carry, the attention economy, hormone replacement therapy, the Clear Pill and beyond, drill music, opiates, the sacred mythology of the digital age, the podcast accent, the Love Islandification of urban dating, psychogeography, nightwalking, meditation, unspoken connections between images, the poor image, the deep-fried meme, North Korea, Britain First, all the best ambient music coming from the former Axis powers, the inner life, the outer life, Discord, weird Twitter, the Zoomer Laureate, athleisure, myopia, espionage, Chinese ballet, reptilian overlords, vanilla normalcy as fetish, sensory deprivation, dopamine fasting, the postinternet revival of bowling and indoor mini golf, stationary viral dances based on hand and arm movements, Funko Pop collectors, minute power struggles, Hostess snack cakes, vape addiction, the perpetual cheapening, sleep paralysis, the love of your life, metacognitive autofiction, kpop performers committing suicide, the looming ghost of Freud, liveblogging, file sharing, Skype call dysmorphia, the death of cinema, shitting in your own hand, ants. All of life so far, condensed. I can feel it. Yes, I can feel it.

♛

He kept staring at me at the bar, very pointedly. Whenever he would catch me looking he would smile. He did this for maybe half an hour before coming over, then murmured in my ear. He said there was something very beautiful about me, more than any of the other girls there, what a lonely girl who does not feel beautiful longs to hear.

He said we should leave, with his hand on the small of my back. I said sure, we went out walking through the campus, it would have been after midnight, everything looked different but I guess I wasn't that familiar with it yet, the lake seemed to simmer like it was boiling, the sky was very clear. We saw a large statue of the Buddha in the lotus pose, we stopped and stared for a while. I felt greatly moved, I turned to him and he looked bored, waiting for something, so we just went back to mine.

He was very rough taking off my clothes, he wouldn't kiss me tenderly. I guess I was still missing the ex-junkie. I cried, he yelled at me, told me not to lead people on, told me to get on the bed. I was drunk, he may have been drunk but did not seem it, he fucked me, I bled, I cried, he stopped, I told him to leave, he said he hadn't cum yet, he held me down and fucked my mouth, my eyes were streaming. I had my eyes open staring at the air vent, hearing my flatmates laughing in the kitchen, the dread numbed into just longing for the time to pass. It was double geography with Mr Battrick all over again, I was there for years, in the sand, longing, he finally came, got dressed, and left without saying anything.

I lay on the bed, called my first boyfriend with the porn addiction, talked for a while, slept, woke up, proceeded as normal. I saw him at the supermarket a couple months later, he looked afraid. I had the power to hurt him now, but I did not use it. I had no desire to ruin his life, he did not ruin mine. It would not be getting even. So, I picked up my bag of cherries, I kept proceeding as normal. And I have proceeded as normal ever since.

♛

A little chat with my friend Will last night. He is a flake and a scatterbrain, which annoyed Alex. I always enjoyed Will's energy and passion, even if it meant he would arrive to dinner two hours late because he got into an argument about Wittgenstein at the pub. To an outsider it probably would have made more sense for me and Will to date and live in warm comfortable disarray. That probably wouldn't have worked either. I never even fancied Will. You rarely fancy the people you should.

"Have you heard from Alex recently?"

"Yeah, he seems okay. I think he's feeling better about the two of you now. I think he knows it was the right thing."

"That's good to hear."

"Are you going to talk anytime?"

"I have a feeling I'm going to have to find a way to contact him soon. I have something I need to talk to him about. He's probably not going to like it."

§

Alex, very stoned, trying to get his mother to stop talking.

Alex, very stoned, ashing a cigarette into a glass of milk.

Alex, very stoned, making small anxious noises.

Alex, very stoned, noodling on a piano in a shopping mall.

♚

It's the partitioning, the surface tension of categories, while the whole thing roars useless and unnoticed, it's the cutting up of life into stuff that we can tell each other, the bare minimum that can be made known, "yes, I too was there, I too was that person..." when asked eventually in looking back, down a busy street of takeaways on a Friday night, while the rain slathers everything in a cold mirror, when you walk past yourself leaning your chin on the top of a girl's head, eyes dilating before the red and yellow price list above this Libyan's chef hat, there's the pause, the lacuna snaps open, and they are already welcoming in this memory that no one cares about, but for some reason that pavement in the early morning, you just reiterate something you read scribbled above the shitter, and the wet slabs which were probably not there on that street, but were down a different street on a different day, the texture of the rock is wham in your face, what the fuck, then you walk back or get a taxi and sweat the grimmy weather out in some girl's bed, and there's no going back and you're not sure it was that great to begin with, there's no going back, once you've walked past yourself you nod your fucking head or you shake it, either way, you didn't have a choice, and I didn't even do anything with her, maybe slapped her arse as she got out of bed, maybe just bit her neck once to let her know it was alright, that I wasn't a puss but I was conflicted I mean, at least I was conflicted, at least I had the manners to be conflicted. Yeah, if I could just be human for enough time I'd get it out, all of it, the fucking, each and every fucking thing, all those scattering colours and the adjustments of space as I walk to the toilets in the student accommodation, those little corridors, those blue fuzzy carpets, that ugly air that dries out the soul, those dawdles, those harrowing pits of prior to's. I was hounded, the panic was bright, the greatest dread in those times when I considered myself falling in love, I forgot so much, girl one, girl two, girl three... it's all more or less gone... now I have to deal with all these cunts, these other tiring cunts, pale cunts, vampire cunts, empty cunts who want to cuntify the whole of life, for what fucking purpose just to gobble gobble turkey-esque on some unabating test of transcendence, a vector of perspective. A long black river, and a concrete slabbed pathway on the side, or a sea, or little bugs everywhere, and I was always being kicked about or waiting for another section of my life, now there's just a grey stretch as far as my inner eye takes me, a wasteland of time. That's why we're writing this see? For the money, for the book. Something to do. So many times, I've wanted to take you all the way in, past the little partitions and the etiquette of normal time, to let you sit inside me. We could sit inside each other and finally eat the stars. For me it's about what just happened, the last 20+ years, what the fuck just happened... that black river yawning, propelled up to here, queasy, properly fucked now, praying for a metaphor, or a fundamental ontology, some new-fangled take intended for eternity that everyone will just forget about in two or three clicks.

Δ

At the weekend I closed my eyes and pointed to a map. I drove to the point, a golden field in between Broomhead Reservoir and Moor Hall Reservoir, near a village called Wigtwizzle. As I entered three crows flew away and I was left there, myself and two beautiful dark-haired horses. It started to rain.

It was wonderful and I am not made of sugar.

Well, well, well...

First of all: Congratulations! I am so happy for the two of you for writing something that you are so proud of. I have always had deep faith in you both, you are sensitive and brilliant and things can be so difficult.

Secondly, Jesus guys, please be more careful with your messages. You unloaded a big truck of bad vibes at my door full of negativity, passivity and self-hatred. I had to have a few days to process it all especially with all the silence preceding it. I do wish you would have told me much sooner but maybe now was the right time all along. All is to say this is in the past, I lead us all to draw a line under it. I forgive you both and I do hope you have the ability to forgive yourselves.

Thirdly you should send me whatever draft you are on right now. I am aware that this may be difficult for you both, and for me, and may be raw and uncomfortable but no matter: it is the only way. Only then can we have a proper chat about things and I can decide how I feel about the project from a personal angle. Only then can the book be truly finished. Only the three of us together can turn all our lead into gold.

I will always love you both from the bottom of my heart, but please be careful and do not try to take advantage of that, it will bite us all in the ass in the end. I know things will be hard but our souls are tied up together somehow so bring both your vibes up uP UP!!!

Alex
(not a pussy, just a badass person)
x x x

§

q: did you get the email?

r: cortisol spike

q: fr
q: not sure how to process it tbh

r: omg

q: unconditional love eh

r: just got it
r: reading
r: i am completely disarmed
r: he's coming at it from the jesus angle

r: [voice message] i.... er..... pfffff...... well i'm glad he's not mad

q: hahahahahaha
q: we were right!
q: aye but like

r: [v] god, ... it's baby jesus alex
r [v] i'm sorry, i'm drunk, woah this caught me in a weird moment

q: this is going to be based

r: [v] yeah i'm thinking its based.

q: [v] especially the last bit, i'm not a pussy just a badass person

r: [v] i'm honestly... i'm proud of him... it was his new

year's resolution to be a badass person and not a pussy, and he's driving! my god

q: yo we're definitely including this in the end
q: new man alex

r: absolutely

q: big man

r: [v] baby jesus alex resurrected, it's easter all over again

q: redemption arc
q: he went full christ tho
q: i was never into like total christ shit but whatevs
q: yeah pretty safe

r: [v] yeah this being said i guess he hasn't seen it yet... erm... uuuuhh

q: true
q: [expressionless emoji]
q: he hasn't erm
q: read the title

r: [video in bath] we could just put a dummy title or you know no title at all until he's completely aware of the situation and knows what's going on with the whole thing

q: nah we putting the real one
q: we gotta own our complete arseholeness
q: [video] i actually feel like alex has erm... alex has saved me, he's saved my soul

r: feel like a disciple of jesus christ

q: aye

q: i'm getting mary magdelene and jesus back together after this, i'm judas

r: i'm sorry judas, mummy and daddy aren't getting back together after this
r: i'm just trying to like, imagine the sensation of, there's no comparable sensation for me, like if two people were to write a book about me in this way, but the sensation of reading it, it probably wouldn't be wholly unpleasant, it would just be ego death, maybe he'll enjoy it, maybe he'll really enjoy it.

q: mummy no!

r: sorry sweetie

q: i think this might save our friendship though, i hope it does

r: yeah i hope it does too

q: i think he will

r: maybe the holiday to bruges can happen after all, the happy ending, where we all go to bruges!

q: i think there's a very good possibility he'll totally understand why it was done, especially if we're completely, i dunno, i think that if it's just... completely honest then that's the most important, like yeah we're evil, we're fucked up, we're all shit. And i guess when you put it out there, when you watch yourself do it, maybe it helps, maybe it's like... funny or like.
q: but can we forgive ourselves roz
q: can we forgive ourselves

r: i honestly don't know

q: well i'm typing this all out it's gold
q: nothing is safe anymore

r: you know i just keep swinging between feeling great and i wrote a thing about this in preparation for tomorrow where we thought we were containing the book but now the book is containing us and nothing we say is exempt from potentially ending up in the book and i feel a bit like any text i send any offhand comment i made at your house, like anything can come up at any time and i feel like now the book is the egg rather than you know the book being inside the egg.
r: it all lends itself to the ultimate honesty, we're completely transparent at this point. feels weird.

q: jesus f'in christo
q: we in the book

r: yes
r: i had that feeling too

q: alex can do the diagrams

r: such a nice idea he loves diagrams

r: [gregorian chant in background] Now it feels like he's watching us.

q: yes my child, that is because... he is
q: raises head to heaven

r: yeah i thought of that just as i finished filming, yes he is watching, he watches over us... always

q: alright i'm going to finish writing this out

r: ok good

REBIRTH

§

Baby Alex emerged from the sea at 12:22, Tuesday the 21st of July, 2020. When asked where he had been in the four months prior, his eyes would turn off, becoming those of an insect, and he would whisper something misty and incomprehensible beneath his breath.

♕

The first conceived thing, scraped apart, washed out, laid somewhere on a hard metal dish, then incinerated. Difficult to speak about. It would have been her second. Her first she had undergone when she was 13, after being raped by her boyfriend, who would later distribute her nudes, revenge-porn style, around the school. The year before she met me, she had also been pregnant, but had suffered an early-term miscarriage. She was tremendously concerned about having a child and the effect it would have on the tightness of her vagina. She was 21, dyed her hair a lot of odd colours, had several body and face piercings, wore red fishnet tights underneath black ripped jeans, and wanted to pursue a career in stick-and-poke tattooing.

On a Friday night in Bingley, Jennifer drank heavily with her friends. 2 am she would impulsively blow an additional wad of cash for an Uber to my house. I'd be notified while lying in bed, get up, shake my head, unlock the door, and message her to remember to lock it back up. An unashamed volume of banging would be heard, the fucker creeping through to my room in the dark, then she would flash her teeth with glee as she jumped onto me in the bed. After a short wrestling match, with me spanking her several times, we would finally settle down to sleep.

The majority of our meetings were punctuated by some intense detail of conflict: me holding a knife to her throat while pushing her up on the kitchen cabinets; me ripping the black jeans off her legs, forcing her to go home in borrowed tracksuit bottoms; me rugby tackling her in the park and pouring water over her face and hair, smearing that excessive BPD/daddy-issues eyeliner over her pink and livid expression; me teasing her labia with my prick endlessly, telling her to bark like a dog if she wanted me inside her, to which she would eventually let out a surly "woof". It all came under the broad cheeky chappie umbrella. I felt very free with Jenni, and no matter to what degree I took the piss and she threw ultimatums back, there would always be a final twinkle in the eye passed between us, all fun and games.

When walking through the park one day I had mentioned that, due to my forays in the astral beyond, the DNA of my sperm had been altered. The fiery nature of both our personalities would forge a bloodline of demonic Chieftains, Leaders of Men, foretold by some inter-dimensional augur — bringing about the revitalised age of something or other. Jenni, sensitive to magical thinking and easily spooked by this sort of thing, was not impressed.

A month of tantrums passed, nothing too out of the ordinary. She noted to me that there had been one weekend when her implant had been removed. I responded, "guess we were doing it the old-fashioned way." She took five tests; they all came back negative. She continued drinking, snorting lines of cheap beak and taking Ubers; I continued pissing about making YouTube videos. (There's even two marks on my face in the Mishima video where she scratched me in an especially feisty rumble.) One evening she turned up, we were doing our Mortal Kombat thing in the kitchen, I lifted her high in the air and something fell out of her pocket. She said "Don't look at that." in her broad Yorkshire accent, suddenly serious, and put her foot over it. I forced the foot away and grabbed what was beneath it. White plastic, the size and shape of a large pen. "Pregnant" — written in blue letters on the side.

"I didn't want you to know."
"What?"
I felt the magnetic poles of the earth being switched.
"I didn't want you to know because I knew you'd be weird about it."
I realised what she was going to do, that my destiny would be in no ways affected. I felt guilt, raw guilt, and something inside me broke.

At around 8 weeks the "bundle of cells" has a freakishly large head compared to its body, some limb stumps, and a developing ear and eye. You're not supposed to cry over an aborted foetus. You're not even supposed to get slightly upset I don't think. You're supposed to be relieved: skipped that responsibility again, yippee, more fuck-world for me...

My child, my baby: doesn't exist, didn't exist. I get close to the thought of it and then I'm ordered to turn back. Here, this thing, I am not allowed to think. I am not even allowed to stare into it, the blank non-event. That other place, that room where the killing and the extracting is done, where the blood-soaked bundle of cells, cells inscribed with Jenni and I, is scraped out of her and flushed away, that room is forbidden. I neither enter nor approach.

From the moment she had discovered it, her decision had been made. I told her that I wanted her to keep it, or maybe I said "I'm not telling you to get rid of it", but of course there was no weight to that, it was just lip service to absolve myself of the guilt. I was in no place to raise a child: I had practically no income, still lived in my mum's house. I made high-quality shitpost YouTube videos.

I began to feel strange around her. She hadn't had the abortion yet, but I couldn't see us having sex after she had removed it. It all seemed pointless, and big turn off. She became a symbol for that other thing, and it sapped me of all joy, of all understanding and all certainty. I did some more stupid shit, pushed the idiocy a little too far. She blocked me one day after an argument about Monica where I wouldn't apologise, I just mocked her and said she looked like something out of Ru Paul's Drag Race. And now my bundle of cells is dead. I don't blame her. I hope this doesn't come across like that. It's not her I blame. I don't blame anyone.

I walk past fathers in their late thirties on the canal, surrounded by toddlers with bright blond hair jumping in puddles, bumbling out fresh vocab and pointing their little dewy fingers at ducks. The men look tired and boring, clad in functional windbreakers, sporting salt-and-pepper beards. I walk past and I shudder.

Sometimes when I play piano, I feel it watching me.

♕

Back home. Out walking, deep in the multiverse, music fades out, watch starts vibrating. Phone call. Flash of cortisol. Is it him? No, it's my mother. I'm making sausage rolls. Take them out of the oven in fifteen minutes. Catch reflection in greenhouse on the field. Little skirt again. Clips in my hair again. She's asking what I've eaten again. 23 years old. Brief compulsion to kill, stab with a knife, her and then myself.

She had work friends over for drinks. The vegetarian-friendly sausage rolls were just for me, so that I couldn't not eat them by saying I'm avoiding pork. She had also asked me to bake cookies so I did. They came around, I had 2 glasses of rosé and listened to grown adults gossip about children not doing their homework. I stared into the candle flame.

Why can't you talk about sex? Or guns? You're all interesting people, why talk about work?

I ate the cookies and vegetarian-friendly sausage rolls under mum's quiet authoritative gaze, feeling fucking disgusting, and momentarily longed for death. Walked for an hour listening to nothing. Came back and sat at the dining table alone in the dark, feeling my freedom dampen and crumple. The walking, it wasn't enough this time. I have to walk and not come back.

And then, like a black shroud, a new command billowed down onto me. Purge. Ok. I got up, robotically walked to the bathroom and looked at myself in the mirror. The more I accepted the command, the more I actually felt like I was about to be sick: the pulse of cold sweat, the shaky hands. I took off my cardigan, took off my earrings, breathed deeply, I knelt in front of the toilet.

You might think now that it's just this once, but if you do this, it will probably become a regular thing. It is very addictive, and incredibly dangerous. Are you sure?

Yes. Don't care. Have to do it.

Jabbed middle and ring finger of left hand down my throat, curling fingers inwards, pressing hard against the root of my tongue. Visualised sesame seeds in the eye of the dead coal tit. Full body retching, whole torso undulating like one spasmodic muscle, salivating, eyes watering, suffocating, I kept my fingers there until my vision blacked out. Nothing. I tried three more times. Still nothing. The nausea overwhelmed me but I couldn't throw up. Thank god.

I gave up, sat slumped on the floor, shaking, weak, hugging my knees. I stared at the wall where my mother had placed a huge laminated map of Suffolk.

☽

I looked hideous. I looked like a ball of uncooked dough.

I looked huge. It took a while for me to actually do something about it, after a good period of trying to blame other things. Intermittent fasting is free, try that. Lose a little weight, feel good. Try alternate day fasting, just eat moderately and count calories on one day, fast on the next. Not bad, surprisingly easy once you get into the swing of it. Feel the weight come off faster. Get compliments. Eat healthier. Stop smoking weed. Drink more water. Feel the weight come off faster. Go hiking. You didn't eat yesterday but you could just not eat today either. You could just not eat until you think you're going to die. Feel the weight come off faster. No longer plus size. New clothes. Eat as little as possible without courting attention. Weight keeps going. Now normal sized. I have always wanted to be called skinny. Tiny. I have always wanted to be picked up by a man. Just keep going. Size 10 now. Size 8 now. Comments at work. Called skinny. Can fit into anything I want. Can't stop counting calories. Feel the weight come off. Can't sit on a chair. Can't lie in the bathtub. Can't go to the bakery. Ribs showing through t-shirt. Size 6 now. Called tiny. You lift me over the railings of the bridge. Old clothes far too loose. Mother is asking questions. Can't stop counting calories. Don't want to stop. What if I get fat again? Can't wear anything that shows my shoulders around my mother. 80 for small banana. Hair is frizzy. 160 for half cup of oats. Chest bones are showing. 63 for slice of Danish-style bread. Nails are blue. 22 for a single prune. Waiting indefinitely for my period. Size 4 now. Size 4 jeans from Urban Outfitters fit me perfectly. That's a US size 0. Still not satisfied. 30 for a flat peach. 25 for half cup of Aldi almond milk. It's fucking unbearable. Constant concerned questions now. But don't want to stop. What if I get fat again? Eating more because I'm being watched at mealtimes. Having a single biscuit in front of my mother in the evenings in a way that appears nonchalant. Exercising more to compensate.

Feeling insane. Occasionally just eating maintenance calories is enough to make me feel so bad, so fucking fat again, like nothing has changed, sometimes I feel like nothing is wrong but sometimes I want to scream, right now I'm in the woods, on my knees, retching, breathing hard, so overwhelmed, it's been so bad the past couple days, I don't know why, I want to leave the world, I don't want to die I just want to leave, I want to lift my eye and escape, on my knees in the woods.

Talked to myself in the dark for about half an hour as if you were there listening, and it made me feel a lot better.

♔

The horror. The vanishing point of all of the things that are stressing me out: I just remembered the exact moment. Food, acid, weed, and Baby Alex.

There was this 24-hour showcase that the comedy society put on every year. "Comedians" would spend weeks preparing exclusive material, be it stand-up, sketches, panel shows, or weird multimedia shit to be performed there. The committee would rake through all the proposals, pick the ones they thought looked the best, and timetable a non-stop, day-long bill of "Content", from 5pm until 5pm the next day. People paid £5 for entry, stayed up all night, drank Jägerbombs, and laughed at all the in-jokes that were written specifically for them.

Alex and I would always be in at least one improv show, ideally the "after dark" slot that took place at about 1am; where you could do African accents and joke about rape. We would always pitch our own show, which would be accepted, but put at a dead time when most of the audience had given up and gone home, usually at 4 or 5 in the morning. This would not stop us from working incredibly hard on it, me honing some intricate script, him tweaking away on AfterEffects, making a detailed lightshow maybe 7 people would end up seeing. The run-up to those shows, when we had a common goal, no matter how arbitrary, this was when we were happiest.

Everyone was just doing sketch comedy about Tinder, or imitating the shit you hear on Radio 4. So, we would try and freak people out. We'd put jump-scares in, or poetry, or scenes where nothing funny happened, just to try and get a rise out of people. We would be writing this stuff, it would seem so good at the time, but no one else was in on it. All that preparation would go into this singular piece that was performed once to almost no one, and no one gave a shit. At the end, if people said anything at all, all we'd get is "wow that was like The Mighty Boosh" or, even more commonly, "you guys must have been on drugs when you wrote that". Ironically, in those times of concentration, it was pretty much the only time we spent together when we weren't on drugs.

So, one time we said fuck it, if they think we're on drugs, we may as well be, and just before we were due to perform, we took 2 tabs each. It was all over before they kicked in, but as people came to approach us, I started to feel it. Their eyes like shiny coins, their mouths wide and moist. Colours were getting brighter. I smiled and giggled, nothing they were saying seemed to matter at that point, even though I was comprehending it. Yes, I guess it was like The Mighty Boosh. Whatever. We stayed around for another couple hours, before our cockney friend doing impressions of Brian Blessed became too much, and then we got a taxi back to my house at 11am. We smoked a joint.

We were both suddenly ravenous. Pizza Express had just opened for lunch. We ordered delivery, way too much food, an absolutely irresponsible amount of food: pizza, pasta, bread, £8 salads I could have easily made myself, soda, tiramisu, fudge cake, coffee. It arrived, we sat in my bed and devoured it all, tripping balls. At one point, alternating eating cake and pizza, taking one bite of something and then immediately requesting to take a bite of whatever Alex had, constantly swapping all this overpriced slop around totally mindlessly, I fell off the edge of tripping and started the slow descent back to sobriety. Then it was the comedown of the show and an actual comedown combined.

Oh my god. Nothing we're doing makes any sense. Nothing we're making is of any value. We think we're bohemians, we think we're in the early stages of some illustrious creative trajectory, something scholars will be writing about in 50 years, but we're not, we're just fucking wasters, posturing and uppity, a narcissism of small differences away from the other wasters we laugh at for not understanding us. We think we're creators but we're not, we're consumers, the consumption vastly outweighs the production, we make a 20-minute-long video that no one watches, get fucked up on drugs of unknown origin, and eat. We don't even fuck when we're high anymore, we just eat and watch videos. We don't even create that one thing that couples are meant to create. We are less creative than we would be if we were normal, if we made nothing at all. I felt disgusted with myself. I felt very, very, depressed. I said nothing. We watched Adventure Time. I ate until I fell asleep.

Blah blah blah Anorexia... Ok, we get it. Let's make this about me now.

§

Mousetopia, Universe-25. A perfect mouse-world, albeit in a limited area, where mice could live 'til old age took them peacefully in their sleep. Zero predators, and as much food as they wanted: a Mouse Heaven that soon became... a Mouse Hell. After the first few generations each and every mouse lost the will to live in its own way, each mouse forgot how to breed or take care of young. They were nowhere near population cap before their numbers began to dwindle to extinction.

Gangs of ostracised hyper-aggressive mice roamed about the middle, picking fights. A large number of male mice simply gave up on trying to mate or engage in dominance displays. Preening themselves all day, looking otherwise very healthy, they were known as the 'beautiful ones'. Same-sex mounting became more common. Foetuses were reabsorbed. Female mice with young began to move their children constantly from one nest to the other, then forgot about them, leaving them in odd places or badly constructed nests, even biting them in random bouts of violence. By the end, the mice — even those removed from Mousetopia and placed with normal members of the opposite sex — had absolutely no desire to procreate, or, if they did, could not raise their pups past weaning.

I quote from the conclusion of Calhoun's Study Death Squared: The Explosive Growth and Demise of a Mouse Population :

"...the continuing high survival of many individuals to sexual and behavioural maturity culminates in the presence of many young adults capable of involvement in appropriate species-specific activities.
... [The] competition is so severe that it simultaneously leads to the nearly total breakdown of all normal behaviour by both the contestors and the established adults of both sexes. Normal social organisation breaks down, it dies.

Young born during such social dissolution are rejected by their mothers and other adult associates. This early failure of social bonding becomes compounded by interruption of action cycles due to the mechanical interference resulting from the high contact rate among individuals living in a high density population [...] Autistic-like creatures, capable only of the most simple behaviours compatible with physiological survival, emerge out of the process. Their spirit has died."

♔

Mother calls. "[...] well I didn't know that Alex hadn't been involved already! That's great!"
"Yeah, he didn't know, so we're glad we now have his knack for logistics on the... erm... team."
"Wonderful."
"So, we're balancing out the edit right now between the styles... between that weird one and the more documentary style."
"Oh good, like a balance between the documentary style and the Joycean one. As long as you make it a bit like that Monica story you did, the documentary style bits, yeah..."
"Yeah."
"Ok great, now don't go anywhere on Monday I need you

to send three faxes to the bank."
"Cool. No problem."

I laid on the edge of the massage table and did body-
weight neck exercises that I had just seen demonstrated
on a YouTube video by a man in a white vest emblazoned
with a garish logo of an alien and two barbells. The
channel's name: Anabolic Aliens. His neck seemed very
thick. His face went red while he swivelled his head: left,
right, one, left, right, two, left, right, three, don't forget
the consistency of speed, left, right, four. His hairline had
norwooded to a three but he kept it at a medium length,
he had 757k subscribers. I wondered how much money he
made on sales of those vest tops. He was probably juicing
by the size of his trapezius muscles: the triangular
muscles, "traps", that extend from the shoulder to the
neck are very sensitive to androgens, so steroid users tend
to have these exaggerated slopes from the head
downward. Traps of Terror I believe they are called. His
eyes were kind, a pale grey that caught the light, and he
made too many rehearsed hand gestures while he spoke so
he came across as a little moronic. I got to the third set of
exercises when my neck felt unable to hold my head and I
thought I was going to throw up. I rested on the table for
a minute, incapacitated, but glad that I had found a body-
weight exercise for my neck that seemed effective. I
thought briefly about calling my father but decided
against it.

§

Message from James Cooper:

Listen Dickhead I fucking hate you you total piece of shit
you are a dick stream you little gay boy fuck you fuck you
fuck you im a lover boy i love you man i think you're ace
you're willing to come down with me i just told a guy

what i thought was happening bro love the jewels we're
gonna be conquering diamond mines mate funny you're a
short pip so you have to join the army before
Fuck you
Mate what's Alex's number
I'm sorry

♛

There were points when it felt like he was an extension of
my mind. He would know exactly what I was going to say
just before I said it.

He went downstairs to get a glass of water and I stayed
upstairs. I saw him through the walls, an orb of orangey
glow, moving between rooms. Pure joy. I felt him drink
the water.

There were other times when I'd look at him, he'd look
just like a spider: beady, instinctual, like at any point he
could unhinge his jaw and pounce at me. I'd have no idea
what he was thinking, nor him me. It seemed like he
replicated emotions rather than feeling them. It made me
nervous. Towards the end I had the latter intuition a lot
of the time I was around him. I'd let it slip into being
tangible. That night with you at the campus gallery in
January, we were at the bar, you were hitting on that cute
girl with the butterfly clips in her hair. I was standing
against the wall, finding it bizarrely difficult to look at
him then, instead preferring watching you and her, the
sociological study of your body languages and facial
expressions. He pulled my attention back, I looked at
him again, a little irritated.

He said "sometimes when you look at me, it feels like
you're embarrassed by me."

I said "sometimes when you look at me, it feels like you have never seen me before."

♛

It was as if his house was set in formaldehyde. Preserved and immaculate. So many pictures of him, of literal Baby Alex, with his huge blue eyes. It was almost as if he had been killed in a tragic accident. In a way he had. The tragedy of time. No longer baby. His parents never recovered.

Specifically, so many pictures of him at school, with his friends and bandmates, on the side of the cabinet in the kitchen. However, none of you. This always stuck out to me. They bristled at the mention of you.

Upright piano. Tiny fridge. Apple TV. I can't remember the colour of the carpet, in the rooms that weren't hardwood or lino. I wasn't there that long ago. I want to say it was that muted, cool green. Or it could have been that tea-stain, beige colour so many carpets tend to be. But it was definitely clean. Not a speck of dust in the place. His mother had nothing to do but clean. Clean and wait around.

Did you know his father had no sense of smell? But he did all the cooking. And because smell affects taste so much, he would make the most fucked up meals. There was something about a curry with orange squash. I remember one night he made enchiladas, they appeared to have been seasoned with most of the things in the spice rack, very geographically inconsistent, not to mention disgusting. He had put cashews inside. I remember I had been ravenous that night, I had fasted all day, and I still could not stomach it.

The bar that held the toilet roll in the holder in the upstairs bathroom was made of cheap hollow plastic. It could barely support the weight of the roll. Whenever I would unconsciously push down on the roll to tear off a sheet, as I would at home, the whole thing would fall out, make a big crash on the lino, waking everyone up. They slept with their door open.

His bedroom was blue. Dinosaur sheets. Everything cringes. Giant teddy bear, a gift from Mary, watching me from the top of the wardrobe while I sucked him off as quietly as possible. Sorry.
I liked his father. I am often unsettled by friends' and boyfriends' fathers. Not familiar with the dynamic. Don't know how to act. But he struck a chord with me. He was avoidant, he would go out jogging so he wouldn't have to talk to people, just like me.

His mother. I cannot even tease her light-heartedly. She was tragic. A ball of anxiety with no outlet. She would watch pimple-popping videos on YouTube for two hours every day. His father was patient with her. The way Alex would talk to her sometimes would make me flinch. He would never call her stupid, or naive, but he may as well have. He was so demeaning sometimes. I never knew how to react. It must have been so frustrating to have a mother like that, always hovering, incapable of deep communication. But all she needs is tenderness, and I so rarely saw him give it to her.

The whole place was a shrine to him. A reliquary. To the special one.

♔

Baby Alex once said that he had stayed up all night in horror at the thought of his parents dying in a meteor strike. His band Monochrome made a music video for their first single "Fly Away" in the front room of his house, and my mother after watching it made an offhand comment that if she lived in Alex's house she would want to fly away as well.

I never paid Alex's parents that much attention. It's just amusing that they clearly have a problem with me. They were the source of all his problems. If I were Alex, I too would be horrified: not at the thought of their death by meteor strike, but at the thought that I was composed of a mixture of their genetic information.

§

Email from the Replicator:

The things I've witnessed my boy... The things I've put on the out pile... The Algorithm races to the bottom, sans scruples. We are stood symmetrical in a sphere, pointing our nukes, prodding the other's eardrum. Forty days at sea, my friends, forty days at sea! Forty days on the golden dunes, where the scorpions spill under sand-framed moons. The virus does the can-can. From the Euphrates to the Indus, Baby Alex is winning. The Barbarian West surrenders to the Baby Alex Fever. Da da DA da da-da... *dancing oddly* ... Da da DA da da-da...

I was an accident. You were an accident. Who else here was an accident? *Looks around for raised hands*. Come come now, don't be shy. People seem to forget that the British Empire was also an accident, a Mr. Bean moment... *Slips on banana peel*. Halberds, arbalests, drones. Sticks and stones, crucifixes, nigromancy.

Psychological momentum and battle formation. When the crusaders met with the Saracens in the field, the Christian knights took the shape of a cross; the Muslims: a crescent moon. Curious, no? May I draw your attention to item A: the Medieval depiction of a siege, the slaughtering of the vanquished, all faces bored out of their skulls...

A fell fortress: gates of obsidian and ash; Stygian banners for a long-submerged Goddess — oh if only, my little unborn chum, you could have seen... that Golden Age of Death.

♛

"Aren't you going to have breakfast?"

"... I'm literally eating an Activia in front of you."

"That's not breakfast."

"...What would be an acceptable breakfast to you? What's the cut-off?"

"Don't use that tone—"

"I am an adult. I bought these Activias with my own money. I can have one for breakfast."

"How much do you weigh?"

"..."

"..."

"I don't weigh myself. I haven't weighed myself in ages."

"Then how do you know you aren't losing weight anymore?"

"..."

"You said you weren't losing any more weight. How do you know if you aren't weighing yourself?"

"..."

"How much do you weigh, Rosie?"

"That's literally none of your business."

"Well, it kind of is."

"How on earth is it?"

"If you have nothing to hide, come into the bathroom and stand on the scale, right now, in front of me."

"How is it your business?"

"Come into the bathroom."

"This is ridiculous. Listen to yourself. I'm going out. Have a great time in Bristol. I love you."

"Rosie—"

☦

Edinburgh. I am sat in Cooper's room after having smoked half a henry of Amnesia Haze in two joints. Cooper is lying on his bed, where he has been all day. It is 6pm, already very dark outside. The room is cold.

"Bro..." he says, with an excitement that doesn't bode well.

"Mmm?"

"Bro, I've figured it out." His voice quietens, slows in pace.

"Yeah?"

"It's like Voltaire bro..." Silence. "He who dares, wins. We've got to risk everything."

"Sure."

"I mean it man. It's the only way. We've got to like..." He is speaking very quietly, and very seriously.

"Uh huh?"

"We've got to buy a gun bro," he whispers. "We've got to play Russian Roulette. It's the only way to level-up."

I'm too high to disagree, I just say "sure..." again, without really comprehending the action he's suggesting, nor the deathly exactitude of his tone.

"And you know, playing one bullet in the barrel, that's like... one in six. But we should play one in two. Or even... The riskier the better."

"It's the only way…" I say, repeating what he said. "It must be done."

This didn't come out of nowhere. We'd been grappling with this thing all year. The question: How does one become the 2.0 version of oneself? How do we release ourselves from all that weakness, all that shame, and all that hate? Then Cooper arrived at his final solution — an ultimate irreverence for life, a clean-cut gamble, all or nothing: Rebirth.

As I began to understand the magnitude of what he was saying, to truly fathom its logic, I saw this black thing descend over the world, over any and all positive emotion and light, this tremendous dark cloak: a flag of emptiness, a black flag of nothing. I had seen this once before, stood over the kitchen hot-patch, age two or three, my mother explaining to me what it means to die: "You just become nothing. It all ends." I burst into tears and fell down, all my muscles gave up, and the empty flag was born, rippling behind everything. Now, hearing Cooper's conclusion, the faraway thing I had learnt to ignore was once again in the room with me, draped over every surface. I was all the more afraid, because what he said made total sense. I felt sick, I got up from where I was sitting and opened his door to leave. I turned back to Cooper and said "it must be done…", my voice completely hollow.

☙

Watching Weezer perform The Sweater Song live on the Conan Show in 1994 (reupload). Chewing and spitting fig rolls directly into the trash.

4 days late. No sign of it coming. I taste of nothing. Used to taste of maybe yoghurt.

Short stabs of canned laughter reverberating from downstairs.

Mum and Matthew were meant to be going camping on Monday. Then their ETA changed to Wednesday. And now Thursday. My sentences are staccato. My skin is crawling. Please leave. Please leave the house now. Please just clear out woman. I need to smoke cigarettes and blast Oneohtrix Point Never. I need to unplug the router and walk around in my underwear. I need to write like no one's watching.

♛/♛

Die. Look in the mirror. Purple. Jaw hanging off. Black smoke. White python on the floor. Basement. Layer of grime.

The moment. Oh god. I was wrong. I was wrong the whole time. It was the right thing to do. Wrong. I did it wrong. It sent me here.

You. Behind me. Green. Eye hanging out. Stench. No longer cumin. Now death. We did it wrong. We died. We were sent here.

Your fist in my wet hair. Your knee to my back. Push to floor. Where is hole. Hole in ground with metal spike. Fifty feet. I try to speak. Mould in the throat. I scream. Your fist my head. Hover over. Metal spike. I scream.

He is like the evil version of me. You cannot trust him. Hair begins detach from head. Spike calls to me. The point crowned with cartoon star. He was right.

Bellows down the hall. The walking upstairs. No stairs now. Dead. No longer human. I repent. I think of you every day. Lies.

You laugh. Pull me up. Lower me down again. Pull me up. Never drop me on the spike.

You long to kill. I long to die. The sadist and the masochist. Hover over. Camera running. Metal spike.

§

A woman tazing herself on the pussy and passing out.

♖

They're going to put me in that white room, there's going to be a woman with glasses and a turtleneck, she's going to be holding a small ring bound notepad with a clicky pen; she's going to look at me like she hates me, she's going to ask me lots of leading questions. I'm going to stutter, it's going to keep going and eventually I will get tired and head for the door, only to realise it is locked. It feels like the solution is so simple and yet impossible, and it's going to happen soon, my mother's face hardening, pride melting to nervousness, to concern, and finally to something resolute and frightening. She is going to take me to that white room, she warned me today, she said it aloud.

§

Lids of alien metal, hovering miles of radius. Green-tinged sculptures of black meteorite. Pink flames aligned on Broadway like palms. Stalagmite cityscape, a vast sprawl, all lit up with red and white and gold. Labyrinthine sewers connecting the whole, going deeper and deeper, gates upon gates, dividing and hiding each complex. The termite planet, the endgame, the berserk swivelling function. "The things I do are not enough," I say. The termites ignore me.

§

Men falling to their deaths. Men jumping from cliffs, from bridges, from buildings. The waves foaming beneath them over the rocks. Men jumping, splattering red, turning to things emptied out. Men choosing to jump, the air taking them, swimming through the air, their mind made up; men thrown to the great doom. Men in bathtubs of blood. Men throwing themselves onto the railroad tracks, splattering red, the spike of decision, the choosing to die. The choice to no longer choose. Men falling, flailing, or gracefully diving, into their nothing. To leave this place, this termite's nest, to leave this cage, this strange hell. Men falling, dark stars of flesh falling, to their cipher, their hard surface, their escape. Men walking into the sea, into those cold caresses, into the touch of what is not. Men falling until the end of the universe. Until time is done. Men falling.

Just to get to that place, that one clean thought. To get there in one clean motion. The apple's core, the immaculate white cave, far from the nuisance of clouds.

♣/♤

I'm fucking lost! I'm fucking lost! I'm fucking lost! I'm fucking lost! One million three thousand twenty-two six hundred and eighty-nine thousand! I'm fucking lost! One million eight hundred and ninety-four six billion thousand and twenty-three! I'm fucking lost! I'm fucking lost! I'm fucking lost! I'm fucking lost! I'm fucking lost! I'm fucking lost! I'm fucking lost! One hundred and sixty-four thousand two hundred and ninety-four! I'm fucking lost! I'm fucking lost! I'm fucking lost! I'm fucking lost! I'm fucking lost! I'm fucking lost! Yeah! Yeah! Yeah! Yeah! Yeah! Yeah! Yeah! Yeah! Yeah! Yeah! Yeah! Yeah! Yeah! There was no need. There was no need. There was no need. There was no need. There was no need. I'm fucking lost! I'm fucking lost! There was no need. There was no need. Two hundred and eight. There was no need. Two hundred and eight. I'm fucking lost! Two hundred. Two hundred and eighty-eight. There was no need.

Tide. Even she won't kiss me now. Even she won't kiss me now. Even she won't kiss me now. Even she won't kiss me now. Even she won't kiss me now. Even she won't kiss me now. Even she. Even she. Even she. Even she. Two hundred and ninety-four. Watch the film. Watch the film. Watch the film. Watch the film. Watch the film. Watch the film. Watch the film. Watch the film. Watch the film. Make an excuse. The time is. Five hundred and eighty-eight.

Who? Who? Who? Who? Who? Who? Who? Who? Who? Who? Who? Who? Who? Four hundred. Who? Who? Who? Who? Eight hundred. Who? Who? Who? Who? Who? Who? Who? Who? Who? Nine hundred and nine. Who? Who? Who and six thousand and seventy-three and nine billion. Who?

Drum solo. Drum solo. Drum solo. Drum solo. Drum solo. Drum solo. Drum solo. Drum solo. Drum solo. Drum solo. Solo drum. Solo drum. Solo drum solo drum. Solo drum. Solo drum. Solo drum. Solo drum. Solo drum. Solo drum. Solo drum. Solo drum. Solo drum. Solo drum. Solo drum. Solo drum. A single. Drum solo, drum, solo. Something on the gaze of the water. Something on the gaze of the water. Something on the gaze of the water. Something on the gaze of the water. I could just go do it now. I could walk into the sea. I could just go do it now. No more eyes upon me. I could just go do it now. I will do it soon. I will walk into the sea. Tell me how we did it. How did we remove evil again? Tell me now baby. Tell me oh sweet little baby. Tell me oh sweet little baby. Tell me now baby. Oh sweet little baby. Whatever I was. Whatever I could be. Whatever I was. Whatever I could be. No more truth and no more honesty. Seven billion nine hundred and three. All the things we did here. All the things we did there. The future: an erased memory. How will I kill myself? How will I kill myself? How will I kill myself? I will kill myself. I will kill myself. I will kill myself. I will kill myself.

Two thousand seven hundred fifty-four thousand six million and twenty-nine point oh oh oh oh oh one seven hundred and fifty-three. I want to die. I want to die. I want to die. I want to die. I want to die. I want to die. I want to die. I want to die. I want to die. I want to die. I want to die. I want to die. I want to die. I want to die. Seven hundred and eighty-nine point six six four two nine. I want to die. I want to die. I want to die. I want to die. I want to die. I want to die. I want to die. Now I don't want to die. I don't want to die. I don't want to die. I don't want to die. I want to die. I want to die. I don't want to die. I want to die. I don't want to die. I don't want to die! I want to die. I don't want to die! I want to die. I would like to go to sleep. I would like to finish this book. I don't know how to finish this book. I would like to publish the book. I would like to sleep with the attractive ladies the ones that didn't sleep with me before who will of course when they finally read the book will want to sleep with me I want to put my penis inside them and wriggle it around until I ejaculate either inside them or outside them on their belly in my hand I want to die. I don't want to die! I want to finish this book. I would like to go to bed then tomorrow morning wake up and finish this book. I would like to, tomorrow morning, wake up with a really good idea and a way of finishing this book. I would like to finish this book, then publish this book. Then after publishing this book I would like to have sex with all the women who refused to have sex with me up until this point because I was too weird and insecure or just plain ugly for them then as soon as they see that I published this book and this book was immensely successful they will sleep with me. I would like to put my penis inside them and move it in and out until I shoot my semen into their vagina hole and the cervix dips down and lifts the semen up or I will shoot the semen over their belly and they will hold me after its done and tell me its ok and that I did a really good job, a really great job, of the book and of the sex and that I'm a really proficient writer and really good in bed and in my mind I will move up places on some imaginary ladder where I place everyone in my life but I don't really that doesn't really happen in that moment I'm not comparing myself to anyone or maybe I am I will wake up tomorrow and the book will magically finish itself because now Alex is involved and once Alex is involved we don't have to worry because he's saved us all all we have to do is pray to the Jesus man pray to the Jesus man pray to the Jesus man and it's ok because Alex is involved and all we have to do is pray to the Jesus man and it's a-ok because Alex is involved and when Alex is involved finally we can finish the book and one thousand three hundred and eighty nine million four thousand six hundred and ninety two point eight four four four prayers to Jesus. I would like to go to bed then tomorrow I would like to wake up.

Nothing beautiful, nothing sensical. Nothing beautiful, nothing sensical. Nothing beautiful, nothing sensical. A dream. It was a dream. It was a dream. It was a dream. It was a dream. It was a dream. It was a dream. It was a dream. It was a dream. It was a dream. It was a dream. It was a dream. It was a dream. Nothing is real now. Nothing is in the middle. It was a dream. It was a dream. The state of his mind could not corroborate. The state of his mind could not corroborate. The state of his mind was a dream. His mind was the shape of a dream. His mind was the same shape that his mind was. He was in the dream where his mind was. It was a dream where his mind was. It was a dream. It was a dream. It was a dream. The dream. A dream. The dream. A dream. The dream. A dream. It was a dream. It was the dream. It was a dream. It was the dream. When he says he cannot understand that is it, that is what is that cannot understand. He is "I cannot understand" and that is what he understands himself as being. It was a dream. Seven billion five thousand and forty-eight point nine nine nine nine nine nine recurring. All people carry spores. All people carry spores. All people carry spores. All people carry spores. Everything turns to ash. Everything turns to ash. Everything turns to ash. Everything turns to ash. Everything turns to ash. Everything turns to ash. Everything turns to ash. Everything turns to ash. Sleeping fully clothed. Sleeping fully clothed. Sleeping fully clothed. Sleeping fully clothed. Sleeping fully clothed. Sleeping fully clothed. Sleeping fully clothed. Sleeping fully clothed. Sleeping fully clothed. Sleeping fully clothed and having a dream fully clothed. Dreaming fully clothed, while sleeping fully clothed. It was a dream he had had while dreaming fully clothed and sleeping fully clothed. Five hundred and twenty-seven point eight four six two one seven three five reoccurring. By the time you read this, it will be zero zero colon four five. Therefore, I will be dreaming, without my trousers on, without my jumper on, with my t-shirt on, with my t-shirt on. Tomorrow morning, I will wake up and write seven thousand eight million two hundred and eighty-nine thousand four million and twenty-eight. Everything beautiful turns to ash. Everything beautiful. All the most wretched thoughts. Everything beautiful. All the worst thoughts, the most wretched thoughts, the most boring thoughts, the most asinine and idiotic thoughts, all the worst thoughts, the most treacherous thoughts, the most insane and disturbed thoughts, all the worst thoughts, the most wretched thoughts. All the things that are bad and all the ways I am bad. All the things that are bad and all the ways I am bad. All the things that are bad and all the ways that are bad. Not even killing myself, instead getting cancer and dying. Getting a bad illness and dying. All the worst thoughts, the most wretched pitiful thoughts, all the thoughts of dying, all the thoughts of tumours, all the thoughts of sudden chronic pain, all the thoughts of dying but not dead, dying but not dead, dying but not dead, not even killing myself. All the worst thoughts, the most wretched stomach-churning thoughts, all the worst thoughts, the cheapest, most wide-spread thoughts. All the things I have forgotten. All the things I have forgotten. The huge tracts of time, the smallest indications of love, the smallest indications of hate, all the things I have forgotten. I don't care about the things I have forgotten. I cannot care about the things I have forgotten.

☙

Crystal-clear memory, as if it was yesterday, of the New Year's Eve before last, 2018. Cannabis seems to dissect time into scenes for me: the unacknowledged, predetermined stage directions that run alongside the obtuse happenings are made apparent. Someone new enters the room: new scene. The lights are switched on or off: new scene.

The closing scene of the night, and it was a very pomo production, one with a tense and pregnant non-ending that leaves the audience unsettled. You were the highest of the three of us, not having a good time of it, spacing out, making contact with the deep despair that is always on the peripheral. He and I might just have been enjoying the silence, or maybe talking about something stupid, when you piped up with the question. The big thing. The big thing was not my doubts about him, nor my directionless anxiety, nor my starvation. This question, yes, was the big thing.

"Why is there separation?"

None of us could find it in us to even say something placating. You got up and went to bed.

☙

John and I were sat in my bedroom. He was sober, save for a single fruity cider he brought along with his picnic, and was anxious to smoke. I gestured to my glass bong, mumbled something about help yourself but you'll have to load it. He left to get fresh water, returned, stuffed a sticky little sativa nug into the bowl, lit it up and hit it a couple times before handing it to me. As I struggled with the lighter, he began animatedly talking about the sensation of skiing. I finally managed to take a rip, and only about five seconds after the first exhale did I feel my diminishing trip swell into a second wind: the walls pulsating with the bluish almond eyes of Egyptian sarcophagi, rendering every surface with the pattern. John's pretty face suddenly composed of smaller versions of his face. My tongue felt very weird. It was then, in that swell, that I got the text.

The service is starting at 7:30, I will meet you at the entrance.

I had forgotten completely.

I got up and left without saying where I was going.

As I stepped out the door and began to walk, the streets rendered in front of me like pages of a pop-up book, everything folding out and becoming fully actualised after a second delay. As I passed people, weaving through the square and the proceeding high street, it felt as if I were actually stationary, on a treadmill, that the environment was passing through me, rather than the inverse. People's conversations were visual, clouds of emojis and spider-charts swivelling and clustering above their heads, tinted different hues. There was a kind of mechanical feverishness to it, the paving and storefronts whirring like overheating computers, unable to process the load. I walked faster. Soon I saw the spire, poking up above the historical skyline, and headed straight for it.

There Alex waited for me, smiling, on the steps to the colossal opening of the York Minster, and beckoned me inside.

He led me down into the crypt where other people were also gathering; taking off their sensible coats and putting down their sensible bags. The room was tiny but impossibly beautiful, magical. Every surface clad in stone and dripping with gold, with a small wooden altar decorated with flowers, candles, and a gilded Medieval triptych of Christ placed in the middle. My eyes were wide, my heart was fast. The chants started. A long prayer was said, and as the words sank into me, I stared into the central image of Christ. He glowed. I was on the Tron bike, moving at hyperspeed into him, still stationary, huge, inarticulable thoughts generating and exploding, dissipating before I could grab hold of them. All of it was there, and all of it went unsaid. We sang. Tears of joy rolled down my cheeks. Men in white robes appeared and sprinkled us with holy water, it was so cold, it sizzled when it touched my face, cooled me down, washing away the city. The room was all gold then, swimming in it, ageless and outside of time. And then, seemingly without any cue, everyone stood up at once, still singing, and moved single file up the stairs from the crypt and back into the cathedral. The flight of stairs again moved through me, and the light of the candles was replaced with the miraculous purple of the summer evening, hazy in its potency, diffusing through the colossal panes of glass. I was born. I was crying. I had no idea who I was and didn't care. I was brand new, and he was there.

♛/♛

It's all about him. It's not all about him. He barely exists. I am agnostic. This is just about you and me. It's about the fusion of space and the separation of time. It is all about him. He is literally The Son and this is literally the

Bible. This is about replication. This is my book. This is your book and I'm just in it. This is a disco ball. This is by and for everyone and no one. This is for him. I never want him to read it. Give him a dummy book with nothing but pictures of cars and horses inside. I do not trust him. This is the most human novel of the 21st Century because it reads like it was compiled through machine learning. This is the scroll. This is basically alt-lit. This is garbage. I am literally Eve and you are literally the snake. This is Finnegans Wake. You are the toxic mushroom. This is the garbled manifesto of two failed mass shooters. I trust him wholeheartedly. I still love him. The 21st Century doesn't exist. I am Doubting Thomas. I hate you. I still love you. I hate him. He is still a pussy. I am Cooper in female form. You paint the picture and it's like I'm there. We've done it. This is Russian roulette. This is the letter bomb. You are me in male form. Alex is so important. It is all stacking up. This is self-actualising kompromat. This is literary gay chicken. This is torture. I just wanted to do one thing that didn't end up involving him. Let's involve him. I want to spit more food into the trash. We're geniuses. We're all geniuses. I love us all. This is our perpetual birthday card written by and for each other. This is neo-primitivist supertechnology. This is just one word after another. This is scripture. This is the Quran for doomers. We should attempt a threesome again. It is all about you. I almost wanted him to just be angry. Hail Mary. I barely exist. I'm just a voice. This is a book that you and he wrote about me and I only exist in the book. It's all dross. It's all true. It's all for you. It's a Rubik's cube. It's like anything.

✠

Myself, Baby Alex and Cooper: stood very upright, in height order, front row of Christian Assembly; Year 9. Mr Robert Edmonds, the Chaplain, looks at us a little disapprovingly. We are singing Shine Jesus Shine and the sheer volume our trio of voices drowns out the rest of the congregation. We look back at him with very serious expressions, our eyes wide and unblinking.

§

The pictogram of the letter "Q". Looks like a sperm penetrating an egg, or the on/off symbol. The pictogram of the letter "A". Looks like a snow-capped mountain, or a triangle walking around with two legs.

§

The notorious intubation process practiced at eating disorder treatment facilities: a woman being held down and a long clear tube being forced up her nose and down her throat, into which a thick, white, calorically dense liquid is pumped. She groans and sobs.

§

A woman getting skullfucked: the back of her head pressed down onto an anonymous penis until she vomits, penis still in mouth.

§

Quentin, aged six: putting a girl in a headlock at the Wacky Warehouse.

♔

I am excited but wary. Read his email again. It had the grandiose and easy-going tone that one hears from a person on the morning of the day they will kill themselves. Also: an aftertaste of intense condescension. He is wearing masks again.

§

The smartphone erupts. It's Baby Alex.

We talked for a very long time. In the 24 hours between
11pm on Monday and 11pm on Tuesday, we talked for 10.
Most of it was joyous, and all of it was easy. He laughed
and forgave me as if it was nothing. As if it had been no
time at all.

At one point at around 3pm yesterday, the house was
empty, and I was sitting on a broken deckchair in the
garden, staring up into the sky.

"I guess we should talk about what happened the day we
all met."
"Yes."
"We never even really spoke about it. But it seemed so
important."
"Almost too important to talk about."
"I think it traumatised me in a way. Like, I could have
probably made myself feel better about it all if I had just
spoken to you. But I didn't. And I think you did
something similar."
"Yeah, I definitely did."
"I just felt like... I brought him into your house. And I
didn't have to do that. But I unleashed this thing, this
part of me, and I knew I couldn't undo it. It fucking
scared me."
"I know what you mean."
"How did it make you feel?"
I remember I paused for a second.
"...He came through the door, walked down the hall into
the dining room where I was sitting, and I got up and
shook his hand. And we just shook hands and stared at
each other. Then it was like everything expanded. I felt
like I understood it instantly. He was a part of you that

you had let me see, and I felt the significance of it right then. I looked at him and saw you, and then saw the part of myself that is in you in him, and kind of... it was like right then, I loved him. I knew I loved him, right from that moment."

§

A large gathering of LUFC supporters in front of the Leeds City Museum. One single Man U supporter, a woman, wearing the red kit, stood in front of them, dancing. They chant at her and point their fingers: "You're Leeds, and you know you are... You're Leeds, and you know you are..." or "If you love Man U, fuck off... If you love Man U, fuck off..."

♔

Baby Alex pulling out super-hairs from his face, quasi-twigs that have nestled into his skin. Me, asked by the year sperg in PE why I didn't have any hair under my armpits at the age of 16. Even the gremlin sperg had hair there. Asking my Dad if by sweating more I could accelerate the growth of hair under my armpits, him laughing and saying "don't be daft", and me feeling ashamed. Baby Alex in the changing rooms with fully grown pubic hair at the age of 13. Me at 21 growing my first chest hair, long and lonely between my pecs. Me gripping my hard erection in the bathroom and looking at its thickness in the mirror, this morning, age 25. Length obsession has transmuted to girth obsession. Looking at Roz's extra skin and thinking "well babes, you asked for it". Looking at Roz's skeleton wrists and the disproportionate bone mass of her knees to her leg.

"The strangest thing," you say, while we drank jasmine tea

at the reopened Mrs Atha's café in Leeds, "is that he's not even that different from what he was like before."
Experimental volumetric clouds morph silently above.
"Hmm. But the sea did change him a little. He's now dating a thirty-year-old Brazilian chick..." I'm spitting on a tissue and wiping my new AF1s.
"I know. And he's driving!"

He emailed both of us a week after the circus of media and police reports had died down. Faith moves mountains, he said. Also, he received a first in sociology from the University of York. No mention of his re-emergence from the ocean.

Took retarded uncle Steven to Morrison's and let him point out all the deals. He seems to be repeating things more as he gets older. He was wearing a black neoprene mask, and I said I was jealous. He said corrr only 70p for a Battenberg! 70p for a Battenberg!

I could spend hours in supermarkets, just staring at things, picking them up and putting them down. On good days the internal monologue is meticulous but purely anthropological, as though I am an alien who has closely studied the snack foods of the human race. On bad days it is hell, pure misery, and the longer I dawdle the angrier and more savage it gets, until it becomes a single loud tone, a siren, and I have to leave without buying anything at all.

The endless variations that now exist as the snake begins to eat itself. Rhubarb and custard cream biscuits. Cotton candy flavoured GMO grapes. Marmite peanut butter. Lemon cheesecake flavoured 10-calorie jelly. Almond

milk mocha cold brew. Lotus cookie butter donuts.
Miniature watermelons. Katsu curry kettle crisps. Salted
caramel rice cakes. Giant Starbursts. Vegan barbecue
burgers stuffed with vegan cheese. Sugarloaf white
pineapple. Dairy Milk chocolate with Oreos sandwiched
around the outside. Parma Violet cider. Mini frosted
wheats filled with blueberry compote. Diet cherry 7up.
Red pesto hummus. Tiny ball-shaped Jaffa Cakes that
come in a bag. Cauliflower hash browns. Cookies and
cream sugar-free whey protein bars. Coronation chicken
crackers. White Skittles for pride month. M&Ms
chocolate spread. Starbucks skinny caramel latte. Sloe gin
ice cream. Gingerbread avocados. Chocolate chai organic
instant coffee. Soy kielbasa. Mayonnaise and ketchup
mixed and combined in a squeezy bottle. Chickpea
brownies. Salted caramel pretzels. Microwavable pre-
seasoned quinoa. Jelly Bean ice lollies. Ecuadorian dark
chocolate with chilli flakes. Green coffee extract. Sticks
of mature cheddar with a dipping pot of Branston pickle.
Cookie dough Kit-Kats. Sparkly jam infused with
prosecco. Rocky road trifle. Cheeseburger pizza.

♛

His escargots reluctance on New Year's. For all my
freakishness at least I'm adventurous with food. A
gourmand. I like that you like oysters and blue cheese. It
sounds fatuous but I think there's something in it. Same
with how you like animals and he only pretends to. He
had limited tastes. And he would chew distractedly,
mouth open, like a child. Like... a baby. I am a good cook.
I could have cooked him anything he wanted. But he
usually just wanted fish finger sandwiches. I made him
one when I was drunk and he became obsessed. I haven't
had one since I last saw him.

Baby food. Food for babies. Three seven zero plus two five for the V8 equals three nine five plus for the celery probably three equals three nine eight and then one grape to round it up and then a walk minus two hundred and a cup of almond milk. He thought it was cute, how long I started to flail for in the supermarket, he thought I was just excited, or indecisive, and I could never tell him what I was really thinking about. I knew back then, just after Christmas, that there was probably something wrong. But I didn't feel like I was crazy enough, thin enough to have that conversation, so I never said anything about it. I never gave him an opportunity to do something. What could he have even done? But we'd be fucking and I'd just be out of it, worrying about having to go to Nando's with his parents two days from then. I think I just knew I wanted out but also that he would probably thrive with the project of having a girlfriend with a discernible issue. That's why he loved perpetually broken Amy and nervous Mary. I would become a thing he could tinker with but never fully fix, he would get to LARP as some kind of breadwinner, winning me bread, and I couldn't imagine anything worse. So, I said nothing. I do not want to be coddled, kept, I want to be left to my own devices. I want to be a little evil. Five for the two rice cakes in the trash.

♕

The thinner I get, the more breast augmentation ads play before videos.

Three girls sitting by a pool in a hot country. One is talking. She is one of those girls who, even with all the grooming money can buy, is just not a looker. She should give up her pursuit. Chubby with a weirdly masculine, hard face. Covered in such a thick layer of makeup she has somehow made herself more andro, like a drag queen. A pantomime dame. Speaking in a broad Birmingham accent: "everyone keeps saying, oh, you only got your boobs done to get attention, you only did it for the lads. Uh, actually, I did it for lots of reasons. I did it for me, and... I did it for my mental health, and like... because it's 2020."

♛

Phone call intervention with mother and grandparents. My grandmother's defensiveness and flippant tone of voice that she reverts to whenever she talks about something serious, and my grandfather's tendency to just go straight to shouting. No compassion in their voices, only anger, doggedness, a determination to be proved right that was so strong it completely overshadowed the delicate point they were trying to make. And they can only get so mad when they initially praised my losing weight more, and with a higher level of sincerity, than they have any other achievement of mine. I almost wanted to say that. Their issue is wholly an aesthetic one. They and my mother have no idea that I do in fact feel bad sometimes. They just think I look too thin, and that's all they really care about, the appearance, so why should I warrant them with some kind of teary admittance that I can't help but feel they don't deserve. And my mother only allowed them to shout at me for so long because she's secretly afraid of them, always the least favourite of the brood, the lone girl who has done nothing but try and prove herself to them. They never approved of how she raised me. So maybe she is also unconsciously letting them have their constant, two very loud cents on this little food episode to validate to them that she can handle it correctly, and maybe win some kind of respect from them which is simultaneously wholly important and totally meaningless. In conclusion: the whole thing pissed me off. They told me to gain weight and I said "I'll see what I can do" then hung up.

On all fours in the bathroom, quietly panicking, trying to get the egg out. Forgot how difficult this is.

I've got it.

§

Message from James Cooper:

Muuuundia
do you know what it's like to not be able to trust anything your dad says?
in muuuuundia

2019, sometime in the spring, stood by the bus-stop in Leeds City Centre: awaiting a bus that I have never taken before. The bus comes, I get on, press my contactless card to the reader, take my ticket and sit on one of the upstairs seats, right at the front to enjoy the view. The bus drives out of the city, to the south, further and further into the more forgotten areas of West Yorkshire, little knots of suburban towns indistinct from each other, that may at one point have been alive with industry, making steel or textiles, but now seem to be the places where people live because they have no other choice. The white communities from these towns have vanished, almost everyone is brown, and each person looks either unhappy or too stupid to be unhappy. Following the bus on Google Maps, I figure the next bend in the road should be my stop, I get up from my seat, feeling the mass of metal sway, and bing the STOP button. I descend the stairs in galloped clumps of three steps, arrive by the left of the driver. The bus brakes, the door's pneumatics phssst open, and I say "Thanks a lot" to the driver's sleepy face.

I am carrying in my hand a copy of Joyce's Ulysses, of which I have only read the first ten pages. I cross the road, walk down a street of grey houses, the sky overcast as usual. I come up to a large building, an NHS sign somewhere at the front that I don't read, and I walk straight in, through the two sets of automatic doors, into a reception area, heavily carpeted, smelling clinical and sour.

"Hi there." The receptionist smiles at me.
"Hi." I smile back, "I'm here to see er... Brian Scobie?"
"Ok well, that's great. Just sign in here on the register and I'll send you through."
"Sure thing." I sign my name and wait at the door for her to unlock it.
"I'll just ask you to go in quite quickly because we're having some problems with one resident."
"Yeah, no problem." I smile at her. I smile at her to show that I am bringing happiness into her building.

The door opens and I go through, immediately finding an elderly woman to my right, white hair frazzled, barely any of it left on her scalp, mouth open and eyes facing in a strange direction, attempting to get past a middle-aged nurse wearing blue, who is holding her by the shoulder and saying "Margaret, come on, let's go to the TV room, why don't we watch some TV?" Margaret, with no desire to watch TV, lunges for the open door, then the wall — unsteady on her feet, holding her grey plastic walking-stick slightly in the air. I close the door, am thanked by the nurse, and walk to the elevator.

In the elevator I stand next to two nurses, one wearing blue and another wearing pink. The one wearing blue is a skinny Pakistani girl with a hijab who looks worried; the one wearing pink is white, in her mid-forties, a plump arse, a nice face, and a general air of maternal business, that soothing voice and authentic up-beat attitude — just a mastery of what it means to care, a genius of hospitality — that makes me want to crawl into bed with her and be patted on the head. The elevator doors open, I walk down the corridor, thick lino floor, walls painted a muted lime, framed photographs of things from the 50s and 40s, and one particularly large photograph of a mountain vista behind a window frame, and, disturbingly, some real mini-curtains in front.

I arrive at a large area with three deranged old people milling around, one watching television sat by the window, another walking at a very slow pace in one direction then turning and walking back, doing this hobbled loop, a third grinning idiotically, sat at a dining table. I go to the small nurse's kitchen area, with posters on the doors explicitly asking residents not to enter, and ask if they know where Brian Scobie is. "Oh, I think he's in his room. He had a bit of a... moment, earlier today."

I walk up to my dad's room, opening the door slowly. There he is: similar hairstyle to Margaret, sat on the side of the bed, doing nothing but staring outwards with a slightly shocked expression on his face. They seem to have shaven his beard in the three days since I last saw him, leaving him with just a moustache, which unsettles me more than anything else. I have never really seen my dad without a full-beard. One end of his plaid shirt is sticking out the half-opened top of his fly, but this is normal.

"Hey dad... heard you were being a wee bit of a trouble-maker."

"Trouble? Well son..." He laughs a little beneath his breath, but it's almost all reflex, he has very little idea to what I'm referring to. There's also something about the tone of his voice that suggests he doesn't know if the last time he has spoken to me is five minutes ago, five days ago, or five years. "No, I'm not... well if it did..." He sighs, smiling slightly, perhaps pleased that his speaking duty is over.

"I've brought some... Joyce. Ulysses. I know you can't read so I thought maybe..."

"Joyce?!" His eyes brighten, his mouth pops open, then he smiles. He is completely shocked this time, the name clicking onto a compartment of his mind that has lain dormant, a crystallised set of memories that somehow refused deletion. "Yes, Joyce is quite... Yes... there's something..."

I look across at his desk. Books, four of them in a stack: pointless books for an English Professor who cannot read. Ilona has also left a framed photograph of Hugh MacDiarmid.

"I see you've got your MacDiarmid picture nicely propped up to keep you company."

"MacDiarmid!?" Shocked again, my father's voice suddenly becomes doubly Scottish and almost belligerent, and he raises his eyebrow at me as though to say watch what yer aboot tae say jimmy. "It's not quite... Ah..." He chuckles in a reminiscence that may or may not be authentic. "Christopher. And his wife would always..." He laughs again.

He cannot exactly remember his stories of the Scottish Nationalist and Communist poet, Hugh MacDiarmid. MacDiarmid's wife would explicitly command: "No Whiskey", before my dad was to drive MacDiarmid on speaking tours of Universities in England. As they reached the Scottish borders, about to enter England, MacDiarmid would always repeat a joke, looking out at the sky in the distance, saying with a foreboding tone: "Looks like bad weather up ahead..."

I glance at the photograph again, then at my father, remarking on the similarity of phenotype, that wizened old Scot quality, kind eyes that have been squashed in by a perpetual grumpiness. "Why don't we go outside, the sky's clearing up a little, I can read you some Ulysses."

Dad smiles again. We start the old person shuffle, down the corridors, into the elevator, past beaming nurses glad to see a young man taking care of his confused white-haired father. In a room with six or so senile people and a nurse, attempting to get through one of the glass doors into the garden, I almost feel the impulse to protect my father, to shield him with my body, from the vegetation of the elderly around him, to say "No! He is not one of you! He is not going to become like you!" They look back at me with their vapid, utterly cretinous faces: either smiling or totally vacant. One of the nurses defends the doorway as we go in the garden, to prevent any of the demented zombies from following us.

Once in the garden we sit on a bench, after a bit of herding-cats difficulty with the three-quarters blind and fully stubborn father. I turn to see that the care home has placed an exact replica of a bus stop in the middle of the path, next to the greenhouse. "Buses towards: Dewsbury, Huddersfield, Leeds."

"So apparently there was an issue," I say.
"There was an issue."
"But it's been resolved."
"Yes... well. They've... conceded."
I laugh and begin to read Ulysses to him. Every now and

then he will correct my pronunciation of a certain word. These moments of acuity surprise me, I try and milk them for all they are worth. I delve into these points, attempting to understand what part of the file is still uncorrupted, asking a follow-up question, but the responses are always dissatisfying, completely unrelated, or so mumbled and syntactically chaotic that they are impossible to decipher. In any case most moments with parents, lucid or not, could rarely be described as satisfactory.

A memory: possibly the closest I remember feeling to my father, the closest I came to relieving the tension of our relationship. I was in my early teens, and my dad, having understood my growing interest in the written word, sat down with me to give a personal father-son lecture on how to write. Of course, there was the slight pretence of stuffiness, of authoritarian business-as-usual — and still that gulf, that coolness — but I appreciated that moment with him more than any other. We sat on the sofa in his cold house in Bradford, and he, in a rare mood of openness and calm, took out a copy of Shakespeare's Sonnets. "Sonnet 12, like the twelve hours on a clock-face. Ok son, now listen to this..."

When I do count the clock that tells the time,
And see the brave day sunk in hideous night;
When I behold the violet past prime,
And sable curls all silver'd o'er with white;
When lofty trees I see barren of leaves,
Which erst from heat did canopy the herd,
And summer's green all girded up in sheaves,
Borne on the bier with white and bristly beard,
Then of thy beauty do I question make,
That thou among the wastes of time must go,
Since sweets and beauties do themselves forsake
And die as fast as they see others grow;

And nothing 'gainst Time's scythe can make defence
Save breed, to brave him when he takes thee hence.

§

"sucking sage leaf on a balcony"
"drank two sips of beer and gave up"
"i'm in bed like a piece of shit"
"i posted this selfie for my crush and he didn't interact. why doesn't he LIKE me"
"chamomile tea to hopefully allow me to sleep w minimal anxiety about bugs crawling all over me :-)"
"i wish i had a yard"
"me (reading philosophy): what"
"every new Dairy Queen flavor is a technological leap that shits on the grave of every scientist that worked on the Manhattan Project"
"tried rollerblading but forgot to bring socks w me :-(.."

♕

My occasional phone sex partner from New Zealand has been messaging me again in the past couple of days. Strangely enough, this is my longest surviving friendship, having met him in the golden age of novelty Facebook groups. A perfect example of those liminal connections you make texting someone you don't know irl: in those periods of heavy talking you pine for them so viscerally, so vividly... and then it ceases overnight and you quickly forget they ever existed. They slide back into the DMs months later and the cycle repeats. Pretty much nobody in my life knows about him, and I doubt anybody in his knows about me.

He has just gotten out of his last relationship and is feeling sad, which is why he is speaking to me again.

While we do talk about a lot of things, the crux of the relationship is sexual, and we never get smutty when one of us is seeing someone. I had sent him a mirror selfie of my outfit that morning just as I was getting ready to leave the house. He had said something about me looking like a snack and him wanting a piece which I had ignored, not feeling the dopamine spike I usually do when I hear from him. As I sank into the bathwater at midnight he messaged me again, just rising from bed on the other side of the world.

a: fell asleep thinking of you, woke up thinking of you

r: [selfie, breasts obscured by bubbles, hand placed thoughtfully on chin]
r: how intriguing
r: that's me looking intrigued

a: oh my god
a: look at you
a: as lovely as a peach

r: [hopeful eyes emoji] a peach?

a: yes you
a: love your big eyes and your bare shoulders
a: your collarbone turns me on

r: [selfie, with more defined angle of collarbones and added cartoon rainbow sticker]

a: oh my god
a: i want you so badly

r: [selfie, sitting sideways in the bath, legs hanging over the edge, breasts obscured by arm, mildly bored expression]

a: you look so delicious
a: going to make me late for work if you keep being so cute

r: [picture of bare legs, one bent one outstretched, foot visible]
r: be late!! see if i CARE
r: hehe

a: i'm going cross eyed
a: your legs look amazing
a: skin looks impossible soft

r: [selfie, stroking leg, breasts obscured by leg, more bored expression]
r: it's pretty soft ngl

a: no bath for me
a: 30 second shower for the working man

r: that's miserable

a: that's life

♔

I felt completely removed from the situation, I wasn't aware it was me taking the selfies. I was instead a third party, a lurker, the proverbial "FBI agent" silently observing everyone's private online interactions. In that train of thought, I found myself getting a little turned on at the thought of watching two people flirt, and then I remembered one of the people was me. I got up and went to bed, my phone still buzzing as he asked for more.

♕

Queued for 20 minutes for world famous fried haddock from a chip shop in Aldeburgh, stood directly behind an exhausted young mother with a hyperactive child who appeared to be reciting a Disney movie line by line. Mum was sitting by the beach with the dog. When I finally got to the counter I panicked in my fasted state and just asked for fish, and then fish and chips for mum. I walked all the way back to the beach, gave mum her fish and chips, took two bites of my fish. A seagull swooped down from a nearby rooftop and snatched the entire piece of fish from my hand. I did not react. We walked on the beach for two hours, and then I got home, went to the bathroom, and passed out cold on the floor for 10 minutes.

§

"Only a being that is essentially futural in its being so that it can let itself be thrown back upon its factical there, free for its death and shattering itself on it, that is, only a being that, as futural, is equiprimordially having-been, can hand down to itself its inherited possibility, take over its own thrownness and be in the Moment for 'its time.' Only authentic temporality that is at the same time finite makes something like fate, that is, authentic historicity, possible."

♔

We turn up to Baby Alex's new-build house, recently bought, a month or two after his rebirth from the sea. His new girlfriend Lecia opens the door.

"Hi guys! So glad you could come! Alex is waiting for you

in the gym."

"The gym?"

"Yes, he told me to send you right in. Do you want anything to drink, with have green tea, yerba maté..."

"I'll have a jasmine tea."

"I'll also have a jasmine tea."

"Excellent, ok, go on through..."

The place is immaculate. The walls are painted a mixture of aqua blues, platinum white and cool greys. The floor is varnished sandalwood. Two cream sofas in front of a sheepskin rug face a vintage stove, with no television. We move slowly through the house, every ten seconds or so giving each other odd looks. The art pieces on the walls are all Baby Alex's — seemingly a set of visions, large canvas oil paintings of apocalyptic scenarios, salvations, rapture. We arrive at the home gym. Baby Alex is running on the treadmill with white sensors placed over his body, ringed by circles where his body hair has been shaved off. Gregorian chant plays from a state-of-the-art sound system with an additional two subwoofers. He turns, slows down the machine to a walking pace, gets off and walks up to us, taking off a strange pair of glasses and handing them to us.

"Take a look at this."

I take the glasses from his hand and put them on. Suddenly the room is filled with data-points, navigating each other and forming these transient graphs that seem to shift with the movement of Alex's arm. He zips himself into a full white Adidas tracksuit after towelling down his forehead and back.

"Augmented Reality Biometric system. Pretty neat huh?"

"I... guess. Where did you get the money for all this?"

"Well, I have about four or five different income streams

now. Plus the advance from Harper Collins for the book I'm writing."

"Book? But you don't write."

"That's what I told them! But no..." he laughs, then smiles at us with a beaming grin, "it's good to see you."

You look at me, we smile, and we look at Alex and smile.

"It's good to see you too."

I hand him back the glasses. "Been a while. Glad to see you haven't changed."

"Not really, not where it counts. I have so much to tell you."

He leads us out to the garden, smallish, surrounded by a tall wood fence. He managed to get one of the new-builds with the garden that looks out onto the woodland.

"I see you managed to get one of the new-builds with the garden that looks out onto the woodland."

"Yeah. There's a little gate, we can go out later, I'll show you this spot by the river where I go to meditate."

"Nice, very nice."

"I'm currently doing a two-day fast so I'm not going to eat anything but do you guys want something to drink or eat?"

You turn to me quickly, then look back at Alex.

"I think... I think Lecia was going to get us jasmine tea. I'm not hungry."

"Yeah, Roz has decided to go as the boy in the striped pyjamas for Halloween so she's skipping carbs today. I will have a celery stick with peanut butter smeared throughout... the interior. You know."

You look mock-disapprovingly at me.

"I am actually not skipping carbs today, and I will also have a celery stick with peanut butter smeared throughout its interior."

"Great, oh here's Lecia now."

Lecia comes out with the jasmine teas.

"Lecia." His voice goes a number of decibels quieter. "Do we have any peanut butter and celery sticks?"

"Em we have celery sticks of course. I'm not sure we have..."

"Celery stick no peanut butter is fine." I interject.

"Yes," you say, smiling "fine by me."

"Guys..." he looks at us again, smiling. "It's really good to see you."

We sit eating the celery sticks and drinking the jasmine tea before I crush up the final inch of stick, finish my mouthful and turn to Baby Alex.

"So... Roz and I came up with this hypothesis."

"Yes?"

"About your erm... brief stint in the sea."

"Oh..."

"You went into some parallel thingy. Magic parallel thingy. I don't like the idea of parallel thingies, for various reasons, but you know, it seems like in this case, a parallel thingy is the best description we can muster."

"I see..."

"Yes, you do see. The sea. Also, there's the question of all this money. Are the aliens paying you? I mean I get it that you want to grow up and that but erm..." I gesture to one of the odd contemporary art water features in the garden. "Is this necessary? Are you paying for this?"

"I have about four or five different income streams now, it's quite easy. I have patrons, I sell merch, I have a podcast, motivational speaking packages, fitness plans. The money I got from doing some media plugs after I ... I put it straight into a fund that's doing very well. Crypto, etc. Chinese unicorns. And then there's the book deal."

"But the market is down, Alex. The market is down."

"It just takes a little more initiative to make money in a bear market."

You look at me to signal a polite entrance into the conversation, putting on your slightly higher-pitched nurse voice when you want to seem both maternal and assertive. "Well look, personally I don't care about the money and I've very glad that you've got your act together Alex. But what we really came to ask you about is the ... sea ... thing."

"Well yeah, the sea thing is important. And it might explain the fact you've gone from a stoner loser who lives with his parents to this... Elon Musk cult leader."

Baby Alex puts down his cup of jasmine tea, sighs, and walks a couple of steps away from us, facing the woodland. He sighs again.

"I swore I would never tell anyone this..."
"But you're going to tell us."
"Leave the Jasmine tea. Come with me to my meditation spot. I don't want be around the house in case Lecia hears."

♔

He leads us past the garden gate, along a dirt path through brambles and ferns. The path snakes about the woodland before forking, Baby Alex takes the path to the right, and we descend towards the river. There, by the riverside, is the concrete skeleton of some abandoned industrial building. Baby Alex leads us through an open stone doorway into a room covered with broken glass and rotting wood, then through another doorway to a room with half the floor missing, looking out onto the slow-moving river and the forest behind it. Hidden away are a number of fold-out chairs and cushions beneath tarp. Baby Alex looks out at the river and takes a deep breath.

"Someone installed a wind-chime nearby when I first got here. So... I had to do some reconnaissance work and now... let's just say..." he looks at us, taps his nose: "the wind-chime sleeps with the fishes."
"Very cool."
You sit on a fold out chair and begin to roll a cigarette.
"Aye, well speaking of fishes, you were saying... the sea."
Baby Alex's expression goes sombre again. He looks out at the river, his gaze seeming to lock onto its speed completely, somehow his face becoming riverlike.
"Ok erm, well, watch this."
"Watch what?"
"This."

His eyes turn completely white. A wind picks up, twisting and accelerating at him. His hands outstretch, and his body begins to levitate and glow a blinding hot blue. Music, like nothing I've ever heard before, music like all the emotions of the world in perfect representation and harmony, like someone managed to reverse-engineer the brain's experience of the sublime, impossible textures and unknown instruments, voices from other worlds. Something like "Holy! Holy! Holy! King of Kings! King of Kings! Holy! Holy! Holy! King of Kings!" The music fades gradually as Baby Alex returns to the ground, the wind slows and his eyes return to normal.

I'm squinting at him. "What... the actual... fuck? Woah!"
You take a long drag from your cigarette, blinking quickly in a bamboozled fashion.
"So you're Jesus now?"
He sighs. "In a manner of speaking."
"In a manner of speaking, right."
"In a manner of speaking, we're all Jesus," he says, brushing some dirt off of his tarp.
"Well, I suppose, in a manner of speaking, but in another manner of speaking none of us can quite do... that."

"That was quite impressive anyway, Alex."

"Thanks Roz. Look, I can't explain."

"Hey, don't worry bud. We got all day. I think I'll have a ciggie."

"Go ahead," you hand me the baccy.

"The day after Roz broke up with me..."

"Oh, so it's her fault."

You shoot me a look of exasperation.

"No, not quite, it's not her fault. It was perfect. It began the day after Roz broke up with me... I walked into the..."

§

One of the more colourful explanations of Christ's resurrection had been that of an Alien fleet camped out of the Earth's orbit taking the Messiah's body from its tomb and conducting a resuscitation program on the Son of God somewhere in space, returning him three days later. Various passages were referenced for evidence of extra-terrestrial technology and each of the Biblical miracles could then be rationally explained by hard science. Christ was either an alien, or a human who had been bestowed with futuristic alien technology. This didn't seem far-fetched. The homeless mechanic who expounded the hypothesis slept with no sleeping bag, did not shower or bathe, had black fingernails, and paid me ten bucks to debate him.

♔

" ... "

The sound of the river. No one says a word, you ash silently into a broken bottle filled with rainwater.

"If I have told you earthly things, and ye believeth not, how shall ye believe, if I tell you of heavenly things?" He finally whispers. The sound of the river returns.

"Did I tell you I quit sugar?" I say, after a minute of watching the dark ripples grow, undulate and disappear.
"No, you didn't."
"You mentioned it to me a couple of times," you say.
"I quit sugar. I think it's causing my anxiety to play up. That's a thing, right? Something to do with dopamine, the cravings."
"I wouldn't know."
"Apart from that, I feel much better. Much more focussed."
"That's great."

You take a last drag and drop the cigarette into the bottle. Turning to Baby Alex, you look at him for a moment.

"I get it."
"You do?"
"You don't have to explain it. I get it. I've got it."

✚

A neo-cardinal in a red tunic sits at a desk in a white box, light emanating from its walls, looking at ancient parchments with a pair of AR glasses. There is a knock on the wall. It turns transparent, revealing a lanky young man in a beige tunic on the other side, holding a small malleable tablet.

"Father."
"What is it, Anthony."
"Word from analytics."

"Well, say what you must."

"The Replicator made contact, father."

"...Again?"

"Just like his father."

"...Which year?"

The intern looks at his tablet. "Plane Delta, 2020. One of the plagues-"

"Yes, I am familiar, my child."

"At the point of temporal entry it had been less than a month since contact, and he already has his two disciples."

"He has initiated them?"

"Not yet, father. But Alex's power grows each day. They're synergising. He appears to be very... motivational."

"Keep all eyes and hands on him. On the three of them. May they be blessèd."

"May they be blessèd."

"Now back to work. Keep close watch."

"Yes, father."

The wall turns opaque again.

"And Anthony?"

Transparent again.

"Yes father?"

"I would like some cereal. The good kind."

"Yes father."

♛

Right now, I'm sitting by the river with the fancy vape I dug out from my drawer, inhaling artificial abstractions of watermelon, thinking about Richard Brautigan. Feeling pleasantly hollow, like a Fabergé egg, or a golf ball. Heart rate 45bpm. Overcast sky. Light and balmy breeze. Low tide.

Sometimes I feel completely horrified by the tech I have orbiting around me 24/7: the bacteria slab with its inner wormhole, the bigger bacteria slab, the orthorexia watch on my wrist, the several vapes, the headphones and EarPods. It makes me wonder if I should be this horrified all the time. These are the points when I put everything in a drawer and meditate. However, some moments I embrace it fully, enjoying all my things in a way that doesn't seem weak or frivolous, but instead very powerful: accelerationist, alchemical. Sometimes I just relish the freedom I have, the potential for knowledge, a futurist mage in a forest of information, warping with fractals of detail and density. Sometimes I really love my phone and I'm not afraid to say it. Waking up in the middle of the night and listening to ambient music on a quiet volume: it has such a mood to it, such a colour, a beautiful and delicious melancholy.

§

You feel this sudden self-hood. You're three years old at a party and you start to point at the other children: you have a world inside your head, so do you, so do you, so do you. Or: you are stood in the refectory aged seventeen about to have lunch when you feel this surge of awareness, this uncanny sense of a new reality. It happens steadily, and then all at once. The details of yourself, that you knew up to that point as a set of disparate elements, take on a highly formalised structure, something geometric and thus able to be scrutinised even further. It is not a passing moment of lucidity, it is your mind from that point onward, the degree with which you understand life. You think: "Oh, so this is growing up". You think: "Oh, wait, I'm actually alive."

§

"So how did you meet Lecia?"
"Hinge mate."
"Nice. Real nice. Haven't tried that one yet, will do. Roz went on Hinge a little."
"Yeah I did, Rural Hinge."
"Sounds depressing."
"It was."
"Bit presumptuous though don't you think."
"What?"
"I don't know man, like, moving in with her and that."
"Sometimes you just know. I was ready."
"Yeah, I see. You can drive now. It makes sense."

§

A streak of gold in the sky, like a reflection from a pane of glass, sliding in and then out of the clouds.

"Did you see that?"
"What?"
"...I don't know."

♔

There were moments near the end, driving us to and from his house in Bradford, along the M62, when Dad was losing his eyesight. He began to drive by use of touch. He would veer left constantly, maintaining his straight line on the road through following that ominous moaning of the wheel when it hits the texture to alert the sleepy. At first, we didn't notice, we thought it was just his particular, odd style of driving. Then he began to hit things, curbs and wing mirrors. Each trip became fearful, gripping the door handle and nervously saying "erm, Dad, watch out..." He had his major accident without us in the car, and after that my step-mother drove.

☖

They appear rigid and confined, like cows at the edge of the cow-field. There are cows in the cow-field, we pass them, in the "Baby Alex"-mobile.

"Thanks for taking us to the station." you say.
"No problem."
"A pleasant drive in the countryside." I pipe up from the back. "E adesso, il treno."

A looming hooded figure, plodding along the thin line of grass by the drystone wall. I turn quickly to look at him through the rear window.

"I think..."
"Really?"
"Yeah, I think that's Cooper."
"Do we stop?"
"I ... I don't even know. You're Christ now. Would you stop?"
"Where's he walking?"
"He's pretty far from Bradford. I think that's where he's supposed to be."
"We should stop."
"Ok then, stop the car."

Baby Alex brakes slowly and pulls over in a lay-by. I get out of the car, feeling that small trickle of dread spreading over my nervous system, then wave enthusiastically at Cooper shouting "Hey! Fuckface!" He sees me and starts grinning with those oversized lips of his, then suppresses the grin and looks around a little paranoid, before walking up in lumbering steps to me with a facial expression that could interpreted as anything from stifled glee to stifled terror.

"Hey guuuuuuys!" he says, his voice intonation very forced and unnerving as always.

"We're driving to the station. Baby Alex is, he can drive now."

"Woooooow... oooh Alex is a big boy... big boy nice car... ooooh."

"Hey Cooper."

He looks at you and Baby Alex for a second, eyes darting back and forth between you, and there is an uncomfortable silence.

"Alex and his girlfriend."

"She's actually not his girlfriend anymore."

"Ooooooh" he leans on the car.

"Yeah, we broke up."

"Why... was he not fucking you hard enough? Ahahaha..."

Cooper starts to grope the bulge in his tracksuit bottoms.

"Wakawakawakawaka... ahahah"

"Well Alex?" I say, enjoying the fact that I'm not the focus of Cooper's hijinks for once.

"How are you doing James?" says Baby Alex, unphased, still smiling.

Cooper stops laughing and starts looking grumpy and restless. "Fine..."

"Do you need a lift anywhere?"

"Yeah... can you call me a taxi?"

"I can drive dude, where do you need to be?"

"Actually, can I borrow your phone? I need to call my dad."

"Why don't you come to the station with us?"

"Errrrrr...."

"Just get in the car big man."

"Alright alright, but I need to use your phone."

Cooper gets in the back with me, his gangly legs pressing up on the back of your seat. "Move your seat forward errr Alex's girlfriend..."

"Hi, it's Roz."

"Yeah... err... Roz, move your seat forward."

"Sure," you look at me with a slight smile as you adjust the seat and I smile back, secret messages exchanged in the smallest fraction of time.

"Don't doooo that."

"Don't do what big man."

"Don't make fun of me."

"Alright alright, we won't. We weren't."

"Shut the fuck up... bitch."

"Alright," I sigh, "alright. Cunt."

"Bro you don't understand what I've been through..."

Now Cooper is in the back less than a metre from my face I can see his teeth up close, stained yellow with what looks like hard pieces of brown grime stuck to the middle bits. He takes out his baccy and papers and starts to roll a cigarette, loose baccy placed in random places on his tracksuit bottoms, falling onto the car floor. Baby Alex looks around for a second.

"James you can't smoke in here."

"Ok I'll just..."

"James!"

"Ooooh. Alex! Ahahaha. I'll just roll it."

"James..."

"Brew you don't understand, like, I've been... wait" he looks around the car and out of the windows, checking for something, then whispers in a mischievous tone, "I've been getting her dude..."

"Getting who?"

"Getting my grandma, who do you think?"

"Uh huh. And how's that?"

"Great." he says, in a very standoffish childish way. "Breeeew... I've been getting them all brew."

"Uh huh. Did you know Baby Alex is Jesus now?"
"Ooooh Alex... Jesus and driving! Ahahaha. Still can't use that wakawakawakawaka."
"I actually have a girlfriend Coops."
"Oh yeah well, have you fucked your grandma?"
"..."
"Thought not... wakawakwkawakawaka."
I look at his pants bulge.
"Cooper are you getting hard?"
"Yeeeeeah baby."
"You gonna cum big boy?"
"No. Bro they're fucking awful, they got me these pills now I'm all fat and my dick won't work."
"I'm sort of glad."
"Hey Alex?"
"Yeah James?"
"Does your bitch know about my fat cock?"
Baby Alex smiles.
"She doesn't actually."
"Well errr... you should tell her. Oh and I need to call my dad. Ooooh Alex... Alex."
"Coops."
"Put on D12 brew. D12."
"Ask Roz."
"Errr Roz?"
"Yes James."
"Do you have music? Pass me your phone."
"What do you want?"
"D12"
"Which D12?"
"Errrrr... put on 'My Band'... No! Errrrrr... Put on 'Purple Pills'."
"Ok."

The Yorkshire countryside is plunged into an odd juxtaposition with the vintage Eminem project. Dirty dozen, eighty of us, Shady brothers, ladies love us. Detroit blares from the car stereo at the unsuspecting sheep, their heads raised in shock. That's why our baby mothers love us but they hate each other. They probably want to take each other out and date each other, some- something something something something something...

We pull into a service station.
"Would anybody like anything?" I ask.
You nod. "Yeah uhh... can I have a Fanta? Any flavour."
"Sure thing"
I turn to Alex and smile expectantly.
"Just a bottle of water."
"Cooper, anything you want?"
"Fucking... pussy."
"Fanta, water, pussy. Got it."
I shoot you a backwards glance as I open the passenger side door. You are smiling, showing your teeth.

We're stood at the train station. Cooper is moping about the side of the road, looking suspicious and worried. Baby Alex smiles at both of us. I smile back at him, unable to shrug a lingering sense that I am interacting with something only partly human.

"Guys... it's great to see you."
"It's great to see you too, Alex." I say.
"Come here." he smiles, opening his arms wide for a three-way hug. We all huddle up, into the Lord's arms: our redemptive moment. He blinks, eyes flitting to white for split-second, and I feel this orgasmic rush overriding my nervous system, blanking out any and all thought processes. I stagger away, every cell in my body exploding

into a blinding white heat.

❦

Taxidermy seems appropriate for an n-dimensional library, encrypted somewhere beneath the fabric of... whatever. The bear was polar in variety, stood on its hind-legs, claws stretched and fangs exposed. To the left of the bear, an astrolabe. To the left of the astrolabe, a stuffed dodo. To the left of the dodo, an impressive geode. To the left of the geode, an African tribal mask. The left of the mask, a set of flintlock muskets. To the left of the muskets, the assassin known only by the name of Q. He sits on a red leather armchair, facing his consoeur, the assassin known only by the name of Pussycat (you).

"They've devised another mud-tussle for us, Pussycat."
"Mmm?", you are eating a flapjack, the crumbs bouncing down your black leather get-up, while reading a book entitled: The Stonehenge People. You finish the mouthful, "sorry I wasn't listening, what?"
"HQ babykins. Una missione. And they mean it... this one's straight from the top." I slap down a newspaper on the coffee table, take out a small black metal container, click it twice, and snort loudly while pressing my nose up to an appearing tube.
"Top top?"
"Top top."
"Jaco's coming?"
"Naturally."
"Where is that shit-flinger anyway?"
"Billiards room probably."
"He does love his snooker."
"Right well then, I suppose..." you look at a non-existent watch on your wrist, then at the grandfather clock in the corner of the room, both hands removed. "I'll meet you in

about an hour in the armoury?"

"Ok. I'll go take a shower."

"Marvellous."

"Great."

I get up from the armchair and scratch my ankles with an ivory cane.

"He's not wearing the gold Adidas by the way."

$

Weeeeeeeeeee like to drink with Alex, cause Alex is our mate! And when we drink with Alex he gets it down in eight! Seven! Six! Five! Four! Three! Two! Waheeeeey!

♕

I brush granola crumbs from my jumpsuit. I knock on the door.

Silence. This must be where he is.

I open the door. He's vaping by the window. His snooker game has been abandoned halfway. He's wearing the tracksuit.

I sigh.

"Come on, we need to leave soon. You know you can't wear that."

No response. He keeps looking out the window, crouched irritably, pointedly ignoring me. He takes another drag. Banana menthol.

"Jaco."

He puts the tank down and sighs. He looks at me.

"How about the nice little Armani number I picked up for you in Milan? It's very versatile. And I know you're partial to that one."

He looks defeated. He nods solemnly.

"He nods solemnly..." I say solemnly.

He walks across the hall to his room and shuts the door

behind him.

I walk back into the kitchen. You are sat at the breakfast bar, staring at your hands.

"One too many deep-web nose beers?" I ask, returning to my now-cold cup of sencha.

No response. Your eyes are large.

"The dark plum of the world" you say.

"What?"

"That seems like a good line. The dark plum of the world. Poetic."

"...Please put your shoes on."

♜

The armoury: titanium-reinforced door, hand-sensors, eyeball readers, passcode inputters, magic spells, but we leave it unlocked, the door slightly ajar. There's no reason not to: the library is remote enough as it is, like a house in the mountains. People rarely lock their doors in the mountains.

"Any particulars about this one I should know?" you say, practicing some advanced kata with a pair of spike-studded nunchucks.

"Erm, apparently..." I'm holding a spring coil for one of my pistols and boinging it between my fingers. "We're sacrificing someone."

"Sacrificing?"

"For the salvation of humanity."

"So what we always do..." you give me a playful wink and spin the nunchucks a little too close to my face.

"Watch it." I grab the nunchuck mid-spin with a leather-clad hand and make a serious expression, eyes hidden behind mirror-black shades. "This guy is different. This is one of the good guys."

"You mean... one of our own?"

"Yes." Silence. "HQ gave him something... experimental. Absolute Faith. They're testing it, and now it seems they want to abort."

"Absolute Faith... and what can he do with that?"

"There's no upper limit, I checked the stats on the Computatron-9000."

"Hard fella."

"Well you know the saying mon chou... The harder they come..."

"You think we've got what it takes Q?"

I hit my Juul, lower my mirrored shades and look at you sternly.

Jaco patters in, wearing his versatile Armani suit and a black fez.

"Jaco. Good to see you. Thanks for not choosing the gold Adidas."

He squeaks something sarky back.

♔

We would be getting high in the attic, Cooper and I, aged 16: I would start playing Age of Empires II on the computer, or making beats on Fruity Loops, turning back to the narcissistic comfort of the screen. Cooper would pick up one of my notebooks and a pencil. He would scrawl, scribble, just these ugly loops, throughout the whole book, while laughing and talking to himself. He ruined three or four notebooks doing this. Occasionally the scribbling stops and he writes something, some Eminem derivative rap lyric or a sentence about Enlightenment being a ball, barely legible, then the scribbling begins again, hoops within hoops of graphite manifold, wasting as much paper as possible.

§

"The generative network's training objective is to increase the error rate of the discriminative network (i.e. fool the discriminator network by producing novel candidates that the discriminator thinks are not synthesised.)"

§

Chinooks groaning over the Sahara dunes. Baby Alex closes his eyes on the cross trainer. I see them coming, he thinks. The great light summons the dark: as it rises, as it flexes its hope, vaster despairs come forth to test it. Across the garden, behind the wooden fence, near the river, Cooper stands watching him through the window. James' mind is being beamed in real-time to HQ. They're beaming back layers upon layers of glitches and interference, hiding their surveillance under a cacophony of sexual terrors and incestuous garbage.

"Sir, I think he's spotted us."
"The sentinel?"
"Negative sir. Outward astrals completely scrambled sir, there's no chance anyone but us could unpick that. But the target is acting strangely, moving slower, his cross-trainer times are way down. He's sensing the incoming Virus Unit."
"Excellent. An improvement. No need to engage."
"Yes sir."
"Contact Virus Unit. Set a new course for... the North Pole."
"Yes sir."

My mother is wearing Marks and Spencer loungewear.
My mother is washing up and singing.
My mother is refrigerating cans of gin and tonic.
My mother is speaking to the dog as if she is a person.
My mother is eating coleslaw.
My mother is viewing apartments in Felixstowe.
My mother is hiding the food scale.
My mother is asking if the book will be "a little bit meta".
My mother is watching Broadchurch on demand.

"*schkrrrt* The North Pole?! Christ alive, we'll freeze! *schkrrrrt*"

"*schkkrrrrt* You'll be provided with snowsuits upon landing. *schkrrrt*"

"*schkrrrrt* But Jaco? *schkrrt*" I look to the monkey dramatically; we exchange shocked expressions. "*schkrrrt* He's a monkey! *schkrrrt*"

"*schkkrrrrt* The three of you will be provided with snowsuits upon landing. *schkkrrrrt*"

"AREN'T THERE THOSE SNOW MONKEYS ANYWAY, YOU KNOW..." you shout at me over the roar of the chinook rotor, "THE ONE'S THAT SIT IN THE HOT SPRINGS..."

"WHAT?"

"DOESN'T MATTER!"

"WHAT?" I point at my walkie-talkie headset. "TELL ME THROUGH THE WALKIE-TALKIE!"

"*schkrrrt* Q, I was just saying about the snow monkeys that sit in the hot springs, I don't know if Jaco is related to those kinds of monkeys, but it doesn't matter anyway. *schkrrrt*"

"*sckrrrt* Pussycat, he is not that kind of monkey. *sckrrrt* ...

sckrrrt If I had known back in la Bibliothèque we'd be going to the goddamned North Pole, I would have point blank refused *sckrrrt*"

"*sckrrrt* C'mon Q, it's not that bad, wait a sec... *sckrrrt*" Jaco squeals something in your ear, "*sckrrrt* Jaco is asking about the brand of the snowsuit. *sckrrrt*"

§

Baby Alex runs over one hundred miles, shitting himself in the process. HQ are completely astounded. "His numbers are off the charts!" That night he makes love to Lecia, her orgasms refuse to stop, even after he has left the room, washing his face in the ensuite bathroom, in the mirror above the basin he sees her still on the bed, fists clenched on the bedsheet, eyes rolled all the way back. "Oh meu deus querida..." she moans. "Como... Como você faz isso-oh? Oooh... OooOOOh..."

"This little light of mine," he sings, placing little dabs of moisturising cream on his cheeks and nose, "I'm gonna let it shine..."

♛

The chinook lands on the helipad on front of the base. It is slate-grey, everything steel reinforced, with black turrets. It is the size of an entire town centre. A mega-mosque. A temple. Dark smoke curls around the walls. Shadowy gargoyles poke fun from the bartizans.
"That thing looks fucking demonic" I remark.
We unbuckle ourselves. I put on some more lipstick in the mirror.
"I do it to regain control", I sing to myself.
You open the door. I follow. Jaco jumps out of the sun roof.

He wails in surprise at the cold, and scurries into my arms.

"Like I said, I don't know what brand they're going to be."

"Brace yourself, Pussycat." you scowl into the distance, "...It's gonna get a lot colder."

You walk through the whipping snow towards the black main gate. I follow.

I see the outline of a shungite statue of the Buddha.

♔

We stand on the North Yorkshire sea-front, faces locked on the incoming wave, cresting on the right, folding slowly over itself and fizzing, hissing, disappearing into wet sand. Our eyes beam out a brilliant white light.

You grab my hand and we start to power-walk at the waves.

The water reaches the ankles, our shoes are filled with sea.

The cold water shocks, stabs, burns through all the nerves of the skin, but we walk. Our heads go under and we start to swim, deeper and deeper. A dark cloud comes over us, it solidifies to an encasing black sphere. We die.

♔

A blizzard is picking up, somewhere near the northernmost point of the North Pole. In the midst of a snowstorm, a single figure runs topless.

Ice, blasted in from the Arctic wind, fills the stone-engraved letters on each monolithic door of the black gate: HQ. A creaking mechanism fires into action, tar-covered cogs grind their teeth, the letters begin to separate from each other, and the gate slowly opens. The Assassin known only as Q, the Assassin known only as Pussycat, and the Fez-wearing Monkey known only as Jaco, walk through the entrance, past an equanimous shungite Buddha. "It's fucking freezing!" I shout, my voice reverberating over the heavily-fortified black walls.

A neo-cardinal stands smiling in a black winter tunic with additional fur lapel. "Virus Unit. We've been expecting you." Shaven acolytes in beige robes rush to us holding three huge snowsuits, snowboots, and snowgloves — all white, and custom-made by Hugo Boss. We clamber inside them, the numerous zips and fastenings done up with an intense speed by the monks. They scurry off.

"Father, you bloody rerouted us." I say, chewing on a toothpick.
"Hugo Boss, Jaco." You look to him hopefully and he makes a disappointed squeak.
"The virus is inventive, my children."
"The virus is inventive." we drone back.
"I trust Qliphoth has briefed you on what we are up against."
"I gave them the gist. Absolute Faith..." I scowl, and stare into the distance.
"Absolute Faith indeed, my child."
"Q said something about this being one of our guys, a rogue agent." You hit your Juul, and blow the vape smoke seriously.
"Not a rogue agent Sekhmet... He has been chosen."
"Chosen to die..." I rasp, looking wistfully into the distance, the other way.
"Indeed Qliphoth. Chosen to die." His eyes shine bright, the edges of his mouth upturn to the slightest smile. "The snowmobiles are waiting."

Djent Metal.

♔

The immortal sphere, the secret moon. A pinprick of white, the reflection: shines, bellyflops out of orbit, takes on distance, crawls, glimmers into a rainbow glitch, oozing oozing oozing, zooming in from all angles, through itself, onto itself, stabbing us, glassing our faces with stacked hues in crystal frenzy.

A tsunami of communications. White fire and magenta wave. A shower of needles through the skin. Dick in pussy in dick in pussy in dick... Three hundred and eighty-nine thousand four hundred and sixty-five billion two hundred and eighty over nothing. Hordes of diamond mosquitos, malachite beetles, amethyst locusts. Hailstorms of frozen blood. Great leviathans of Atlantean terror sing: "Death! Rejoice! Holy! Holy! Holy!". A spasm in the centre grips it all, jostling and flexing until it snaps. We sit, on two red leather armchairs, in our library.

"Erm... Roz?"
"Yes babes."
"What did we just... I feel like I just... came... for a week..." I lean back, face confused.
You get up, turn slowly, eyes studying the curios that fill the room. You see a mini-fridge in the corner, which you walk up to. You open its door.
"Someone's left... mouldy jam in here."
"Hmmm."
"There are about four or five... of these jam jars. Half an inch of jam left in them, and the top is all mouldy."

♛

The cassette reached its end. The dread sank in as the TV turned to static. The blast consumed the empty house. I was too small to reach the doorknob. The windows were shut. I pulled at my skin. It was the most loathsome sound to ever exist and I did not know how to make it stop. I thought it would kill me. I crammed myself through the cat-flap in the backdoor, scratched, bleeding, wailing, barrelling for my grandmother, who had her back to me, putting washing on the line.

How about this. How about static every day, hours every day, inches away from your face, drying up your eyeballs, haemorrhaging precious time. A spiritual microwave, where the deliciously replicatory microbes of a north pole episode of your espionage novella will be exterminated and your internal monologue becoming nothing more than the mindless hum of your retarded uncle. How about promotional videos for three hundred-dollar beanbags with one-hundred-and-fifty-dollar neck rest attachments. How about fifteen thousand reposts of the same candid picture of Cooper's wife Lana Del Rey, wearing ripped denim shorts and a face mask, approximately thirty pounds heavier than when she was last seen in public. How about snippets of her reading her Rupi Kaur-tier poetry, now the fastest-selling audiobook on iTunes, how about adoring, emoji-laden reviews of the audiobook left by medicated teenage girls. How about two normal people you don't even know publicly arguing for three hours in short explosive bursts accumulated into a linear thread. Memes about films you haven't seen. TikTok witches. Zizek lo-fi. Convenience store discourse. Big titted Euphoria star. I am too small to reach the doorknob. How about static every day, hours every day, inches away from your face, drying up your eyeballs, haemorrhaging precious time, and every night when you go to sleep, you forget it all, and in the morning, you go back to the beginning.

♕

Snowsuited and booted, we crunch our way through the white. The neo-cardinal follows behind, squinting into the sun.

"You know, I was going to guess it would be Hugo Boss but I wasn't sure."
"Always go with your gut, Pussycat. Especially seeing as you don't have the dick to go with." you scowl.
"Mmm. Yours matches your glasses."
"My dick?"
"Your suit."
"I was never one for coordination."
"You don't have to tell me that."

♔

To the right of the bear, a narwhal horn. To the right of the narwhal horn, a set of the Japanese board-game Go. To the right of Go, an iron maiden. To the right of the iron maiden, a vintage television-set from the fifties. You stand in front of it, holding a flapjack you found in the mini-fridge.
"I wonder if it ..."
The TV sparks to life, the grainy image on auto-dial to maximum definition, but it's all white.
"Huh, must be brok."
Then we see him, at first just a silhouette, edges besieged by snow. The camera zooms in, and there's his face, his beard and eyebrows coated with white: Baby Alex.
"You've got to hand it to him... he did grow some balls."

"Do you think he ran all the way to the North Pole?"
"Well you can't run all the way. I guess he must've swam as well."
"That Iron Man shit huh."
"I wonder if his back's still hurting." you say, nibbling.
"That's actually a good question. If his back is still hurting—he's even less of a pussy."

♕

"Haematite-encrusted snowmobiles... A strange choice there Father." I spit, scowl and Juul aggressively.
"Bloodstone, my child." He smiles. "I've always found the benefits conferred by crystals to be rather... trivial... in the grand scheme of things. But in situations such as this one, there is no taking chances — By blood we live, the hot, the cold."
The Neo-Cardinal places his hand inside his tunic, removing a gold flask decorated by a cross-potent engraving. He pours a little liquid on his hands and flicks it in our faces, murmuring prayer in hyper-Aramaic. We squint and make uncomfortable expressions. Jaco grumbles.
"The target is currently ten miles south of here."
"Father," you say, "I can't help but feel we're under-prepared for this. How can we kill him? How can we destroy Absolute Faith?"
"My child, Absolute Faith is powered by absolute certainty in its own demise."
"But that doesn't make any sense!" I shout, beating my fist on the snowmobile handle for emphasis.
"Perhaps." He titters. "But does anything of this make any sense to you, Qliphoth?"
I stare at him, stricken, beads of sweat appearing on my brow. What? A memory sparked from nowhere, a baptism, a crucifix, a pact. Blood raining down. A

separation. Suddenly gone, deleted. I sigh, look across at you and Jaco.

"Let's just kill this fucker and get out of here."

Technical Death Metal.

♔

Two snowmobiles on North Pole snow. The blizzard clearing, the lone figure running. We watch the scene play out on the fifties television in the n-dimensional library.

"Wait a sec... who are these two on the snowmobiles?"

"Baddies..." you say, now with a camomile tea and some cookies.

"Intense. When do you think the action's going to start?"

"Why?"

"I gotta take a shit."

"Well errr... good luck. I hope they have toilets."

"They have a mini-fridge, I'll bet they have toilets."

I get up a little too quickly, feel that rush of brown blobby fractals on my vision, but it's also different, much different: I see animals, scenes, playing out behind it, little pockets of thrumming activity within that microsecond brain-glitch, with odd loops of squelching tribal chants. I put my hand out on the armchair to steady myself.

"You feel that?"

"Yeah. That's why I'm eating."

"Yeah it's like the blood is... pumping weird."

"It gets better if you eat something, trust me. Have a camomile tea."

"Alright, yeah. Urgh" I press on my eyes. Images keep poking in, detailed ones of civilisations, capital cities built across impossible shapes. "Maybe it will get better after I poop."

"Well then go."

I put on my country bumpkin voice: "I'm going ya'll!..."

I open the ornate mahogany door of the library, onto a dimly lit corridor. The corridor: marble-floored, with monochrome geometric patterns, the ceiling is high. The walls are white, lined with tasteful art-nouveau light fittings, and countless framed paintings and photographs. I study the pieces for a moment: Appalachian landscapes with caravans, abstract experimentals, absurdist reimaginings of pastoral English countryside scenes, boudoir erotic stuff with high-contrast lighting, pinned butterflies kept in a glass cabinet frame. I reach one of the photographs and stop, my face scrunched in a cognitive overheating.

"Roz... I think... you'd better come look at this."

"Did you miss the bowl?" you ask, getting out your armchair and padding over the green velvet library carpet.

"Look... at this." I say, face now slack and eyes blinking rapidly.

You walk up to the framed photograph and stare for a second.

"It's us."

"Yeah it's us. With a monkey."

"It's us... wearing fetish gear, holding assault rifles..." You look at me, utterly confused. "With a monkey?"

"A monkey wearing a gold Adidas tracksuit. Hmmm." I close my eyes.

"So the monkey is... our monkey? Huh." You give me a snide look. "That would explain the jam-jars."

"How did we..."
Another cabinet holds a gimp mask and a skull-measurer, along with various small stainless-steel tools. An oil portrait of a sickly-looking bald man in a smoking jacket, holding an Oriental ceramic cup. A manikin in a glass case wearing a bee costume. Stacks of manuscripts marked with runes. A framed stock image of a bird with a hole in the middle of the canvas. Various bank cards and passports on a low table. A longsword on a Persian rug.
I hear a scuttling.
"Did you hear that?"
"Yeah. It was like... a scuttling."
A creature appears at the end of the hall, scaly and ancient, the size of a large dog. Its long forked tongue slithers in and out of its mouth. I drop my cookies on the floor.
"Oh my god, Quentin, what the fuck is that thing?"
Your face is pale with recognition. Your eyes locked on it. It looks at you and, surprisingly, walks away, back into the room it emerged from.
"That... that's a komodo dragon."

Two snowmobiles on the North Pole snow. Jaco holds on tight in the monkey-sidecar. We accelerate towards the target—one of ours, the Neo-Cardinal said. One of ours. We park up on a ledge, I'm unsure how to even describe the landscape here. It's snow: some of the snow forms hills, some of the snow is gullies and valleys, some of it is plains, very flat. We are on this snowhill, looking over a snowplain; the three of us, all with binoculars out, in height order: Q, Pussycat, Jaco.

"You see anything Pussycat?"

"There's a fair amount of snow, but no non-snow objects yet."

"Bande de bâtards"

"Q, honey. Don't get upset."

Jaco squeaks something rude.

"What is up with you two? Come now children, we're professionals."

"Oh yeah, my child. Would you like to suck me off, my child? Oh no, Mr Neo-Cardinal, please, not again..."

"Q..."

Jaco squeaks something excitedly.

"Bingo" I say.

"Where is he?"

"3 o'clock incoming."

The speck on the far horizon, seen through the binoculars, is revealed to be a panting bearded figure with long hair, barechested, hirsute and coated in ice from head to toe, wearing nothing but a pair of white shorts. He is running full pelt at us, with no indication of tiring any time soon. Oh, and he's ripped now.

"That's ... Baby Alex?" you whisper.

"Agent Anus?"

"The very same."

"What is the Jesus of Bureaucracy doing out here in the bloody middle of the bloody... wait take a look at his feet... is he even wearing shoes?"

♚

Argh! Fuck my arsehole is playing up. I pull off two sheets of toilet paper, fold them, and pad the point of exit. I hold the paper out for inspection: hmm, no blood — good news. The bathroom of our secret n-dimensional library is quite nice, white tiles, pink fluffy bathrobes and mats, smells really good. The feminine touch I presume. I soap my hands, soap my arsehole, wash both through with hot water, dry with two pink fluffy hand towels removed from a cream cabinet. I look at the shape of my bald head for a moment in the mirror above the wash basin: "OK, it's not that bad." then I look at the odd twist in my nose and think "OK, it's also not that bad." but I press down on the septum a little in an obsessive compulsion to even it out.

Back in the library you have found some wool and needles and are knitting. Two scones with clotted cream and raspberry jam sit on two little plates, white with blue decoration, beside two mugs of camomile tea. The mugs are Pingu mugs.

"Anything happened yet?"
"Nope, still running."
"Reminds me a little of those times my mum would watch the Olympic marathon at home. Three hours sat in front of the TV just watching these fellas run, well... they were women, she'd watch the elite women. Did you know she even used to do the 'red-button' commentary?"
"Your mum?"
"Yeah, I even went down to London, to the old BBC building, to wait in this appalling-looking studio for four hours plus while she just commented with some other dude on women running."
"Wow..."
"I must've sampled every biscuit known to Britain on that day."
"Ooo, something's happening!"

The camera zooms in on the two assassins with their single snowsuited monkey-assistant on the snowhill. Their faces are now seen up close for the first time, stood in height order in front of the camera, the line caught at a 45° angle: Q, Pussycat, Jaco. You spit out your tea.

"There's the bloody monkey!"
"Who the fuck are these guys? Man... my head looks weird."
"No, it doesn't. Your head looks fine."
"They, erm — we look confused about something."
"We look a little... conflicted."

✞

The Neo-Cardinal walks through the black metal corridors of HQ, acolytes on either side of him bowing their heads. He stops, turning to the right. In front of him: a large titanium door, inscribed with a sigil, a planetary egg upon which sits a tiny bacteriophage structure, almost bearing a resemblance to a crucifix. He nods his head and the door grinds open, the bacteriophage going up, the egg descending.

A cave: a womb; a complex of uterine echoes; a cacophony of screams vaguely heard, twisting about each other. The Neo-Cardinal walks onward, into the black throat. Before him stretches a dark lake — he places his feet on the liquid but does not fall beneath its surface: he walks upon the water. The wails grow in volume, their definitions sharpen, they separate to delight, to pain, to anguish, to despair, to pleasure. Then the light is seen. Green and purple, dancing along the cave walls, across the Neo-Cardinal's black robes. Green and purple light emitting from an enormous, beautiful, glowing egg.

Absolute Resource, the Neo-Cardinal thinks. Strange... one would have thought that an organisation that has everything — that is everything — would have nothing to protect. And yet, here it is, beneath layers and layers of fortification and labyrinth. God waiting to engender itself. Doesn't really make sense. But something clicks on an emotional level. The Neo-Cardinal smiles. The game continues, as always.

♛

"How about a warning shot?"

"Maybe he'll stop if we just drive up to him."

"But we're supposed to kill him. Pussycat, we kill people. And Agent A... he kills people too."

Jaco nervously squeaks a point of information.

"Jaco says he's getting faster. Maybe he's seen us. Wait..." you look down your binoculars, "Yep. He's yelling. He's screaming at us."

"OK, listen. This is what is going to happen. I am going to shoot him in the leg. Then we're going to drive over there and see what all this nonsense is about."

" ... "

"Agreed?"

"Just don't miss."

"I don't miss."

I load the Dragunov, and settle my scope, slowly easing on him, controlling my breath. Then a memory, a warm one, comes back to me.

"Did I ever tell you, Pussycat, that Agent A and I were at public school together?"

"No... but I knew you knew each other before entering the service."

"We were even in the same house actually. Harrison. Red. Something of a dream-team in terms of providing music for the House Choir. Anyway... Sayonara Baby Alex. Forgive me."

A shot rings out over the Arctic waste.

REBIRTH

✠

"Holy shit."

We look at each other, mouths open, then back at the screen, then back at each other.

"They fucking shot him!"

"Fuck!"

"They just fucking... shot him!"

The camera zooms in on Baby Alex writhing on the snow in agony, blood trickling from a gunshot wound on his knee. "My knee! Aaaaaaargh!"

"They shot his knee!"

We look at each other again, pogchamp moment, totally flabbergasted.

"We shot his knee!"

Baby Alex is wailing, crawling in circles on the snow leaving a trail of blood, "Aaaaaaargh! Aaaaaargh! Aaaaaargh!"

I suck in air through my teeth, "Man that looks painful."

"Aaaaaaargh!"

❦

Camera cuts to the face of Pussycat, also wincing, looking through her binoculars.

"Jesus Q, did you have to shoot him through the bloody knee?"

"He was running!"

"I know but..." you suck in air through your teeth, "God that looks really painful."

I pick up my binoculars and take another look. There he is: Baby Alex, sobbing on the snow, in enormous pain. He calms down, sits up, looks directly at me. His eyes are furious, he's hyperventilating, his cheeks ruddy from the cold.

"Alright. Let's just get in the snowmobiles, ride up to him, and apologise."

"Wait a sec, check him out now."

Down the binoculars I see Baby Alex stood up, still huffing, staring right at our position. He closes his eyes for a moment, then opens them with a roar that trembles the snow-hill we are stood on. He starts running again.

"Uh oh. This isn't good."

"I told you, we should have just... gone and spoken to him."

"How the fuck is he still running?"

Jaco squeaks.

"Jaco, I don't see how shooting the other one will do us any good."

"I'm going to speak to him."

"What? What if he kills you?"

"He won't. At least I hope he won't."

"I'm coming with you then."

"No! You just shot him in the knee."

"I didn't mean to shoot him in the knee."

"I think... that this peace mission will go much better if you just stay here."

"Ok, but leave Jaco."

"Fine."

♛

I finish the last bit of my scone, then, as my eye veers left a little, another of the library's treasures catches my attention.

"Oh man Roz, look. They've got every single Now That's What I Call Music."

"Wow..."

♛

One snowmobile on the North Pole snow. You are revving the engine vrrr-vrrr-vroooooom and the snow looks magnificent, crisp, brilliant white glittering, and the sun is setting and the light is perfect for selfies. Baby Alex runs at you. You slow down the snowmobile to a stop, waving at him. Baby Alex keeps charging, screaming.

"Baby Alex, I mean, Agent A! We're sorry!" you shout.

Baby Alex is still screaming.

"We don't want to fight!"

Baby Alex is still screaming; he is louder, he is closer.

"Q didn't mean to shoot you in the kneecap!"

Baby Alex is about ten metres away.

"Alex just…"

Baby Alex lunges at you, throttling your neck, throwing you to the ground.

"Sto-"

Baby Alex starts to punch at your face, hitting you again and again, breaking your nose, breaking your jaw, teeth flying in all directions, caving in your forehead, mashing your face into a red pulp, hitting, hitting, hitting, his fists impervious to bone. When he is finished, blood covers his arms all the way up to the elbow, his face is covered in splattered brains, above your shoulders there is just a gored-out stump where a head used to be. He looks up, sees me watching all this in the distance through my binoculars, and starts running again.

"Holy mother of God…" my face is pale, turning a shade of green and I vomit onto the snow in front of me. Jaco shrieks in panic. "I can't believe he… Pussycat…"

I break down on top of the snowmobile, gasping for air. Jaco is clawing at my snowsuit, imploring me to do something in little monkey screams.

♛

"Did you fucking see that?"

"Wait… I died? I can't die!"

"I'm not sure I'm Team Baby Alex anymore…"

"He just… killed me."

"To be fair, you were trying to kill him."

"No, I wasn't! YOU shot him! I was going up to him with no guns, no nothing. I even said sorry!"

"Hey, I don't understand this situation very well. Maybe Baby Alex has his justifications here."

"Unbe-fucking-lievable. Now you're defending him…"

"I'm just saying we don't know the full context!"

"Urgh this is… urgh."

♛

I'm reloading the Dragunov, monkey on my back, screeching. Baby Alex is on the warpath, blood dripping from his hands, smeared across his face and dotting the icy coat over his body hair, sprinting closer, emitting his endless Aaaaaaaargh.

Jaco squeaks angrily.

I get him in sight, slow the breath, then say in a sandpapery resolute tone: "This one's for Pussycat."

Blam. Baby Alex flies back five metres onto the snow, blood pelting out of his eye socket, a chunk of the back of his head gone. He lies there, mouthing words, a croak jittering over his vocal cords. I watch him through the binoculars, wary.

"Don't get up you motherfucker." I whisper, then spit.

♗

You look hurt, and your skin is a little grey.

"Roz, you don't look so good."

"Why are we..."

"Roz, you really don't look good."

"I think... I'm going... to be sick."

"Go to the toilet then, it's third on the right, past the armoury."

"There's an armoury? Of course there's an armoury. Urgh." You get up from the armchair, hands flailing from the blood pressure shift. A strange procession of things dances on your inner vision. You swivel to me. I'm staring at you, a little sheepish.

"What? What is it?"

"Roz, you're erm... I don't know how to say this."

"What?"

"Big."

You look down at your body, your stomach has grown to

triple its regular size, your breasts are gigantic, and your arse is fat.

"Oh my GOD! I'm FAT! AAAAAAA—"

"Roz calm down..."

"AAAAAAAAARGH!!! NO NO NO NO!"

"Jesus Roz..."

"I knew that fucking scone was... blurgh.." you go another shade green and projectile vomit onto a Persian rug in front of the fireplace.

"C'mon Roz! Man..."

"That fucking scone was..." you spew again, sway for a moment, mouth hanging open with dregs of spittle and sick clinging to your lips. You make a groaning noise and your trousers go wet, liquid drenching you all the way down to your shoes.

"Oh dude, did you just... piss yourself? Bro..."

"Quentin... what's... happening? Aaaaargh..." you clutch your stomach and moan.

"Holy mother of... Roz, I thi-"

"Uuuuuuuurgh.... Uuuuuuuuuuurgh..."

"You're going into labour Roz!"

"Uuuuuuuurgh..."

"Push! No... wait... I don't know... Push? Wait, lie down on the floor, not on the sick, wait... I'll get some pillows."

"Uuuuuuurgh..." you lie down, beads of sweat across your face, mixing with the sick and the sputum. I pull off your moist trousers.

"Ok Roz, you're going to have to trust me, I'm not a doctor but..." I look down at your vagina. "Holy... it's crowning! Fuck, I thought it was like... ok, woah... it's fucking crowning Roz, Major Crowning!"

"DO SOMETHING YOU FUCKING PRICK!!!"

"Ok, ok... erm. Push Roz! C'mon big girl I mean, skinny girl, formerly big... Push!"

You let out a chthonic tone, the purple head of the baby squeezes out of the dilating hole into my hands. I pull it up by the legs, give it a smack on the back, it starts to scream.

"You did it Roz! Baby! ... erm.. wow... Baby." I'm holding it in my arms, take a look at its genitals. "It's... a girl... Haha. Better luck next time."

You pant, eyes half open, hair frazzled, then smile. I hand you the darling babe.

"I guess we gotta chop the umbilical. Wait a sec..." I rush over to a drawer by the mini-fridge, searching through ancient compasses, marbles, antique forks, finally finding a little pocket-sized Stanley knife. I spit on it for sterilisation purposes, and cut the lumpy purple-black cord. The baby girl screams.

♛

Snow and sky frames the ice-world. The Assassin formerly known as Q rides on the single snowmobile with specially-built monkey-sized sidecar, over the North Pole snow. I park the vehicle about fifty metres away from the spread-eagled body of Agent A, also known as Baby Alex, also known as Agent Anus, surrounded by an artful circle of red. I take my katana from its in-built scabbard on the snowmobile, kill the engine, and start to walk, Jaco in tow. Neither of us says anything. We watch the body of Baby Alex from about ten metres away. Fat flakes of snow brush past my face, like falling cherry blossom.

"I ..."

"Agent A... Why were you chosen? What is Absolute Faith?!"

"I..."

"Anus! Speak goddamnit!"

Jaco squeaks.

"Why!? What does it all mean!? Why doesn't it make any sense?"

"I... have..." He coughs up a spray of blood. "Absolute Faith... in the... project."

"Project? What is the project? Anus!"

"Absolute... Faith... in the p-... in the.. project."

I close my eyes, raise the sword above my head, high in the air. I whisper into the artic wind: "Omo yo yurushite" His head separates and rolls into the white drift. I fall to the ground, kneeling on the snow.

"What does it mean Jaco?..."

"Q..."

I turn, face pale, to see Jaco by the snowmobile, pointing his monkey-sized pistol directly at my face. "Jaco?... No!... Not you!"

"I'm sorry it had to be like this Q..." he says, his voice impossibly deep. He cocks the hammer. "You were never supposed to come back."

The bullet flies, slow motion, into my forehead, shattering the world. I see rainbows, Gods, processions of crystal wind; I see billions upon billions of triangles.

♕

12:19

Everyone on the train has AirPods in, specifically AirPods. I am nervous, the day is oppressively hot, I am nibbling my way to Peterborough. Of all the things I remembered to bring, I neglected to bring a single pen. I am borrowing this one from a commuter, who had AirPods in.

There is a man on the phone, via his AirPods, to a woman. He is inquiring the whereabouts of their friend Alex, whom they are both travelling to meet. The man and I make eye contact. I return to my seat.

22:12

It was always going to feel like this on the first day. The shiny red car. The politeness. The non-catch-up. His pseudo-holy breeziness. What is there to say? Something, but it is not being said, because it can't be, not on the first day. Us at the Shell garage with our masks on, him paying for petrol, me across the aisle looking at the protein bars. The growth has been accelerated, fertiliser mainlined to the heart, it was a blink, a flurry of sentences, and we are now suddenly so ahead in time. His hair is long. He has a girlfriend. Last time I saw him his hair was short, and I was his girlfriend.

He had suggested we go to the supermarket together, which on a logical level seemed unnecessary, but he suggested it because it was something, he remembered I enjoyed doing. He suggested increasingly complicated things to make for dinner and my brain switched off entirely. I suggested one thing, Greek salad, which he overturned without explanation. Some things never change.

Your house: The unmoved plate. The jam jars. The coffee stain on the carpet where I last sat, reciting sub rosa. The rug next to the attic's bed, depicting Snoopy playing the saxophone.

—

He is beautiful, he smells good, he has changed in a lot of the ways I hoped he would, he is kind, generous, endlessly understanding, and I feel absolutely no desire for him. No pang of regret, no gnawing jealousy. I feel only the warmth, the love, all the good things, ever so slightly carbonated by a mild inexplicable irritation with his demeanour. Just like the good old days.

It is so great to see you. This goes without saying. It is the first day. I wish we could have talked just the two of us, even just for half an hour, before turning to the kitchen window to see him approaching down the path. I don't really think I had anything in particular to tell you, but that might be because I didn't get the chance.

Within an hour of arriving at your place I got the feeling, the acidic ache in the jaw, the hyper-awareness of my appendages, the shift in gravity, and it seemed like I had already spent the day reading to you again.

The three of us in black, all with different hairstyles. Our new characters. We are all thinner now. What, you're gonna pick on me just because I'm the thinnest? Take a chill pill! :-) No, I know, I know I look like a total freak, I took some flash selfies with the flip phone, I do look like a fucking gremlin, little gremlin nearly crying over a bit of focaccia, I know, I KNOW, but I ate it didn't I? I grabbed the nettles and pulled them out, I hate moths but I'm typing this up with the light on and the window open.

—

Listened to a part of the new Cum Town last night where they were making fun of bad storytellers and it made me feel deeply insecure, they were so shitty and dismissive. Made me understand why you didn't like the small dick thing. ;-)

—

10:13

Quentin is making me coffee. You, Quentin, the person reading this, right now you're making me coffee.

—

While you were upstairs doing something, I wandered into the living room where he was doing some oblique holistic stretching and breathing exercises. He inquired about my health, how my posture's doing. He asked me to take off my shirt so he can check the alignment of my torso. I did it because I am surrendering my will for the benefit of this important week. He feels my tailbone. He says I look good. Even I don't think I look good anymore. It's in moments like this, or when I read him a piece I had mentioned and think is weak, and he insists that it's "good", that I do not trust his judgment, and become even more thankful that I have your perspective. You tell me I look like an Auschwitz corpse, you poke at my bones, you laugh at my Replicator jive monologue, scrunch it up, and toss it into the corner of the room. Your criticisms of me and my work feel genuine, and therefore rarely actually hurt me, and also make your occasional praise much more affecting. He thinks everything I do is "good", out of either love or weakness, and therefore nothing actually ends up seeming as if it's good.

I lay on his chiropractic bed of nails. I watched you enter the room and call me Skeletor, and the two of you flit masculinely about the room, shirtless, warm, sizing each other up. The gendered dynamic feels more established in this visit, even if I am a dyke, even if I am one of the boys. I'm still a woman in her bra, lying on the floor, and you are still two shirtless men, pacing around. I sat on the leather armchair and watched you make him do many more press-ups than he believed he could, by the end he was releasing primal shrieks of exertion, and I didn't know whether I wanted to laugh, or be shocked, or something else. Then it was my turn. A meagre effort, but very psychedelic for me, my vision ripples as the ornate rug came closer to my face and then shrank away again. As my arms began to shake, you supported me, your hands on my hips, and whenever I dropped to the floor you would hoist me back up, and it would keep going. Then I shrieked too. It felt great. I carry a lot of tension in my neck and shoulders, and I could sense it opening up like a window, a breeze flowing in.

12:07

We talk about our respective experiences of cosmopolitan busyness; he chimes in with feeling left out at school "for being Catholic". We ask for his opinion on the book's purpose and he makes a you-derivative sound with his mouth while waving his arms around. We prepare lunch for ourselves quietly and unceremoniously, he uses three different bowls and an unclear amount of utensils just to make scrambled eggs, finishing his meal with a metrosexual flourish of Parmesan that he grates from a great height, saying something about dude, I had lost my appetite for a whole year, and now it's back. I agree with you: in these moments, even the ones between press-ups, writing, and intense conversation, he is endlessly loggable. I had somehow forgotten how much attention he demands. Even when wordless and silent, he is also somehow extremely loud. Not a complaint per se, just an observation. I don't want to be mean. Now I will get changed, and we will go running.

17:49

The run was joyous agony. I don't think I've ever ran

more than a mile non-stop in my life. My breath quickly eased into a very even rhythm, perfectly aligned with my feet, my ears locked in on the sound, my eyes taking in a new sight: the two of you running, tunnelling through some green terrain, some video-game landscape, and me following you faithfully. And then my chest started burning, and then really burning.

I would have started walking much earlier if you had not been there, pushing me, both emotionally and literally, your hand driving me forward whenever I slowed. I ran until I thought my heart would burst, with elastic saliva that pooled in my mouth and refused to be spat. The rest of my body didn't hurt, my legs felt fine, I didn't have a stitch, it was just my chest. I really wanted to keep up. But the bridge where we stopped to catch our breath, that was my limit for the day. I watched you both jog on, you turned a corner, and then you were gone. I followed the way I thought you must have ran, but couldn't see you all the way down the line of the canal, and figured I must have gone the wrong way. I turned back and walked into a nearby street, figuring I could find my way back to your house. All I'll say was it was a hell of a detour, one that took me down main roads and over bridges, and into more than one neighbouring village. A kind and chubby family giving their Boston terrier a breather on a bench let me use their phone to look at Google Maps. I walked for what felt like over an hour back to Horsforth. When I saw Sophie's Choice on the high street, I knew I was where I needed to be.

We had our half an hour, over PBJs and glasses of cold milk, while Alex made his way back after sneakily attempting to escape your influence. We had a harmless little gossip. All I had to do was look bemused and say what is it with him, because you get it.

But I don't want to poke fun at him pointlessly. As I had said later about his online seminar, he's enjoying himself, and I don't want to come in with the wrong energy.

Even the way he was sitting though, god, sitting there cross legged, and totally neutral, endlessly loggable.

23:19

He cooked while you wrote in your room, and it was your turn to be gossiped about. Your concern that your Goggins awakening would be belittled by him manifested itself mere hours after you expressed it. He is pushing us too hard. He doesn't get it. We need to work up to it. I was diplomatic. I am enjoying being truly pushed. I'm enjoying the tasty glint of self-loathing. I could see myself running regularly. I could see myself writing 2k daily. So, I am going to do both. I have spent too much time fucking around. I want to see what I'm actually capable of. I love Alex, but I am tired of the Alex School of Being Kind to Yourself. I am a little concerned about you developing "exercise bulimia" though. Please just walk instead of running, if only once a week.

———

I'm thoroughly enjoying spending time with the two of you, floating between rooms, dipping into your tough love and his New Age-y acceptance, then feeling them mesh together when the three of us talk. However, I currently feel much more connected to you, much more likely to side with you in an argument, much more likely to mirror your sentiments on the topic of discussion. Each glance I shoot you in the kitchen, in the attic, in the parking lot of Hobbycraft, each could be its own 1k. So when you got grouchy, just as I returned from Tesco to the two of you aggravating each other about The Goggins Question, then when I inevitably put up a bit of a fight about eating a bowl of pasta, and you started talking about "you two", I felt a little irritated. Not at you, more at myself, and the inescapable multitudes of the religion of three. I don't want to be lumped in with him, although I guess that's the way perception works. I might be annoying and he might be annoying, but I am with you, of course, I'm either with you or I'm not, and I'm with you. I'm writing a book with you, about him. You dictate the rhythm and I accept that. I will be as compliant as I can with your way of doing things without my anorexic heart giving out.

09:58

Sitting in some grass near Hunter's Greave. I took a bath last night. It was late, past midnight, so I tried to be quiet. I didn't know if you were still awake. Just as I was drying off and getting my things together, I heard you leave your room and send my name down the hall. I opened the bathroom door.

"I can't sleep until you get out of the bathroom. Try and keep the midnight baths... pre midnight."

I apologised quietly, you turned back around and shut your door. I went back up into the attic. A tiny interaction that should have meant nothing except that I should bathe earlier. And yet I lay awake for at least half an hour, cringing, agonising over me being me, and me and him being "you two": nuisances, these unpleasant little knots of tension in the body of your house. The dynamic is different. I could tell you were very irritated, despite your tone being even and cool. My insecurity snowballed until it felt as if that bath was so inconsiderate that it scrubbed away the pleasantness of our evening walk, leaving only a long day of the two of us pissing you off in our separate ways. Tears of exhausted frustration welled in my eyes.

I woke in the morning still remembering it, curdling internally, and, as I gathered my stuff to go downstairs, I dropped the flip phone on the floor, and another wave of shame coursed through me. On the one hand, being this nervous about making a human amount of sound seems psychotic, and on the other hand it makes total sense. I know who you are, and how you feel about noise.

I made myself tea and Alex appeared. He had a scone with cream and jam for breakfast. We spoke and drank. He asked if I wanted another cup when I finished mine and I said yes, but it took him absolutely ages to make it, and then when he finally did, he placed it down in front of me half-made, i.e. with no milk and the bag still in the water. These small things in turn annoyed me. We had a nice talk though, and he had brought a poetry collection that I read a little of and found interesting, I would like to hear your opinions on it. We discussed white Buddhists, the Dalai Lama's opinion on white Buddhists, his Brazilian gf's potential Jewish ancestry, and inevitably, you. He slowly forgot the spatial-temporal context of our conversation and began to talk at the normal, slightly stagey volume he uses when in an upbeat mood, and I winced remembering my bath again, not wanting your sleep to be bookended with noise complaints. His anecdotes became a little too much for the early hour in the day, and I excused myself to go for a walk. Partially because the weather was good, partially because I needed a moment alone, and partially because if you did wake to the sound of his voice I didn't want to be there when you came downstairs.

My body hurts immensely. My arms are veiny and sore. My lower back is emitting a creaky ache. I might run a little bit, but I need you to go easy on me. Already terrified at the prospect of what I'll eat today.

—

21:57

We had a laugh about the bath thing. I read your log, and the birth scene, which I really enjoyed. At one point Alex came into your room, and it felt very fun and devious to read what you had to say about him while he was standing right there, by the window, looking at us neutrally. A bottomless well of patience for our bullshit.
You, me, and him had a chuckle about the idea of hiring random Africans on Fiverr to read sections of the book for promotional purposes. He he he, we went, he he he.

Later the two of you lifted and I watched, feeling mildly uncomfortable watching his suddenly-thin-again arm wriggle up to the sky with the hostile-looking metal weight, and feeling mildly x watching you stoically doing bicep curls sitting on the couch. What of it. I tried to be as passive a presence as possible, but I couldn't help but wonder if the tone would have been different if I hadn't been there at all. Can't lie, I was impressed at how many of those pull-ups he could do though. He surprises me frequently.

I went to Tesco and got potatoes for the Sunday lunch he had suggested we make, and, as I returned back down the lane, I saw the dreamy glow of your tiny distant torsos, leaving the house and bobbing down towards the canal. Note left for me on the door:

Key on lock
gone 4 run
ur 2 skinny
can't roll with us...
x Q

Slight relief and slight disappointment. I was readying myself for pain and it didn't come. I let myself in, wandered around aimlessly, tried on your big blazer with the shoulder pads and listened to Born Under Punches, took it off, and wrote on the note:

Gone for a long skinny walk...
R x

Left and went for a long skinny walk, which was uneventful and mostly thoughtless. The tension of the anticipated pain went unreleased.

—

I came back to the house after a couple of hours, feeling the burn in my legs, to the sight of Alex freshly bathed and looking sleepy in the kitchen, you nowhere to be seen. He started asking potato-related questions, chicken-related questions, and it was slowly made apparent he had in fact never cooked a roast dinner before. I gave him more and more suggestions until I ended up doing most of the preparation myself. However, he did know the tricks for seasoning and stuffing the bird. I stood peeling the potatoes as he watched from the table. Any love or tenderness I had hoped to feel while preparing a meal for the two people I care about most was placed in the background to accommodate a throbbing, housewifely resentment. I don't want this food, it wasn't my idea to make it, it's going to end up being some kind of awkward performance to present it to you, and I'm not even hungry. While I peeled and chopped and boiled and tidied he very messily told the story of the year the two of you won the house music competition at school, a story I hadn't heard before, and if it had been told more concisely and when I had been in a better mood it would have probably moved me. Instead I was just throwing out oh hahas and that's crazy that only worsened my irritation. You flitted in and out of the kitchen intermittently. He chomped on a raw carrot like a child. Soon before the food was done, he suggested the two of you "do some stretches", which seemed to be his attempt at getting you to do something you were less good at than him, some kind of payback for all the lifting and running, rather than him actually wanting you to stretch. I had a moment of thinking that this whole thread of you and him going on about touching your toes was spawned by my late-night-questions email from a few days ago, where I asked you if you could touch your toes. Have you been worrying about it because of that? I hope not. It literally doesn't matter. Either way you guys went off to stretch in the other room while I played house, sulkily knifing the chicken to check its juices. Whatever he did in that time clearly rubbed you the wrong way, because you returned looking even more tense than before, and we had an almost wordless moment in the garden, us both seeming very inflamed, before you disappeared to the shops just as the food was about to be served. We are animals, I forget that we are animals and that we can smell tension and hostility, and that any attempt to suppress it just leads to it swelling until someone is bitten. I stirred the gravy and quietly said to him that I felt like crying.

We ate when you returned. The potatoes and vegetables, which I prepared, were mostly tasteless, because I had been unhappy when I prepared them. The chicken, which he prepared, tasted much better, both because he had been in a gentler mood and because it was covered in butter. The mealtime itself was kind of fraught. You were mad at him, I was somewhat mad at him, you were somewhat mad at me, I was mad at myself for giving you reasons to be somewhat mad at me, and he was chewing very loudly. You stated that you would like "us two" to leave in two days. You left soon after the food was done to go for another solitary walk.

—

Two pieces of context for the following passage:

1: In the phone conversations leading to this visit, Alex and I floated the idea of platonically renting an apartment together as a way of escaping our parents.

2: When we went for the evening walk the day previously, and I grabbed the nettles, they had barely stung me, but in that moment, I felt compelled to lie and say that they did.

He and I talked while we cleaned a little. I can't even remember half of it, I was in such a haze by that point, the thousand-potato-stare across the room as I registered every articulation coming from him as either obtuse or blatantly inauthentic. Self-help shit. Self-care shit. It was someone else's words. Why couldn't we just be quiet together. And I had been lumped in with him. It kind of broke my heart, it felt as if he just didn't get the whole thing, I wanted to grab him by the shoulders and shout "don't you get it, you keep just saying you love us, but it's all fake, you don't truly believe anything you're saying, it's all flat, there's no substance! There's no fucking duende! Don't you get it, you fucking moron, we are making fun of you, because you are so you, and you're still doing the same shit!"

I did not do this.

I very clearly remember just one thing he said:

"I'm not Baby Alex anymore."

Yes. Yes, you are. You are unchanged. It's just like when I was going to come back from Sedona, and he promised all these things, how he'd changed, and on the phone after an extended period of no communication it all felt so believable, that same teary relief washed over me as it did the other week, and then after a day and a half of actually being with him, him being fake and rolling feebly around on the floor I realised that no progress had really been made. It's just like my parents.

I can't live with him. He might know me better than anyone, he might truly believe in me, we might be forever connected, but there is something about him that in these moments I absolutely cannot bear. His bullshit is a maze with no exit or entrance, and I am doomed to scramble in it forever, oscillating between deep and thankful love for his existence and unexplainable fury that he is even breathing. There is no way out of him. And there is no way out of me. I felt my voice cracking. I wanted to stick my fingers down my throat again. I went for another solitary walk.

I took the iPod and listened to Tomboy by Panda Bear. I stormed desperately down the canal, feeling so overwhelmed, and not like last time anymore, like I was tripping, or like I was on the verge of an incredible idea, but instead like I was teetering on the realisation that all was somehow lost: there was no way for me to leave Suffolk, and the book will never make any sense, seeing as the person central to it doesn't even seem to understand why he's in it. I marched past families and couples who looked at me concernedly. At one point I just wanted to properly turn on the waterworks, slump into the grass and blubber like I did when you first sent him that draft, but the tears did not come. I slowed at the top of a path leading to a meadow, looking at the ditsy flowers in the grass. The sorrow subsided, and was immediately replaced with a brilliant rage. I was sick of myself. I was surrounded by nettles.

I lied and said he and I could live together. I lied and told him he had changed. I lied and told you the nettles stung me. I am as fake as he is.

—

I grabbed them by the fistful. The pain came. They stabbed me in the palms of my hands, the quicks of my nails, the insides of my wrists. I bared my teeth. I pulled a whole bush of them out as people stared. Enough stings for an entire childhood spent outside.

The rage left as quickly as it came. Suddenly everything felt fine again. My hands flickered like embers. I turned around and walked back to the house, grabbing more bunches of nettles as I passed them, ripping them up and throwing them on the pavement, enjoying the occasional pedestrian's disturbed glances.

I walked through the door, through the empty kitchen, to find you in the living room, eating granola and talking to Peter. You seemed to have had an equally refreshing time of it while you were out. You took my hands in yours and examined them. We ate Peter's bird food and described the flavours of the different colours. We laughed a lot. We had a quiet moment of appreciation of Peter's Deleuzian difference. We fed him a prune. You let him pick granola out of your teeth as I watched with a deep sense of peace.

Whatever it is, it is fine. If the book is shit, I'll write another.

The scene changed again, and you went upstairs to log

whatever the fuck this day was, and Alex reappeared to talk with me. He seemed lovely again. I gave him a hug, and kissed him on the chest through his shirt. Muscle memory. We walked to Tesco in the mid-summer dusk. He said he was happy, and that he felt he had the easiest role to play out of the three of us. He has changed. Maybe I could live with him. He surprises me frequently.

—

We were cracking a safe, time was running out. You shouted strings of numbers and letters. Sweat beaded on my forehead as the guards closed in outside. The scene fizzled out at its climax. Rectangle of soft blue above my head. Checked my watch. 5am. Closed my eyes again. A void. Rectangle of white above my head. Parrot sounds. Coffee sounds. Checked my watch. 8:45am. Got up.

Upon rising to my feet, I felt very bad. My hands burned from yesterday's nettle abuse. The soreness from the press ups was even more aggressive. I made my way downstairs very slowly. Any kind of movement was challenging, I felt as if I had been fasting again despite having eaten twice as much as I usually would the day before. I passed you on the way to the bathroom and meekly mumbled something in response to a sound you made. I got ready and went to the living room to listen to Alex recount a dream about his grandmother dying. Unless dreams are juicy, sexy, or concern the interlocutor personally, descriptions of them should be brief, which his was not. You arrived with the cafetière, and it felt a little like when you're at a party and someone pulls out a joint: you try and remain blasé while locked in on the thing, waiting for it to be offered to you. You teased him for somehow having used up all of his data after only being here for two days. Just forget about the internet, bro. Then you went back up to your room to continue writing. I pulled myself back up the stairs to get in on the coffee, only for you to say you had left it on the piano, and I walked back down, vision blurring. Chugged a cup. Felt even worse. Sat in the kitchen vaping, willing myself to muster energy. Alex had mentioned wanting to have breakfast with us and seemed hungry, but I knew you would most likely do your usual egg routine closer to noon, so I offered to make us porridge. My hands shook as I stirred the slop, feeling extremely close to passing out. As I separated the oats into two dishes, a huge glob of them fell and smacked on the floor. I got a sudden flashback to the abject meals I would see people make in halls, and cleaned it up while biting the inside of my cheek. It's cool man, he said, still sitting. Of course, it was cool, but it didn't feel at all cool at that moment, it felt impossibly frustrating, and I fought the urge to tell him to shut the fuck up. Gave him his bowl, violently sliced a banana onto mine, and devoured it in feral silence while avoiding his friendly gaze. If I were asked to rate that dining experience out of 10, I simply would not.

—

I read your log in your room. Your log is now in my log. We are log-docking. I find it funny that we're here mostly just to be around each other, but we cut the time short to excuse ourselves and slink away to separate rooms to render written replications of the moments we just experienced while he does yoga. I don't know if I've ever passed someone in a hallway to go get dressed, and then half an hour later read a rendition of that interaction. Our feelings about yesterday's dinner were very similar. Alex is often fake or superficial, or has a grating je ne sais quoi that is all the more grating for being so unexplainable. Any attempt to articulate how he is when he's like that runs the risk of sounding so petty that you don't deserve to have friends at all. Yeah, I have this friend, and he's very sweet and smart and accepting and loving, but it kind of feels like he is missing a layer of his soul, like he's just an artificial amalgamation of every other person he's ever seen with no tangible defining self-ness, and also he chews food really loudly, and breathes weird, and says "fucking" too much when telling anecdotes, and sometimes even the way he looks at you is somehow also fake and annoying.

We walked to the car to go for a drive, the porridge slowly replenishing my life force, but still with the metacognition floating around. You dropped into the back seat of the Alexmobile with a cheeky grin on your face, and I wondered if the disciples ever made fun of Christ like this.

Was it Ilkley Moor we went to, or the other one, with the funny name? It seemed as if we just went to one place out of the two we were going to visit, and then to a confusing supermarket, and then back to the house again. Either way we drove and you governed the music from Alex's highly curated selection of /mu/core via the backseat. As we ascended the hill and the trees stretched out in aerial perspective, the landscape turning hazy-blue, the tense minimalist groove building, I was suddenly a year in the past: looking out of the passenger seat of the khaki Subaru over miles of red rock and evergreen, as Carson would extract me from my father's house and pull me up the mountain into Flagstaff. Then I was further in the past: in the flatness of the Norfolk countryside, going to some random village on a Sunday afternoon to glumly look around charity shops with my mother.

You would start playing an album and then skip through it, or change a song halfway, which I knew is one of his pet peeves, at least it was in our bong-ripping days. He was mostly silent on the drive there, concentrating on the winding roads, squinting, seeming stressed. I didn't know what to say, so I said nothing.

I enjoyed the walk in the forest, the actual walking, a lot. What can I say, I'm really into trees at the moment. I loved that lush, savage moss that colonised their trunks. I loved the subtle comedy of his cream linen suit, so ridiculously inappropriate for the terrain. I loved your quiet tenor renditions of French lullabies sang for no one in particular. And I loved the photos he took of you, and the two of us, standing on that rock, with my mask concealing most of your face. He has a good eye.

"You should abandon all these flirtations with being a priest and just be an ad man. You would be so good at it. And if you totally resign yourself to it, it would probably give you more meaning than being a priest. Being a priest is basically just being an ad man for God."

"But I'd want to be an ad man for God, not for fucking Cheerios."

"I don't know though; Cheerios are pretty good."

We were so quickly back in the car, and it was that Sunday drive feeling again, when you don't seem to get out of the house soon enough and everything is already starting to close. I could tell this oppressive sensation was also on your mind, which you would later confirm back at the house. You spoke a lot about school, what everyone must be up to, if anyone else went crazy like Cooper. You imagined a leader board: every quantifiable area of each ex-pupil's life rated for its success and assigned an overall numerical score, who would be near the top, where the two of you would be. The conversation picked up speed again and we laughed a lot conceptualising new branding for GSAL, such as "Leeds Grammar School for Boyz and Bitchez, est. 2BC" and "The New Leeds Academy for Upwardly Mobile Pakis Whose Parents Made Money Doing Whatever". Then we laughed more imagining each other as different races, simply saying things like "Nigerian Q" and "Eskimo Roz" in between bouts of giddy cackling. The biggest laughs, however, came immediately after this, when we stumbled upon a goldmine.

"Saudi Alex."
"Yes. YES."
"It makes sense, man. Those flowing, minimalist clothes, the fasting–"
"The lying down on the carpet."
"Oh my god, dude, you're literally Muslim."
I could see it all so clearly. The immaculate beard. The cologne. The call to prayer. The hooka. The hijabi wife. The sobriety. He said one of his favourite days of school was when they showed the kids a VHS of Mecca. We kept repeating "that was your favourite day?", doubling over.

——

We came back and wordlessly splintered up: Alex to nap, you to write, me to walk. After I returned and milled around for a while I found you in the living room, talking to Peter once again, lifting weights. We talked about the drive, and you talked about your father. The melancholy of a childhood Sunday afternoon spent in a neighbouring town, melancholy that does not yet have an explanation nor a name. The difference between our fathers: mine barely ever saw me, so wanted to think he'd made me happy even if he didn't have the power to, yours saw you from time to time, but did not seem to care.

You went for a run and Alex and I talked hot air. He stood at the sink and scrubbed at a tiny stain on his suit trousers. He referenced the jokes on the drive as "worthy of us having a podcast." I reiterated, in as kind a way as possible, that he probably would make an exceptional ad man. The other week while on the phone he talked about how you had once told him that his music is very well produced but lacking duende, whereas yours was rawer but more evocative, and he said he believed the opposite was true. I can't imagine how he could think that.

We ate cheese and bread and matzo crackers. I did a kind of "tell them we drank toilet water to settle the score" thing where I purposefully ate what felt like a lot of food in front of him, announcing it as I did it, hoping he'd provide me with an alibi if you ended up coming back dragging a bison behind you that you expected me to chow down on for dinner. This did not work.

You returned in a lucid mood and pan-fried a steak in a lot of butter. Alex asked about how I was going to escape my mother's house in such a pointed way that I experienced a flash of paranoia about him sneaking up to the attic to read last night's log. He probably just thought it would be a good thing to talk about, and I had been meaning to bring it up. I felt relieved by your responses. Just leave. Who cares? Leave in the middle of the night and don't come back. Mind if I take that poetically? I would probably end up telling her. But I am fully accepting of needing to leave, or quit my job at the bare minimum. I may be doomed to be a medium sized person in a medium sized space no matter where I am, but I can at least hope to feed myself with a job that does not exhaust my brain. It is clear to me that writing is what it's about.

Alex's mother could be her own 1k, 2k, her own book. Baby Cinta. Her hours of pimple-popping YouTube videos watched from the bed. Her Nando's indecision. Her slumped on the couch, saying in her thick Yorkshire accent: "I've lived my life all wrong". Then when he and I went to Tesco, the conversation turned to Mary, and then Mary's father, a wealthy businessman who unexpectedly dropped down dead from a heart attack a day before his retirement. Stuff like that, man. Man oh man oh man. It sends a chill through my whole body, fans out at the neck. Anything but that. On the way back, Alex looked at me very pointedly, with a wobble of real concern in his eyes.

"...You seem like you've turned a corner. You know, mentally."

"I hope so. I'm not certain I fully have though."

"I don't want you to die."

"I'm not going to die. Don't worry about that."

"...You know, in those places... they put tubes in people."

Merry Christmas, bitch. More pasta. The densest, briniest rendition of dad's tuna caper pasta I have ever tasted. Good, very good, but felt like a lot, especially seeing as I was already full of Jewish crackers. That's another thing: when you're fat as a young girl, your female relatives drill into you the mantra of you're not hungry, you're just bored. To the point that even now I still feel immense guilt for ever eating anything when I don't feel like I need it. But I know I need it. And I'm thankful for both of you making me eat it.

—

Another evening walk through the trees. On the bridge you stated that you felt older than the two of us. You seem older, yes, but that's because you feel older, and that's because you think you should feel older. It's not an ideal situation, but I guess it's better than thinking you're still a teenager, which a lot of men your age seem to do. The solution is to just keep doing something. Do it until your kidney ruptures.

Discussion of baby names. Quentin Scobie Jr.

Homunculus Counelis. Mohammed Baghdad. Ascending up another hill at magic hour, me behind you, fixated on the red soles of your sneakers leaving trails in the dark. Post-tuna hallucinations. Laughter. I stopped occasionally, such as when someone suggested naming a child "Ant Andec", and crouched on the ground. I was trying not to pee. That might have been the first time on this trip, as it already neared the end, that the dynamic felt like it used to. Everyone just walking, smiling, saying words. Medium sized people in a medium sized space.

We got back to the house again and splintered off once more, night consuming the cobwebbed corners.

—

10:57

Sometimes when he talks it's almost impossible to actually understand him. Of course everyone sounds a little messy while trying to articulate a thought as it comes to you, but 70% of what he says appears to be I just want to like, tap into that, and like, go onto the inside to get a general consensus of what's fucking going down, and like, I'm good, I'm good and I want to just build on that, like go in there and just be like, yo man, what's up, I just wanna figure it out and get to the bottom of that whole thing. What?

15:33

He and I took a walk on the canal. We crossed the tow bridge and went through the woods. I'm enjoying his company on a bodily level, it feels like a fantastical expedition, two ageless will o'wisps floating through the forest, one leading for a little while and then them swivelling around, the other taking over. He talks about becoming a psychoanalyst, says that he thinks he is smart enough to go to medical school, and theorises "what angle" he would treat his patients from, making shapes with his hands. I have the hood of my jumper up, hands clasped in the kangaroo pocket at the front, cutting paths through the undergrowth with my trainers, eyes on the ground.

"But it's just more school. You only just got out of university. Is that really what you want?"

"I don't know, I just think, I've always been drawn to that. Something about my demeanour. I have therapist vibes, people always tell me that, they say 'oh Alex, you should be a therapist.'"

Sometimes a conversation seems interesting in theory, but you find yourself completely unable to keep it going: the whole thing feels too self-aware, or too constricted to a framework of imperfect language, the things you can say in response to someone suddenly appear limited to a drop-down menu of video-game dialogue.

"Mmm. Something about your voice" I say.

We came home and he had his Zoom interview with the head of digital content for the BBC. You and I sat in the kitchen and you showed me images from the downloads folder of your MacBook: various pictures of star-nosed moles, HD photographic portraits of American vagrants, shots of the sky at sunset. This experience, seeing the crumbs of external stimuli that someone else saves purely for their own enjoyment or inspiration, removed from that person's original context, always seems strangely intimate. We were near each other at the table, eyes on the same still colours, contented and mostly wordless.

You show me the introduction to one of your videos that you never uploaded. You had written about it before. Murmurations of starlings in a white sky, clustering into cannonballs and boomerangs before stretching back out.

How the mind warps with it, trying to make sense of the shapes themselves, then how they could ever possibly be formed in the first place. It started off as a thin oblong with rounded edges and slowly elongated out horizontally to form a wide window. The rounded edges gave it the sense of something that wasn't a thumbnail, wasn't just an image on a screen, but something organic, physical, an actual window to the world outside. A call to reality. I got goosebumps on my arms. That's what pisses me off about The Book Club: YouTube is a distraction, and becoming popular on YouTube has appeared to cause you a decent amount of existential anguish, but your videos have the power to affect me in a way nothing else I've seen on there has. You more than anyone should be the person making videos for YouTube, and therefore you more than anyone should get as far away from YouTube as you can.

I sat at the table in silence, eyes closed, dreading dinner. I visualised a hippo contentedly wallowing in mud while listening to Alex chew a mini Scotch egg. He swallowed. "What are your opinions on Moby's new tattoos?"
I smiled.

♔

I was in the living room stretching when I heard the distinctive voice of Baby Alex that he normally puts on when he enters my house: "Hello-ooooooh". I had prepared something to say in the minute before you turned up, but there would be no point in saying it if the delivery wasn't perfect: Two travellers, from a distant land. I felt devious, cheeky, and sagacious from the yoga stretches. Something had also changed in my mind that I hoped would come through, something very recent — the work ethic, the David-Goggins-Berocca moment, a kind of furious attack of not-so-much "inspiration" following a period of depression and self-hatred, but a deeply felt sense of the reality of what this all takes, the extent to which one must exert.

There is no secret, it's like Kung Fu Panda.

Alex says "Hello-ooooh", I get up from my seated stretch on the floor, smiling, feeling very bald: wearing the black shirt with the top three buttons undone with the gold crucifix around my neck. I walk through the corridor slowly, grinning, listening to you two in the kitchen make little comments about where I am in the house. I say my line: "Two travellers... from a distant land" just out of sight. You laugh a little at the tension of the scene. I go up to hug Alex: he seems very tall; I'm not wearing shoes and he has his lifts on. I hug you, fingering your bony shoulders, amused by the skeleton you have become, not too worried about it, trying to make you feel that I'm not worried about it. I mention it and you do this little pained face, like you keep messing something up, a trivial task that is causing you a great amount of inconvenience.

Alex, of course, has bags of shopping, and bags of "his shit", which we need to get from the car, so he can logistically have it, and move it about this house. I feel quiet around you two. I'm moving between two characters, versions, within myself: a brash and high-t me who tries to dominate the space, and a quiet, smiling me who watches it all and doesn't give a fuck either way. I sense I am becoming this second one more.

I am wondering now if you were thinking the same kind of thing: whether you felt you were bridging two versions of yourself. You were navigating Alex, whom you had not seen since you broke up; you were navigating me, whom you saw a number of weeks prior in a much different mood and circumstance. You were navigating the "I'm anorexic/I'm not anorexic, and everyone's mentioning it/not mentioning it" axis. You were much quieter as well.

Baby Alex is talking the logistics of everything and where it will all go. I know I do this as well: I have my businessman slots. There doesn't seem to be enough time for two people to speak when three people are speaking. Baby Alex says: "I keep remembering I'm the third person here. Like I'm counting, one, two, oh wait I'm the third." The trinity is complete. It is nice, it feels mostly harmonious, I feel like there isn't the intensity of the two-way back and forth we had before. It makes it less tiring, less scary.

We stopped talking for the first time that evening, walking by the Himalayan triffids next to the river. Alex said: "Has that sign always been there?", pointing to some incongruous signpost in the wood noting Horsforth and Kirkstall Abbey, while directing us implicitly to a newly-built café.

Baby Alex's North Face rucksack and luggage bag, professional explorer Baby Alex. Baby Alex brand mastermind: The Year 8 English assignment, Trainers for girls, blue, simply named — Jayne. "It was average University level shit; I've always been that guy for branding".

Where does he come up with these fucking self-assessments? I'm guilty of the same bullshit, no doubt, constantly moaning about minor YouTube fame like it's some venereal disease I've only just gotten rid of. It's probably not even that, that's the thing. I can't even see what I'm really acting like. Maybe neither of you can see it, or maybe if you compared notes you'd see completely valid, completely different edges of whatever that inconsequential nonsense is we spout about ourselves; a force field, a cloud, smoke and mirrors to keep something hidden within. We don't even understand why we are hiding it. It's just too easy to speak, it's too easy to fall back into what we've always said. We're like Peter — if Roz squawk, I squawk; if Baby Alex squawk, Roz squawk. If me whistle, you whistle, Alex whistle: we all whistle.

I didn't feel so much an anxiety at you all being in the house, just an animal discomfort at seeing Alex using up my surfaces and you leading me back to whatever my earlier self had been, the one who ate things with peanut butter, who had sugary coffee with cigarettes. Alex's hair looks really nice, I'm quite jealous, or maybe I'm not, I don't know. I just remember when I had hair, I guess. I'm not going to make a big deal out of it. I feel strangely richer in having no hair, and I sense it a lot more now I'm actually in his presence. I'm walking around with this perpetual discomfort, something that forces me to confront my end.

The salad, Alex's weird looking salad in the casserole dish. I made a comment. All this autism vis a vis plates and dishes is just a direct download from my mother. I put a slab of ... what's it called? the fucking Italian bread... focaccia, on your plate. You look at me, horrified. Probably the realest moment between us that evening. I can feel you despising me for it, shooting me this you're not my mum, you're not my dad, fuck off fuck off fuck off. I'm trying my best to not give a fuck. There's about 95% no-fucks-given coming off me but there's also a secret little thought, Jesus I hope she doesn't flip out. I feel like I'm the only one that wants to address this shit. I go to the bathroom. This dude even has a North Face wash-bag. The smells have also shifted ever so slightly, Alex has a much stronger aroma than yours, but yours is not quite completely drowned out. I smile in the mirror, thinking it's quite pleasant to analyse friends, and look at my bald af fucking tête and my tired looking eyes.

—

I'm not sure jumping in the river was a good idea. My skin is burning a little. Baby Alex was right not to jump, on that level, wrong on the other level. I think he's gone out to look for you. He wanted us to split up in the middle of the run to find you after you started walking, but I said that you were a big girl and knew how to find your way home. He was secretly doing it to avoid running further with me. We talk about the fact that you probably don't even have the energy sources to create endorphins from running. Just pure flat pain. My eyes are stinging, like I've been in a chlorinated pool. I think I better go wash them. Baby Alex doing the last set of press-ups, I'm shouting to say thugs are coming to kill his family if he doesn't go for that final one, he roars in deep man.

I am now in a Justin Murphy Zoom seminar, at the left side of Baby Alex's square, totally unprepared, giving my opinion on something I have no clue about. I am only talking because I see a fit girl is talking about Bataille. It is very... Bataillean? "Erm yes well, these are naïve notions of an interior... erm yes well, I find isomorphisms with ahem cellular biology to be rather suspect..." I am using the best words at my disposal: "emancipatory", "exteriorisation", throwing them out there to see if anyone nods their head. I realise I probably sound very stupid. I'm barely keeping up with their words — "disaggregate", "Kantian agency" — I couldn't tell you what that means. I am himbo, pure himbo, himbo enlightened. What is Baby Alex doing in this seminar? He is a professional bullshitter, of course he is in this seminar. Did I learn anything? No. No one said anything that I hadn't heard before. No. I refuse to learn. No one said anything that I was like... woah, white-hot take broski. I am better than all of them: I'm at the back of the class, writing something cool on the side of the desk.

Maybe I should try and be smarter, get me some of these Zoom seminar bitches.

——

Baby Alex is stood in the doorway of The Card Factory Superstore, and we are both walking away from him, and I am walking away from him faster, towards his little red car. On the back seat of the little red car I have put the sunglasses and the can of white spray paint. The two rib-eye steaks I bought cost £8, the spray-paint cost £7. It has been an expensive day. I was in the car saying ideas of what I will spray-paint: "PEACEFUL EXISTENCE", "THE LORD'S PRAYER", ... "They'll be sort of oblique strategies without the strategy", "Just oblique..." Alex said. I was sat in front of the computer before we set off, thinking: I have to fucking write, but also feeling like a trip somewhere I had never been before was a bit of a shitty thing to miss out on, even if it was Hobbycraft. So, I got up and went, complaining half the time. "TRUTH".

Baby Alex comes downstairs and starts to cook his meal, I do my confrontation, my intervention, telling him that I think his intellectual posturing is very fake and reflective of a complex about his intelligence — leading him to pursue this nonsense path of academia and not dedicate his time to really trying to understand himself. Maybe I'm just dumb. Maybe I just didn't understand what the seminar was about and felt a bit insecure. But I don't feel like anyone understood what they were talking about. They were all saying the exact same thing that everyone has said since the beginning of time, like words be kinda stoopid, aha, let's address that, with some more words.

At the height of the shit-flinging, Alex pulls some pretty irrelevant things out of his bag because he probably feels so under-attack from me, something about my being an autistic weirdo whenever I actually have to meet normal people. This is very true. I'm glad he brought it up. I accuse him of being an inauthentic schmoozer, again. In as much as I'm doing this, part of me doesn't want Baby Alex to grow up and get real, get wise to his own faults, to start to really buckle down and get his shit together, because that means more competition. But whatever, that could work as well. I know now that all I have to do is be the one of the duo who is working harder. I merely have to work harder than every other person I've ever met.

My hands have gone from the tingly stage to the itchy stage — the worst stage — of nettle stings. I am enjoying sternly making you eat normal meals, and I am just hoping you're not throwing it up or doing clandestine star-jumps somewhere when I'm not looking.

You're actually both at your least funny when you're riffing, but I don't mind it, I'm the worst rifferer of the three — I don't know, it has the aftertaste of Comedy Soc to it. You're both funniest when you're doing your little defences against the world, when you're looking at the table, miles away from the conversation, staring at your finished plate with dread. Baby Alex does not amuse me because of the contents of anything he says, but he's funny when he's not trying to be funny, when he's being boastful then immediately afterwards a little vulnerable. He's just such a happy smiley boy that's out of the loop in some strangely basic way. Quasi-normie. There's just no darkness to Alex. He's not dark when he's depressed, he's just flat, superficially stressed, hammered into robo-mode. I think that's why he sucks at music, why he's so good at branding. He doesn't have the duende. He's a capitalist, he's a salesman. He should go fully into advertising. I think he'd be great at that. The priest thing is like eh, I wouldn't want to impose Priest Alex on anyone, not really. There are probably loads of worser priests than Alex, not to say he would be bad, I just think that advertising is his true calling.

I stood in the kitchen and said something along the lines of "I think I've figured out how to combine my depressed side and my happy side, by making my suicide my work, by using work to completely clear myself, to hack away at the excessive energy that would otherwise provide me with fuel to hate myself; to work so hard that I don't even have the time to consider how people might think of me, how I should be this or that." If you know in your heart that you've worked hard, no one can really touch you. Argh fuck this platitude shit. Sometimes I can't help but think I've surrounded myself with dumbfucks and then I get that fucking thought urgh fuck that means that I really am the dumbfuck. But whatever, who cares about natural intelligence.

I'm willing to be a talentless hack. We should all become talentless hacks. A talentless hack is the only way to conceive of yourself, whether talented or not. Like urgh urgh I need to make a video to be validated by my community of pseuds, exactly the same impulse that drives Baby Alex to sit there, in dingus position, with my bookcases as his background — chatting b.s. he hasn't even read up on in a Justin Murphy Zoom seminar. Sweet Lord, that image, when we came up the spiral staircase. I know that somewhere in the back of his mind he is ashamed of what he's doing, but he's built up such a strong system to override that shame that he acts out the character perfectly. He's sat all upright in front of the webcam, like a well-behaved schoolboy with his packed lunch. That shame is the truth: stick with the shame Alex, the shame is the beginning.

Just on the brink of releasing my gorilla-grip-coochie hold of the present, I hear Roz Counelis coming down the attic stairs, oh no oh no the horror, oh fucking hell she's running a bath. My heart twinges into heat and I feel myself slowly waking up into a very pissed-off state, imagining Roz Counelis just lying there, minding her own business, dedicating this late-night moment to a bit of self-care; Boney Robbins in the tub, soaking, hands out, arms at right angles, like a Necromancer princess, cucumbers over her sunken eyes. Even though it is silent now, the bath has stopped running, my body will not allow itself to sleep until she goes back upstairs, and it is very tired, so it becomes wide-awake and pissy. I repeat to myself: "Don't go over there, don't make a scene out of it, just tell her tomorrow, don't go and tell her to go to bed." I realise that the code-switching thing we talked about even operates on the level of the mental chatter, I will have these moments of analysis, moments of trying new age affirmations to calm myself down, moments of pure red alert, where the rage goes down the upper part of my arm, all the way to my hands, like a mantle of fire. I get up and in what I hope sounds like a very measured and reasonable voice tell you "Please keep the midnights soaks pre-midnight." Even after you're back upstairs I'm swirling my duvet into ropes, twisting and gnashing my teeth while another voice repeats "sleep, sleep, go to sleep, you are tired, go to sleep."

—

Baby Alex runs along the Leeds-Liverpool canal, then stops. "Come on man, you're not even tired!" I say to him, pushing his back, forcing him into a jog.
"No... I just don't want to run!"
"A-ha! See! They're all excuses."

I'm running in front of him, turning around at him, running backwards, shouting motivational statements like "It's torture, you just have to learn to torture yourself." A middle-aged guy with his family hears this and turns around to look at me with a smile. I send a hot-green beam of recognition his way through my third eye.

—

Baby Alex, talking about my intrusion into the seminar, says "It's so funny watching Q get around a hot girl, he locks in and then his eyes go BAZONGA". Then we're talking about my reaction to girls and maybe you're thinking hey, I'm a chick as well. Nah Wozzo, you're one of the boys now. Lesbian Roz, a Butch Cyberbear, with her badass dog with the eyepatch — we riff on and on.

First thing in the morning I go to the toilet to piss, Baby Alex is lying on my sister's bed, on his phone. As I come out, we look at each other and he says "yoooo" in that funny voice and I go "yoooo" back. Baby Alex comes out of my sister's room, I ask him watcha readin' in an Irish accent, he says book, I look closer aaah "The Real Jesus"? he says Yeeeah this is the reeeal jesus, I say oh I know him well.

There's no death, horror, sin, pain, in close quarters, there's just urgh urgh I'm in this room, urgh urgh, talk to this person for x number of minutes, forcibly remove myself from this room, gotta get to the solitude, but the solitude is never enough, the me time is never truly free of the knowledge that you might intercept someone on the way to the bathroom or that some crazy nut will start running a bath at 20 minutes to 1 am. The good times are funky, but every joke is a compromise, meet me here, meet me here at location y, and we will laugh for x number of minutes.

Baby Alex lying on the hot patch, seemingly doing nothing with his morning, chilling.

—

Come back from very depressed walk, a short complete poem in my head:

Nothing is reserved from me, for I'm in pursuit of dark felt. Lay the fabric on my bones — the murky tones of the general. The conglomerate ever watchful for their small raven prince. Nothing is denied of me, for I'm in pursuit of dark felt.

—

My fictional version of grown-up Baby Alex is much superior to the real-world Baby Alex.

§

Message from James Cooper:

You're the archetypal lives at home artsey fartsey fuck up loser
bare funny

♔

Baby Alex will not stop talking about his Sunday Roast. He is now in managerial mode, making an "empathic" tone with his voice which makes me want to beat the shit out of him. He is telling me how to stretch, how to breathe, he is doing the same voice he uses in the Justin Murphy seminars. From now on, I will refuse to make him exercise, I will just do my exercises by myself, and my runs by myself. I am not a switch; I do not respect Alex's opinion on anything.

Baby Alex shows me how to breathe by making an O with his mouth, sucking in hard, and showing the top-whites of his eyes while staring very intently into mine. The Sanpaku diagram comes to mind: This man wants to have power over you. "Very intently" but I'm uncertain as to what the underlying intentions of this theatric is: for me to acknowledge his yogic brilliance? I've done that party trick before Alex. It isn't going to work on me — and were there any validity to the therapeutic effects of stretching out hidden trauma in the body, I'm not going to do any of it while you're huffing at me like a moron and giving me these Jimmy Saville eyes.

That's just it. I know the real deal, I know what spiritual potency looks like, its name is Cooper, no matter how malformed and disorganised that potency was. Alex is all form, all organisation, zero substance. Cooper is all substance, a Spinozist-Hercules, schizophrenic oneness. I'm just slightly disgusted in myself for straddling the two. Fake fake fake, Baby Alex is fake. And I'm fake from the perspective of the Looney Bin Fuck-Up. I don't have the natural ability. I don't have that McCoy lightning. I am not OG insane, I have not been diddled by Apollo.

This morning Baby Alex tells me about Baby Alex lying in the dark, his mind spewing attacks at me, waking up multiple times, attacking attacking attacking. I know the feeling. I guess I got my comeuppance when I was being huffed at and eyeballed, or when Alex wouldn't stop making this grating comments in an endless unfunny stream over the Sunday roast, his pride and joy.

"Honestly guys, tell me, out of ten, what was the roast. And be honest!"

"Errrr..." you say.

"A six." I say, picking up extra bits of skin from the underside of the chicken. "Wait, if gourmet chef is ten, that would mean that like, best roast I've ever tasted from a home roast is like a seven, then yours would be like... a four."

He doesn't look upset or disappointed, slightly amused but also hesitant at how to respond.

"Okay, well... if a one is like inedible..." I continue, "Well then it doesn't really make sense. Then yours wouldn't be a four either. Hmmm, I'm going to say, a five point eight. But it's still nice to eat."

"Pitchfork scores, nice."

"Haha yeah, not best new roast."

I really didn't know what I was saying, or even what I might expect from a 10/10 roast. But it was the inanity of the question: rate my roast. Fuck your roast dude. If I cook for you guys I don't want a fucking medal for it, or a talkshow: just like a polite thank you, and if it's good give me some feedback on that, or if it's bad we can have laugh about it. There's this cultural residue in him, this manner in which his style of speaking is littered with inorganic ice-breakers, these things that have been programmed into him as good to say, and other things which are bad to say. He's a prescriptive moralist, taking his cues from scripture. He's the opposite of the tragic failed-übermensch manifest by Cooper. He is domestic, civilised. And if he is domestic, then I am domestic. And that is what really pisses me off about my friendship with Baby Alex. If Baby Alex is derivative, then I am somewhat derivative, downstream.

(It is the same agony experienced by Wittgenstein, upon reading Sex and Character. How to be more male, more original, less downstream? All my best ideas I have stolen from James or other lunatics, or more exactly, my best ideas are inhabited by them. That is the truth. To be more male you have to be hit-or-miss more of the time, more willing to lose it all in a gambit for that jackpot. "Being male" is the opposite of playing it safe: it is high risk high reward, inviting of ridicule, singular. It is dangerously alone. In the creativity racket, real men howl and paint with poop before their morning sedation).

—

I walk past you in the morning, I go Ooh! in a loud caveman voice. You barely say anything and go straight forward into the bathroom. Each interaction during your stay here is now rated out of ten, and I have to keep my rating up within the group or fall out of favour in the tacit leader board that hovers in the air. Baby Alex possibly thinks his scores are high: but they are not, they are at an all-time low. Our interaction could have gone better, but I'm sick of trying to make connections with you to counter-balance the stress of Robot Alex executing Socialise.

Baby Alex arrives downstairs in his Cos pyjamas. I don't look at him but say "Alex..." while making the coffee. I walk out of the room almost immediately, singing that Rage Against The Machine song that would appear on Tony Hawk Pro Skater 2 for the Nintendo 64, lights out, guerrilla radio. I check my emails, just notifications about people leaving comments on my videos, the comments are all retarded. I go back to the kitchen to finish the coffee; I can hear his voice talking to you but I'm not sure where from. I walk down the corridor and hear you both from the living room, his voice much louder, yours almost silent, clearly harrowed by something this morning. "Woah that seems like it has a lot of symbolism..." you say, without any emotion.

"Yeah and there was like fire all inside the ..." his voice drones on.

"What is this about?" I say, merely to interrupt Alex, not particularly interested in what this is about. I place the French press on the top of the piano.

"So basically... I had this dream..." he takes the speed which I used to ask the question and decelerates it all the way back down to a rate slower than the one he was speaking in before, as though the latecomer needs extra help in catching up with the information.

"Oh, a dream?" I say, quickening the pace again. "Can you summarise it in one sentence?"

"I had this dream... my whole family were gathered... it was my grandma's house... and we were going through her things..."

I flick my finger at you, interrupting him again, and whisper coffee under my breath, then say out loudly "And it was on fire? Classic."

"Yeah..." you say, hiding an exasperation and a general morning bad mood, "it's quite a common one isn't it."

"No, I know it's like a cliché," Alex says, defending the dream, "but it was so meaningful to me..."

"Uh huh."

Peter makes a sound from underneath the blankets I placed over his cage fifteen minutes earlier. You both start to talk about Peter, Alex rehashing the conversation we had about the bird's tragedy the previous day. "Hello I've spent all my life in a cage" imitating Peter's internal monologue, you mentioning the prune we gave him, "a prune the size of his head" Alex notes. There's something about Alex talking to my bird or about him that feels like a breach, but at this point Alex could say anything and I would be annoyed at it.

Alex says: "Oh, do you know when you're thinking of putting the internet back on?"

"Why?"

"I basically... accidentally used up all of my data trying to

figure out the best way to get there today..."
I give him an unimpressed look.
"No, I know, I know..."
"You could have just asked me," although really, I barely know the way to Ilkley.
"I know but like," he says, "anyway I'm just wondering when you're going to put it on, I just need to buy a new data packet."
"How about you just forget about the internet for a bit." I don't even understand why I'm being this cruel, I just checked my phone two minutes earlier.
"No, I get it," he says.

I think one of the reasons for my complete lack of sympathy at the fact Baby Alex has used up all his data is merely the way he asks. If he had said to me, Bro I need the internet for like one minute, something direct and urgent, I would have been amenable. I might have even gone to do it right then. My issue is the eternal Committee meeting that is holding court in the presence of Baby Alex. Everything is empathic, everything is deep listening, everything is taking other people's feelings into account, when really, he just wants something done, he just has an explicit desire that he can't allow himself to state explicitly, he has to be duplicitous, bendy, all stretchy and yogic about it. The wearisome game of politics: diplomacy. Everything is politics for Baby Alex, and as such any interaction is additionally taxing. He's always trying to get something from you, attention, a laugh, a moment of emotional heft, a hug — and he computes you, understands your signals only according to his own cybernetic system, his inputs. It's all branding. It's Kantian bro.

I cannot stand this much longer. I do not particularly want to write a book about this guy. I remember why I sided with you, post-disintegration. We have made a terrible mistake. I come downstairs, looking for a second cup of coffee, walk in the kitchen. Alex is sat at the table with you, I look at him, he looks at me, eyes wide, face expressionless, pure 100% Robot Alex.

—

As we approach the Chevin, I say something stupid then "that's the way the cookie crumbles..." and realise if I were to log everything I was saying all day I would be unbelievably embarrassed. The road is winding, I have control of Alex's iPod Nano, and I am playing an album by Dawn of Midi, a band that Alex describes as "minimalist, if Roz were describing it she would call it very Alex-y". I think about all the times I have rode in the car with people my age, listening to some new music that I didn't enjoy. I think about using music to describe yourself, or your own name to describe music, and sitting in the ambience of another person. I think about whether Alex will crash the car, that I am in the backseat, and therefore have less to worry about. The pianist is playing one note repeatedly, I want the note to either resolve or stop. We pass a café in Guiseley.

"Oh, that's the café me and my sister stayed at when my dad pissed himself, and then him and my stepmum had to go buy some new trousers down the road..."

"Oh wow..." you say.

I'm wary about telling a boring anecdote that doesn't really go anywhere, especially about my dad.

"Yeah, it's a really awful café, we had to stay there for ages. The sandwiches all looked awful. It was a real mood, that day."

I cut it off. We drive into Otley, doing one long turn around the roundabout when I decide I want to buy water "from somewhere", mid-roundabout. The plan for the day is reiterated by the Alex-bot, "Okay, well we'll go into Otley, get something to drink, then we'll drive up and see if we can find a place to park. Then maybe we'll drive into Ilkley, go on the moor. Even just drive over it." We pass a petrol station, Alex parks. I get out and realise I don't have a face-mask, I walk back to the car and say "face mask", you hand me a black buff-type mask, the kind you can wear as a headband, or just around your neck, that middle-aged cycling dudes in the US wear a lot. I put it on and walk up to the shop, seeing my reflection in the glass of the automatic doors, decked out in black tracksuit bottoms, black tight t-shirt, gold crucifix on a chain, black face-mask, and shaved head. I feel like I am about to rob the place. I grab a water, the shop assistant seems more friendly than normal, and I get back in the car, explaining to you two my new sense of appearing as criminal. Later as we're driving, I say something stupid like "I would actually enjoy robbing a place, you know, armed robbery..." and you say "yeah..." without much feeling either way. Alex parks next to a white Subaru with gold rims which we admire until we see the West Yorkshire Subaru Club sticker on the backseat window. Alex talks about how the blue Subaru with the gold rims is the "classic Subaru".

Walking through the Chevin is almost enjoyable, but not really. Alex takes a picture of me with the face-mask as we riff about how the mossy bark on the pine trees and the pine-needle carpet is perfect for Instagram or High Fashion adverts. "Chevin," I say, pronouncing it like a French word, "pour homme". I pout at the camera, slightly pained at the fact I might have to look at myself afterwards, but more confident in looking "badass" by how I looked in the shop and car windows. I take a look at the picture, and immediately regret posing, or allowing him to take my picture. Branding. PR. Publicity. We walk a little further, up to a rock over a sheer drop, where more pictures are taken. I do some stupid things with the facemask stood on the rock, then you come up

onto the rock. I say to you "hey stand right on the edge
Roz, yeah stand right on the edge" in my ironic voice. I
stand with you right on the edge of the rock, looking at
the drop below, Alex says "don't guys..."
I say to you, "hey ok now push me. Push me bro..." as I
stand right on the edge. I don't feel fun or funny, there's a
heaviness to everything. "Come on bro, push me." I look
over the edge again. "Probably wouldn't even die. Just get
a little... oooh... mangled."
Alex shows us the pictures he took of the both of us. I'm
mostly looking at myself and thinking about how awful I
look and how thin my forearms and neck are, but I
deflect from this in my mind by zooming the picture in
on your face, doing an expression that I think I've seen
your Dad do in a picture you showed me of him. You say,
"Oh, great..."

We walk past a part of the Chevin where there seem to
be about four different large families with small children.
As we move away from them I say to you both "You feel
that?" and I'm about to say Biological Necessity, when
you say "Yes." very definitively, so I don't want to risk
you figuring out perhaps we're referring to two different
things, so I say nothing, as though all has been
understood, and keep walking. We start to talk about
whether or not we would genetically modify our children,
after I bring up the pink Himalayan invasive plant species
that grows along the side of the path, that Alex says is
"Himalayan Balsam". Alex says he would not genetically
modify his children. You would also not genetically
modify your children. I say that I would, maybe just
because the both of you hypothetically refuse to. Alex
tells us about a high-IQ sperm bank in the 70s who
eventually found a female. The child was a prodigy, but at
age 18 became a monk and now just plays sitar. We agree
on the fact that with High IQ people there is little
indication that their elevated intelligence will mean they

will actually do anything singular. We're all being very downstream, unable to get any effervescence in the conversation, and I'm doing exactly the annoying thing that Alex does when he is scared of silence — inputting inorganic questions on the Reddit-tier controversies of the modern age. Elon Musk takes a hit. Do you believe in Free Will?

It's just the idea of driving somewhere for no particular reason: I associate it too much with my dad and having to spend some belaboured Saturday or Sunday with him, walking. He would always drive for an hour to someplace neither I nor my sister wanted to go. It was a walk-in nature, then to the carpark of some supermarket, then to his cold house for dinner, then back home. I'm unsure what he could have done instead, but each of these trips had that same bleak mood, the nausea of the winding road, the uncertain destination, the Waitrose car-park, Ham and Dijon mustard in a roll opened by finger or plastic knife, the ceaseless DFS Sofa Sale ads in between The Simpsons reruns, while he cooks the same risotto dish with a pinch of the paprika he kept in a little box; then that cold drive home, identical turns, clenching my jaw to the rhythm of each passing streetlight. All gone now. My fucking dad, fuck, I'm really sad about my dad.

We get back in the "Baby Alex"-mobile, Alex sits on the edge of the car boot to take off his walking shoes, he gets up and then starts to notice that he has a dark stain on his cream suit, around his arsehole, which he gets very worried and vocal about. As he takes off his walking shoes, I look at the top of his head, at his thinning hair, and think about my own bald head again. We drive to Ilkley, and I end up telling an anecdote that was probably completely uninteresting for the both of you, like recounting a dream, about going to a pub in Ilkley every Thursday evening and doing my homework with a pint of

Coke as my sister finished Drama class next door. The conversation moves to things we did after-school, the kinds of kids who had to stay after-school until the library shut. You talk about watching optical illusions while your mum finished teaching because you had nothing else to do. We end up talking about Ikbir Singh, a Sikh guy who would stay after-school with me. There would be Ikbir Singh and I, and maybe Adam Walker, walking back to our lockers after the library had closed. I liked those guys, but I think that, when you're in the after-school mode, you can become friends with anyone, you develop strong situational friendships that are at odds with the kind of personas you cultivate in normal school hours. I saw some Facebook pictures of Adam recently, he has a hot gf, looks like he has his shit together, the archetypal dude who is a little square in secondary that then enters adulthood with aplomb.

We're at the entrance of Booth's and the guy at the door, who looks younger than us, tells me I can't go in without a mask, not in a way that's authoritarian, just in a really chill sorry but the people inside will be unhappy kind of way. I take off my shirt and wear it around my face, putting on Alex's cream jacket over my bare chest. We're inside the Booth's, on Auto-Pilot, before we realise that we don't even understand why we're there.

"What are we doing here?" you ask the both of us.
"Erm..." I say.
"We're just... you know... getting something to eat, a sandwich." Alex says, as we are browsing the incredibly bougie selection of pasta.

I buy a really bizarre looking pasta I have never seen before. I look at a rainbow coloured pasta shape on the top shelf and decide that I am not prepared to pay four quid for rainbow pasta. I vaguely watch what kinds of things you are going to buy, judging you but not having the energy to insist you buy something with actual macronutrients. You stand in front of the crackers for a long time before picking up a box of matzohs. I go outside the normal shopping section, to the start of the store, pick up a beef and onion sandwich, pay for it and walk all the way out of the shop, without you two, and sit on a stone ledge next to the illegitimate exit I used. El Bad Boy Invisibile. I sit for a while there and think about the way I look, the way I might appear to an old couple getting out of their car in the car-park. I think about ageing, how I will be one of these two people one day. I try to insist to myself that I am different, either I will get out of the car differently, or I will be dead, or I will not be in Ilkley. Is that my fate? I'm shopping in the same place they are shopping; I am buying fancy pasta. Maybe they, at one point in the bloom of their youth, bought fancy pasta in some impulsive, ironic way: then they just never stopped.

Baby Alex comes out and sits with me. He is a lot easier to talk to during this trip. I feel much less "on form", or just I'm out of my element, muted by this weary lack of real effort that is the "day out" — detached. He's talking about the people we knew from school; we speculate where they are at in their lives. As he's talking about these people, mostly in a disparaging way no matter what they have achieved, I think about the way that we are writing this thing with him as the main character, the main analysis — disparaging him. He is lucky, he gets the chance to read the conversations that others have about him.

We talk about how it would be best to have an enormous four-dimensional graph, which we then extrapolate into a system where you can see the manner in which each individual person processes all other leavers into their own hierarchy, with their own weighted values and variables, and an aggregate clout alongside hard figures such as net worth. He says that one particular guy we knew, a now-millionaire named Jordan, would love to make such a programme, because he is a programmer, and because he would appear at the top. We speculate that the only way to oust Jordan from his place would be to go on a killing spree.

Driving home, Baby Alex passes a sheep grazing by the side of the road and beeps his horn. The sheep raises its head very quickly and looks confused. It is the funniest thing he did all day and I keel over in the back with laughter.

—

The fact I know that this experience will end in two days has changed the dynamic between the three of us. Despite not really enjoying the trip to the Chevin, after I went for a run and finished writing for that day, I felt much more able to listen to Alex. Perhaps I've just grown used to the idiosyncrasies; or perhaps he's growing self-aware from my constant neggings.

I hate the way that I look but I don't want to be absolved from that hatred. I feel like I deserve it as punishment for the vanity I had before. I pretty much hate the way I write and the way that I think as well, I'm not even sure why that is. A medium sized person in medium sized space, in the back of the "Baby Alex"-mobile listening to the stories of people I do not know going off to live lives that are summarised in single sentences: She went backpacking around Australia and is now married with two kids to some forty year old Australian Farmer in the Outback. Or: Oh he's in Cyprus now, he texted me, he says he's loving it. The part of life that is not-particularly-mythical, that anyone and everyone gets involved in, x went off to do x, and now x is x, all of them branching out, occluded in their specific tunnels, localised and hidden from each other. It's also the pitiful manner in which that formula could be stretched to accommodate the most bizarre or admirable fates, and we would still barely give a fuck. They would just be a passing statement, and a passing "Oh really? Interesting..." There is not enough time to really consider what sequence of events might cause someone to settle down in the middle of the Outback with a farmer twice her age, there is not enough information. This is one mere human life, one node that is only touched by the node I myself connect with, and I myself connect with countless nodes, intruding in on my tunnel, or brushing its edge. I cannot even really consider the life of Baby Alex, I only ever know half the story at best. I start to explain this thought, the unfathomable enormity of it, at the dinner table until I feel a little sick and rest my forehead over the rim of my glass. You tell me that if your thing is to let go of thinking about food, perhaps mine should be to let go of thinking about this. Unknown agents on unexpected arcs, surrounding me, just outside the walls of my medium sized consciousness.

To progress life is obligatory.

I don't want Baby Alex to be involved with my creative process. I don't want to create by committee. I'm glad he seemed a lot less robotic this evening. It was probably due to the fact that there was no longer the stress of even attempting to do some kind of project while he was around, whether that be literature, multi-media, or physical exercise. Baby Alex is most fun to hang out with when we have nothing to do.

The same old little drama occurs with the pasta. I say,

"You Will Eat A Bowl Of Pasta", you say "No, I will not."
I say, "You Will Eat A Bowl Of Pasta, whether you want
to or not." You say, "I saw you eat a steak an hour ago
and this wash of relief came over me like, oh thank god
he's not going to make me eat a meal..." I ignore that and
say, "You Will Eat A Bowl Of Pasta." You say, "How
about I eat a soup?" I say "Fine, you can have a soup as
appetiser, but afterwards You Will Eat A Bowl Of Pasta."
You say "How ab-" I say, "Shut up." in front of the fridge,
not even facing you. Alex laughs. I'm glad that you can see
the senseless aspect of your anorexia as well as pleading
me to not make you eat a regular bowl of pasta. It's
probably a sign that it's going to get better. I know Alex
was trying to avoid talking about it, maybe he had some
method that he thought was better, more Therapist-Alex,
he kept saying "Let's go for a walk" each time you started
to explain the dreadful exactness with which you can now
taste greasy or fatty foods. I think the more you talk
about it with us, people who aren't going to make you feel
like you're absolutely crazy, when you're only a little nuts,
the better. I don't know, maybe you discussed this with
him, me being a little OTT with the force-feeding and
the "yabber on about it until you've said it all".

I come back from Tesco's with the passata and you two
are hugging in the middle of the kitchen. The image
disturbs me, as though you are betraying our secret gossip
sessions. I forget that you are his ex-girlfriend, and was
his friend before you were mine. I come through the
door, curious as to what might have led to this moment of
tenderness. I'm out of the loop, then this paranoia flares
again when you say you're going for walk to Tesco's "for
no reason" and Alex asks if you're going alone and you say
"you can come if you want", then you both walk out. Did
I do something? Am I being the annoying one today? Am
I the New Baby Alex? These thoughts dribble in for a
moment before I think fuck it, I don't give a fuck. Then

the thoughts come back... Have they gone off to fuck? One of those memoriam-for-a-dead-relationship fucks? Are they going to be back in time for the pasta?

Later, on the walk with the three of us after the pasta, this heavy sadness came over me in little moments when no one was talking, but I liked the way I felt with one hand in my blazer pocket, my shadow from the streetlights splashed onto the road next to yours and Alex's. I say something after seeing the reflection of my head in the car window then looking at the both of you, "I feel like I'm so much older than you guys", and Alex says "This is something me and Roz have been talking about, you're obsessed with getting old." I say, "Okay, maybe that's my anorexia." I don't want to do the equivalent of a food episode, but I suppose it's due to a number of reasons: the large number of meaningful relationships I feel I've gone through in the last two years that all seem to have taken the same shape and now leave me feeling lost with regards to myself, somehow completely unloveable, ugly, and therefore condemned to die alone, the steady decay of my dad and the feeling of youth as just this spasm that lashes out at a world it cannot understand before receding into pain and idiocy, the steady loss of my hair and the extreme and possibly premature measures I took to remove all reminders that I even had it, and that minor internet celebrity I had garnered, which only consolidates the feeling that people find you, digest you, and chuck you when you're no longer relevant or hot, and there's no actual tangibility to their desire for you anyway, it's all just fake, flat, digital. I'm trying to prepare myself psychologically for the inevitable, but yeah, maybe I'm soaking in the dread a little too much. It's not like my life was that much better two years ago or four years ago or six years ago. It changes, it just changes.

The walk transpired into a standard riff on what we would name our children, and on Alex converting to Islam and changing his name to Muhammed. We decided we would all change our names to Muhammed, and henceforth be called The Three Muhammeds. You laughed so much at certain moments that you had to stop and curl up into a squatted ball.

"Humungculus Counelis"
"Helénkeler Scobie"

——

As we descended the road towards the river, I looked at the stones of a wall, their pattern in the mortar, their irregularity, then I looked at the blocks that lined the side of the pavement, equidistant, regular, and I felt my steps attempt to comprehend their distance, locking in to press down where the stones met, to take one step for every one point five length of stone, 2:3. I despaired for a moment, glimpsing an otherwise-repressed aporia, figuring that nothing could ever describe my mathematical relationship to infrastructure and the logic of paths and roads.

——

I sleep well, but jump out of bed in a foul mood after my heart seizes up from hearing Peter's clanking. I look stupid getting so enraged at Peter's plate-scrape sound that I kick a chair and hit a door. The both of you silently watch me, sat around the kitchen table, as I bash inanimate objects. It's very non-theatrical, it's either this or I throttle one of you (probably Peter). I'm doing Gregorian monk chant to calm myself down. I walk back into the kitchen after my outburst and bow to you saying Konichiwa. I then walk up to Peter sat on the top of the cabinet and bow, saying Konichiwa Peter San. Alex seems to have cooked himself a very large meal involving lots of salad in two bowls. I stand at the kitchen sink, filling a glass for my morning Berocca, before saying to you both, "I had an idea... of what we could do today." Alex, sits up, administrative and ready for a formal suggestion, "Yeah?" You look at me with an amused anticipation. "I was thinking... that we could go see Cooper." I smile at the both of you, mischievous, half-expecting these cartoonish gulps of fear in both of your faces. There's an apprehension that is consciously ploughed-through by Alex saying "Yeah... gotta check in with the Big JC." You say, "Gotta check in with the man downstairs." I laugh, repeating that phrase——the man downstairs, our lad in the chasm, in the catacomb; our experiment in the oubliette.

After taking a shit I look at a cartoon woman on your wash-bag and notice how she looks very Mediterranean. I'm plunged into a disorientated pain, a thought of Marseilles, the heat and the frenzy of the Côte D'Azure; all the Meghrebins in packs hollering along the beaches, the aggressive Gypsy toddlers yanking your trouser legs at the Underground entrance. Beautiful women, stupid amounts of beautiful women, crawling like ants between those sun-bleached stones. It's that horny-despair to be expected from day three of NoFap.

I try and ring Cooper, he doesn't pick up; maybe he's got a different number. I am relieved. Everyone is relieved.

"I'm busy between 2 and 3 today," Alex says.
I look at him, tonguing a canine tooth, "huh?"
"I have a meeting with that BBC woman."
I go out of the kitchen with my coffee to write, and when I return, he is in full-swing, holding his hands out doing the ad-man gestures, kinda like, you know like... fucking...

they need to abandon that, and go completely... He quietens down a little when he sees I'm within ear-shot, realising I'm about to call him out if he descends further into bullshit. I consciously keep quiet, waiting for him to say something retarded.

"It's like this guy, was completely... singular, in his field, making documentaries since his early twenties, and now he's in control of the whole thing. But that's what we need. Q, what do you think, if you were in charge of the BBC, what would you do?"

There is this visceral feeling that I am being farmed.

"Erm... I would disband it."

"Yeah I know but like..."

"I would get rid of the Pidgin English version of the BBC."

"Oh, but I love that..." you say, laughing.

"No. It is not good." I turn to you, speaking in a pained moralist tone, like Peter Hitchens. "If it were a joke it would be funny. They are seriously providing news for people who can't speak English. It's just complete idiocy. And all this inclusivity schtick needs to end..."

There is no correct way to respond to this line of questioning.

"... And I would make it excessively imperialist." I add, my low-res rightoid lapse concluded.

"Well that's my idea, really..." Alex interjects, "with BBC Zero."

"BBC Zero? What the fuck is BBC Zero?"

"It's like... my idea for a kind of... this aspirational, ambient art style BBC channel. Avant-garde..."

"Huh..." I smile, remembering something. "Did you see that fucking... what's that guy called... Adam Curtis spoof on YouTube?"

We all smile, knowing that the spoof also pokes fun at ourselves and the easy-access bullshit that politically-engaged art-school types lap up.

"This is some b-roll of the Grand Canyon, which has absolutely no connection to the thing I have just been explaining." I do my Adam Curtis voice, "But the reality was... it was all a lie. It was a fictional account of the truth that had been manufactured for the interests of maintaining power."

"Yeah, I mean... BBC Zero is exactly like that."

"Wait, you're talking about BBC Zero as though it's already a thing."

"That's what you're supposed to do with brands."

I roll my eyes and turn around, nursing my soul from the monstrosity that is Ad-Man Alex.

"No, but seriously, Quentin, how would you fix the BBC?"

I walk from one end of the kitchen to the other, resigned to the fact I have to consider this question "seriously".

"Honestly... they're playing catch-up. So I would just use all that money, go even further into the ungodliness of apps and Snapchat-TikTok nonsense."

"I know, and that's the thing. They're only half doing that. It's like they're stuck between getting up-to-date and being this thing that distracts old people from death."

You, who have tried to say something multiple times, stopping as Alex or I have spoken over you, say, "I think that, no matter what is being outputted, the kinds of people who will watch ambient art films will feel a sense of guilt in actually enjoying anything that is being funded by the BBC. It's such a dying body that any 'good stuff' will be interpreted as a forced attempt to revitalise it."

"That's what I'm saying, disband it. Destroy it completely, say: oh well guys BBC is over. Then people might feel some remorse, there might be a chance that something new being built. Like Christianity. But like, my real issue is, why the fuck are you getting involved with these people in the first place?"

Alex seems more and more agitated by this reversal of the interrogation; from how do we save the BBC but to why would anyone want to save the BBC? His hands go up and he gives me the Ad-Man googly eyes, ramping up the slick-talk, all cylinders firing for oleaginous rhetoric.

His stated defence ends with the question: "yeah, but what would you do if someone from the BBC got in touch with you?"

I thought for a quick moment about this, reminded of my interview with the Fortune500 company connection which petered out to nothing. In the end, you go with your gut, follow your instinct, that is a platitude I have never doubted.

How do I feel about this whole thing, the Baby Alex book? There are plenty of elements within it that make me queasy, that I honestly hate. Particularly the femoid corruptions; efficient rhythms necrotised by the ungodly bathtub-reveries of Lich Queen Roz. As for the BBC, I don't give a fuck about the BBC, or six figure salaries, or branding, if it is not tied in with my throbbing hard erection, my fury and my heat. First the spiritual, both the angel white bead on the crown and the dick, and I mean the TRUE spiritual, free of all material intention — then, whatever happens: happens.

"I just don't think they would get in contact with me."
"Yeah but I didn't go looking for this, they just found my CV, they probably think I'm some normie dude that has done some interesting things. I'm just looking into this out of curiosity."

Huh, I think, just like the cringey Justin Murphy seminars, that you involve yourself with in order to analyse the educational model. I'm also amused that Alex defines himself as being non-normie, there's something so incongruous about that self-assessment, yes, I'm very much NOT a normie, mmm. Imma supa-freak, supa-freak.

"Look mate, I think like, you're all like this..." I put my hand up, quivering, like the beating wings of an insect. "You've got this butterfly thing, all worried, trying to grab ideas, trying to find some validation for your decisions. You're asking us these gay questions, trying to content-farm us. You just need to chill out. Just focus on the colour, not the contents. The colour that arrives from the anus." I get up and walk out with my coffee, asking you if you want to come and read what I wrote the day before.

———

Alex does his bit with the BBC lady, sat in my mum's study with the door closed. While he is speaking, I sneak up, crawling on all-fours outside the door, make as little sound as possible and eavesdrop, grinning, pressing my ear to the thin line of light glowing between the door and the floor. The woman is mentioning how the BBC gauge the effectiveness of their programming by how many hours a day people will veg out and watch it. This seems like a model that is literally Evil, and then hilariously Alex picks up on that, boasting that he and most of the people he knows "never use smartphones, hardly ever consume news, and avoid the internet like the plague." Pfffft. What a load of bollocks, but he is at least correct in terms of what the idealised version of our generation might do. That unsurprising dyad lel: sanctimonious AnPrim in committee with the Satanic Mills of the Spectacle. It disturbs me that even ye wholesome olde BBC would want a world where its average viewer watches for four hours instead of two; but then again, I'm not in any way shocked — it's not like I didn't already know the BBC was fucked.

We're sat around the kitchen table again, at around four, and Alex is making a soup from the leftovers of Sunday's five-point eight roast. Somehow the conversation turns to Heidegger, and Alex nods his head with the "academic" face on, a fount of expertise.

"Well what Heidegger have you read?" I ask him.
"I don't know. Being and Time."
"You read the whole of Being and Time? Wow."
"Yeah maybe some of it."
"Okay well... which bits?" I'm pretty certain that Alex has barely read any of it. I understand that this could be construed as one of those Oh you like X band? Name their three best songs... moments, but the habit of pretending to understand dense philosophical works is something that needs to be excised from everyone, especially myself.
"I can't remember."
"Did you read the bit about temporality temporalizing?"
"Erm..." He closes his eyes, trying to remember. "No."
"Did you read the bit about fear and anxiety?"
"Yeah I think so. That rings a bell."

I get up, stand by the radiator, now having to demonstrate that I know more about Being and Time than Alex. I do a hesitant parade of information: the they, anxiety, inauthentic versus authentic Dasein, existential versus existentiell, the ontic and the ontological... I even get a little excited mid-way from the sense that maybe even I understand it. However, the purpose was to get Alex to stop nodding his head like he knows anything. Thank god no Heidegger scholar was there to watch me.

—

As soon as you mentioned that you had weed, I started to freak out. I hadn't really left the house yet that day and the thought of going through something like that, that might make uncomfortable stuff rise up from the places where I kept it under lock and key, started this familiar white-purple flashing hallucination in my eyes that meant I was getting panicky. I had not yet deserved it.

Alex played music on Spotify; I felt decidedly unsettled at all the warring multiplicities of three-minute moments trying to recalibrate the world, to prove their place in attention. It was all too much, I was starting to drown, termite world sucking me in. I decided I needed to go for a run, to do something very real and somewhat painful, and drank three large glasses of milk before heading out, for the peptides. As I ran I became more and more bloated, then felt unable to fart whilst moving because I could sense it would be very loud and there were many people along the canal. Somewhere over the bridge in the woodlands, I farted eventually, in a high-pitched toot. As I ran the last half, the stitches that normally cleared up in the first 1k didn't subside. But I kept going, the homunculi David Goggins in my brain repeating "Merry Christmas bitch". I walked into the kitchen; Alex's soup was almost ready. I mentioned that I wouldn't drink three glasses of milk right before running again, you laughed and said you were worried it had been a bad idea.

We ate, I served myself soup. Alex said "Have some bread" twice, the second time practically a command. I said "I'll have bread mate; I'm just going to have soup first." The kale salad was nice, at least he's trying on the food side of things. You go upstairs and come down with the weed and smoking paraphernalia in a Tupperware container with stickers on it. I fixate on the box, muted from the feeling that someone is dropping beads of dread into my consciousness from a tiny pipette, hovering above my head.

After the first two tokes, I start to feel that familiar loss of control, the slow movement into something not quite normal, fuzzy and warm. My eyelids close a fraction and stay like that. Feeling it. I stare at Peter to calm myself down. I begin whistling these atonal melodies I think are appropriate to accompany the image of Peter. Sound becomes haptic. As I whistle everyone is staring at the bird, stood on the back of one of the kitchen chairs, as though he is an icon, some object of meditation.

"I could look at him all day," I say.

Alex does some yoga stretches, then he kneels, breathes in deeply and looks at the parrot, "...what?" he asks, completely bewildered, playing it partly for laughs, partly for nothing. I notice that weed makes the execution of my social signalling ever so slightly detached from the intention coming from the centre of my cognitions, due to the fact that the intention is blurred, the information coming in is too great, therefore it is distorted and laps over itself: misaligned. I might say something supposedly sincere, aware halfway through that the tone is uncertain, between a playful mode and a kind of dry intellectual analysis, so I compensate internally by considering it a joke, which confuses the tone even further, until I say something garbled in ways beyond mere sense, and maybe you might nod your head or go "mmm" or say nothing, probably engaged in exactly the same disjunction from your social signalling as me. On the surface I am talking about how Peter is so strange, so grey and alien, derived from a different branch of the tree of life from us, but the question of who is saying these statements about Peter, who is my consistent character in this situation, that is the real mystery, not the bird. I mention that Peter is like a collection of tones, something musical and animated but in a key signature never seen before, then Alex asks "What about objects?" and I go hmm, liquifying, dripping into my philosophical character, picking up my glass of water and inspecting it before me, in a very ontic way. "I suppose it's like, lots of the same thing, singing exactly the same tone, over time." I look at the glass, I see the heated sand, blown, the atomic structure, the topology of the rim, the edges, the base, forming one mass with distinct inside and outside, I see each of the atoms holding each other in that structure, and each atom like a tiny golden mouth, that is singing, "-Oooooo-", a very simple tone, pure, consistent. Then I look back at Peter and see the jumble of textures, the anxiety of his movements, the tragedy of his eyes, flashing between hesitancy and relaxation — tones, chords, densities in perpetual metamorphosis, all under the consistency of him as parrot, as the other animal, which does not really belong in this house, or this country, or this climate. I look down and see a tiny spider with spindly long legs walk across the stone floor, then consider the animal life operating at the edges of everything, in the dirt behind my radiator, in the edges of this room. Then I look up at you, and that seems to be the most terrifying collection of tones yet — not only filled to the brim with complexity, but, beneath that superficial veneer of familiarity as "just another human", the ultimate horror of my own reflection: staring my own staring in the face, a double awareness of tones that sets off a chain reaction of considerations, of possibles. "Yeah but... that," I point at you, "is infinitely more scary than... that," I point at Peter.

Somehow, I end up going on my usual tirade about the presuppositions that bind metalogical laws in a reality system that could be hyperchaotic, and the inherent contradictions in deeming our Being anything at all if hyperchaos proves to be a consistent rule to apply to everything, in that it demands inconsistency. It's all very paradoxical and bad philosophy. It ends with: "There's no point saying anything about anything." Ye Olde Wittgenstein conclusion. I'm watching myself get all animated about this stuff, about the question of negation, of limit, and I'm thinking "What is it to do with getting high that leads me to babble pseudo-Hegelian bullshit?" Perhaps it's only when other people are high that there exists an audience for this kind of stuff, albeit a trapped one.

I remember in LA with Ana, we'd smoked a bowl before going to an Injury Reserve gig, I got out of the Uber and looked at all the model houses, the dollhouses, all the houses in their fresh paint and pastel colours, how computer-generated LA seemed, and I looked at her feverishly, in a moment of epiphany. "Ana, remember this, we do not know what a point is!" Her face said, who is this gimp? Everything was axis and meta-coordination; everything was data and presupposed mathematic — which is funny because I'm pretty shit at STEM.

I sit down besides the fridge; it makes an odd crack which causes the two of you to give off a quick pffft laugh. I consider whether or not the decision to smoke weed was a good one, whether there will be a net benefit, whether I will regret the decision in the days to come. I say "I think this was a good idea." You turn to me and say "Yeah..." in a light warm tone, "this was a good idea."
"It's like the conclusion, the finale. It came at the right point. The save point."
I am enjoying the conceptualisation of weed-smoking as a conscious decision to save the game. I am feeling sort of Robot Quentin. I lie on the floor and laugh about the fact that I feel like a nematode, merely an in-out system, with a mouth and an anus, a single-dimensional object in the belly of some larger organism. I writhe for a short amount of time in disgust at myself, you laugh. I stand up and come over to the table and watch the both of you make

chai tea, then lay the mugs on the table, the vapour rising, the image restful.

We end up talking about Worms 2, and how great a game Worms 2 was. You don't understand at all what we're talking about, thinking we've just invented a game where worms fire bazookas at each other, right there and then. I say "Oh no, it's a real game, it's a really good PC game, and the voices are funny." We watch a play-through of Worms 2 on Alex's laptop very quickly, because I want to show you the funny voices, and I say, "I'd forgotten how shit this game was." The voices are a lot less funny than I remember them being.

I pick up my copy of Fanged Noumena, kept above the table, beneath the cabinet for the plates and you say "Now begins the Nick Land section of the evening..." and we laugh.

"Ok Quentin, tell us about Nick Land." Alex says, bouncing into inorganic Podcast question mode.

"Urgh Nick Land... I don't really know." I'm flicking through the book, catching glimpses of words that might jog my memory, uncertain where to begin a summary without going for the easy route of Capital is Sentient.

"Erm, well... you know how he's into the idea that Capital is like an AI God from the future?" I say, going for the easy route. You both nod.

"Well... errr... there's that." I realise upon flicking through that I still know barely anything about Nick Land. "Ok well, he has this concept of the Outside, and the Human Security System, which is like the Kantian Cogito, and it's also related to Bataille and the Death-Sex thing of transgression. Erm.." I'm flailing. "There's a pretty cool bit concerning like... third-world countries being the noumena of Capital as Kantian subject, that it processes the resources of in order to formalise into its system. Erm.. that's like the first essay. Then he goes all freaky towards the end..." I flick to the back.

"Yeah didn't Roz read some of those.."

"Yeah it's almost like some really fucked up incest poetry written in a wingdings font."

"So yep." I conclude, "There's that. I mean, he has this whole thing about if something can be formalisable, therefore understood by humans, it can then be understood by a robot, then a robot could probably do it better. And that's why Capital is an AI, because Capital seeks to formalise all activity within its... thing... purview and get better at formalising that activity, breaking down things that refuse formalisation, or are inefficient, so that they can be more easily formalised. That's the Deleuzian angle I guess. The deterritorialisation of all top-down hierarchies based on Platonic ideas or you know family, nation-state, err... all these things are broken into nothing by the bottom-up Capital machine, which is just trying to accelerate towards pure value, pure efficiency, and who cares about humans anyway. That's why he's so into Skynet and Terminator, because there are these themes of convergence..." I rub my eyes, cogitating the progression of this very rough-and-ready summary that is incorrect in many ways... but who's checking? "He likes this image when they kill the second Terminator, and then she starts to rebuild herself, all her parts start to animate and compute each other, and they compute and compute until they're finally rebuilding themselves into the full form. But what he's saying is that, we're like watching this convergence process of something that is actively building itself, but from the future... It's a lot like that Quentin Meillassoux thing about God being in the future."

If (Deep-Thinker) Q : [Ad Man] Alex. Def(function): Y is Ad Man, for X... Q is Ad Man, For Thought. Things are swivelling, attempting to click into place. The theory is all wrong, but we're nodding our heads.

"Oh yeah I get that," says Alex. "I totally agree."

"What? About God being in the future?"

"Yeah."

"Eh, I don't really know about God being in the future, or being in any way determined in its being by a vulgar understanding of time. I just don't really see how the metadata for time moving forward could be held at any point in time. And I don't know how the Christian thing, the whole second coming, can like deal with the absence of linear time. I just think that if we are just simply within God, God being the super-intelligence that results in Being, then there can be no complexity in the future attempting to converge through linear time, or even scrambling linear time by creating itself through linear time. There can be no higher complexity because the complexity we understand as complexity is just a by-product of a human idiocy, and there is no more simple moment. It is always the end, always the beginning, always the highest level of 'complexity'."

"Yeah and I think that that is true."

"Which one?"

"I don't know. I just don't see them as being separate. I just don't care."

"Yeah but..." I feel exasperated at him. "I just don't see how you can involve yourself in the Church when you're like, take it or leave it, on most of these things. Like if Islam is closer to your interpretation of God or the Holy, why choose to be a Catholic? Why the Trinity?" We're pushing the Saudi Alex brand hard; he fights back with the entrenched Catholic Priest Alex Brand Identity.

He starts to explain his reasons for being Catholic, and I feel him explaining his spiritual system to me, in these ganglions of fizz across my body. I want it to click. I want to feel that familiar woosh I get when I have locked in with someone, when I realise, they feel the same way, about this thing. But I can't shrug off the arrogance of Alex's spirituality, the glib charisma he tinges all these moments in, the way he wants me to get it. It's like a hard metal cross, a shiny-shiny chrome cross, floating in misty blue-white. I can feel my forehead is building in energy, buzzing swirling into this very particular bead in the middle, ever so slightly to the left, the side that is tingling slightly less, as it does when I talk about these things, but it hasn't yet reached the point of things clicking. I want to brain-cum, but something isn't right.

"Bro, everyone I know is a Catholic. You haven't like, been brought up in a Catholic environment, all my family are Catholic. It's an aesthetic thing, because I'm English. Roz what do you think?"

You face in a neutral direction and put on your very diplomatic voice, clearly thinking very hard to really enunciate the nuance of what you're describing: "I feel like... I understand exactly where you are coming from with regards to it not mattering when you're getting from it what you need to, and how you're in the right particular context and it fits who you are and who is around you, but I also understand Q's point that if there are large aspects of doctrine that you can just basically pick and mix, why not take all that holiness and great feeling and try and interpret it in a way that doesn't have all that baggage?"

"I don't know. The thing is, I just don't care. Like I don't need to understand it, the Trinity, I don't need to get it at all, or doubt it. It is just what it is, it allows me to feel the way I feel, and that's all it is. It's like this gadget I have inside me, it's like this mainframe. It allows me to feel amazing, clear, always good. It's a device."

"Man..." I break out of the sublime mode when I realise this is coming from Robot Alex, then look at you. "You don't even understand how well this fits into everything, man..." I start laughing, astonished. Robot Alex the Hyperstitional Catholic. You get up, freaked out slightly, and go to the bathroom. We look at each other as you return, we laugh but are unable to explain to him exactly why.

"You want to know how I figured it out?" He is stood up, giving me a look, as though slightly worried about what he is going to say, now over the smooth evangelical patina there is a hint of vulnerability, a bubbling-up from the beneath.

"Figured what out... the Trinity?"

"Yeah... I had like... three realisations. One when Roz went off to Sedona, one when Roz broke up with me, and one when you messaged me saying you were writing this book. It was like Father... Son... Holy Spirit." He touches his thumb, index and middle finger, very seriously. "And they were all around Easter... first Roz left, then I was all depressed for a while, I was like wake up, feel like absolute shit, then bit by bit through-out the day I was meditating, meditating on it, bringing it up. I would go to the gym and try and lift weights, I would walk around but it was like I could do hardly anything. Each night I would feel really great for a while, and then I couldn't get to sleep. And I'd wake up and feel bad again. Until one day I just went outside, I saw a tree, I broke down into tears next to the tree and felt this sense of being held, of being loved. And then the next time, when Roz broke up with me, I was feeling bad, really bad all again. And it was around Easter time as well. But I was doing the same thing, meditating and lots of yoga, and I was stood in front of this Hilma af Klimt print that I had actually bought for Roz, and it had this golden triangle in the middle with this black point, and I stood in front of it, and I felt from like the bottom, you know the Logos? From the bottom I felt it, every single cell started saying Yes, Yes Yes Yes, to it, to love, and I felt it coming all the way up from my feet, every cell, until it reached my head and I felt like, my head was unsure about feeling the same way my cells were feeling, until it said Yes, then I was just aglow, awash with all Love, and I just said okay everything is fine. I was just giving; I gave my bedroom to my dad for him to use as his study because all I needed was just a little room with a bed. And then I had this dream, I dreamt that you had written to me that you weren't having sex with Roz but instead you just had this really strong connection and needed to see where that was going. And I was like, plunged back in that paranoia, I couldn't really sleep. I moved into that little room, my first bedroom, from when I had been actual Baby Alex, then I get that text you sent, the first time you spoke in forever. So, I'm back in it, oh no I'm going crazy, I'm going insane. Then three days later I'm driving, I'm driving and I'm thinking about the three of us, the three of our dads, and the sort of, my sort of relationship with the two of you, it's like I'm the father, whatever you do Quentin I'm like yeah it's great, I give you stuff, I support you like I support a son, and whatever you do Roz, it's the same. And then I was thinking about all of our dads and the generational trauma we have and all the kind of ancestral trauma alongside the 'yes yes yes my son, go for it, go for it my son'. And it all linked together and I had the gold moment again, I felt this huge blue, almost like a mother, energy, hug me, wrapped around me. And from that point onwards I knew this thing was the right thing to do, this was the way, I was like yes yes yes."

"Wow..."

I finally feel it, something about the vulnerability of his tone of voice, the Truth of that final statement. I see behind the ad man, behind the robot, behind the immaturity of Baby Alex, someone hurting and calling out to be hugged, but not in a mushy way, not from any rehearsed understanding that emotional intelligence was valuable, he wasn't using his vulnerability for anything, I saw someone so human, I saw someone who understood, I saw a Human — and there was finally a low enough level of bullshit that I felt it, the Trinity, it clicked onto me and I saw it, yes yes yes, go on my son, I am the Father, I am the Son, and I am the Holy Spirit — passed down through all things to all things, and it's all Love, it's all Yes, and by Christ's blood are men made free. The pain, the sacrifice, the salvation, the grace. Amen.

"Yeah that's amazing."
We look at each other, disturbed by how well this fits in with the book.
"This concludes the Nick Land section of the evening."

—

A gordian knot of mantras, devices, mainframes: designed to push only that point forward, no global coordination, but a wriggling mass of worm-like coordinators. None are specifically contradictory to another, as that itself would imply a shared coordination. They press upon and morph, filter, the morass of memory-forgetting, their jungle-thick accumulation. Somehow the termite planet and the Logos are not mutually exclusive. They writhe around each other. Somehow it connects, in the mysteries of three, of two, and of one. Alex's feeling is X, he relies upon the formalised quality of Trinity (iii) — the relations he holds to this feeling, the dream-like half-shape play of its light, are now coordinated according to quantity, to distinct hierarchy and generation, sequence. The father who generates the son. The Holy Spirit as that generation. Everything can be made to fall into its logic. I see it all swivelling. It was just like when we were browsing music on Spotify, every song instantly accessible, all we had to do was remember the name. Every song was its own present tense, seeking to drive its standard into time, every song was vying for attention, to determine itself as the ultimate mood, to coordinate all other times according to its logic as centrepiece. Each locality, each hierarchy, desires its own empire. But it cannot hold on, it is merely an attack and a decay, it flows in, releases us, then calcifies, dies, falls apart. It holds nothing, the moment it takes control, it begins to lose it. Then Alex replays the Trinity, he meditates upon it again, he goes deeper to further the calibration of his experience. Driven to intubation by the Holy Trinity, made isomorphic to Worms 2, drilling, blowtorching, holy-hand-grenading. The cycles of grace, a honeycomb God; like the inside of a Crunchie bar. Whatever can take us to yes yes yes, go on my son, whatever gives us that strength, that release.

———

We hugged as you got into the red "Baby Alex"-mobile, I could tell that you really wanted that hug, you really wanted to interlock, and I did too in a way. I hugged Alex and stroked his furry belly.

———

With Monica in her room in Edinburgh, the finale of our three-year relationship, coming down from a large dose of psilocybin. I looked at her and thought, maybe it wouldn't be so bad, being a woman. Maybe after I die, I'll become a woman. Maybe I've already been one. It seemed almost inevitable. I'll die, I'll let go, I'll turn up in the next one, a medium sized woman in medium sized space. I'm sure it's very nice to be a woman, in a house, with a man who loves you, when things are quiet, at the end of the day.

♔

Domestic bliss in the n-dimensional library; you, your baby, and I: sat in our two red leather armchairs, listening to the fire crackle while you breastfeed. The TV crackles along with the fire, the image is frozen: Baby Alex's mangled head in the snowdrift, unchanging — now the image is an additional ornament in the room, between the iron maiden and the Cherokee canoe.

"Did we miss something?"

"You shot Baby Alex."

"No, but now his head is detached from his body. It wasn't detached before."

"Maybe..." the baby suckles away, "you decapitated him when I was giving birth."

"Maybe... urgh. Wait a sec." I get up, there's this kind of sudden restlessness, a nausea, the combination of the severed head on the TV and the suckling of the baby, I feel like I'm bloating, a balloon slowly filling with air.

"Q, you don't look so good."

"I don't really feel... urgh. I feel terrible..."

I look down at my stomach.

"Oh fuck..."

"Q are you..."

"Yeah... I'm fucking pregnant." I say, disappointed in myself.

"Jesus how are you going to..."

"Oh fuck... urgh... bluu-" I throw up the entire scone with clotted cream and raspberry jam over my shirt and trousers. "Roz, we gotta do something... I don't want to shoot this thing from my di-... bleuurgh" I throw up whatever I had eaten previous to the entire scone with clotted cream and raspberry jam (pasta with tuna?).

"Take down your trousers, Q."

"Ah fucking hell."

"Q... it's the only way."

"Ah f-fuck's sakes."

I lie down on the Persian rug, slightly to the right of a pool of cold vomit. My stomach is that of a heavily pregnant man. My face goes from pigeon grey to a tickled crimson.

"Ayaaaaaaaa it's coming out my arse!"

"Ok Q, ok, breathe, breathe with me baby..."

Your baby (who looks identical to you, and who shall henceforth be referred to as Baby Roz) begins to howl from its swaddled blanket nest on the red leather armchair.

"Arrrrr— FUCK! AAAAAA This is worse than fucking Anusol on HAEMORRHOIDS. Aaaargh!"

"In... Out... In... Out..."

"Oh GOD!... It's ripping through me Roz! It's shredding my insiiiiiide!"

"OK, it's crowning Q, it's crowning..."

"Major Crowning?!"

"It's major leagues crowning Q, Leeds in the Premier League crowning... one last push."

"AAAA—AAAA—AAAAAAAARRRRGHH!!!"

The purple infant shoots out into your hands. You smack it about a little and it begins to bawl. I lie back, nursing the pain of an arsehole that has just stretched for the largest shit in its existence. It probably doesn't even look like an arsehole anymore. Wagwan for batty man. You hand me the screaming child, swaddled in blue blankies.

♕

I had bided my time, not brought it up. On the last evening the topic of cannabis was being discussed. I said, as blasé as possible, well if you guys wanna smoke, just let me know. The mood in the room shifted immediately, the two of you looking in pleasant, slightly nervous surprise to each other and then to me. We had dinner, then an hour or so of anxious, predrinks-style directionless milling around and chatting, then I went up into the attic and brought down the little pink Tupperware of cannabis and cannabis paraphernalia, to roll a spliff at the dinner table. I got an overwhelming sense, as I took two tokes and passed it to you, staring at Peter standing on the back of the chair opposite mine, a cluster of ancient spirals, that this was very much the end of the trip. It was joyous and sweet and at points impossibly frustrating: and now it was done. It kind of didn't make sense, but it was perfect, it was all we needed. The save point. Then you said the save point, and I realised I had forgotten that you are in my head at all times.

There was a long period of quiet, the earthy colours of your kitchen brightening and increasing in depth. We stared at Peter. I was in awe of Peter, of you, of him, the situation. I said nothing. Scene 1.

You picked up Fanged Noumena and leafed through it. Then the conversation got going. You did your normal routine of becoming deeply existential, which does not feel like a performance, instead a place you travel to without even meaning to, inevitably reaching for an object like a mug or a pair of scissors, picking it up, putting it down, and gesturing to the space between your body and the mug. Being and not. 0 and 1. If it is empirically factual that material reality can be, at its base level, reduced to binary code, and if God was the highest possible point of intelligence, of speed and processing, then not only would God be real, but this would all be God, God in the process of becoming God, an ultimate processing speed, moving towards a "future" where He would have the ability to create himself. Scene 2.

Then we talked about God some more. Alex said he agreed, in a sense, and that all was one, all was the pieces of God, moving and becoming together. We nodded in bland agreement, and then a twinge of a different emotion became present on your face.
"Then why the Trinity? Why be a Catholic and believe in the Trinity, isn't that just an unnecessary step?"
"You should just be a Muslim" I reiterated, in a hazy inebriated tone.
"Because I just am, man, I'm a Catholic, it makes sense."
"Well... do you believe in the second coming? Do you

think Christ will come back? Transubstantiation?"

"Not really..."

"Do you believe in Hell?"

"... No, I wouldn't say so..."

"So why be a Catholic? If you don't believe in half of the doctrine?"

"... It's an aesthetic choice."

I blacked out of the conversation and felt a blip of pure anger. He just admitted that it's insincere. There is no duende. There is only aesthetic. Of course.

"-You know, like I was raised Catholic, everyone I knew was Catholic. And this is working for me now, maybe I'll find something better in the future..."

I thought about my parents again. I thought of my father doing reiki on my mother. I thought of my father doing yoga in our council flat. I thought of Alex's processing of so many significant moments in his life being informed by "an aesthetic", one that he just admitted to not truly believing in, one that could be replaced by a better match at any moment. I willed myself not to say something I'd regret in the heat of the moment. I fade back in.

"That feeling of oneness, of yes yes yes, I use the Trinity to get there. It is the thing that works best for me. It's like a tool I can use to tap into that state.."

I see a flash of significance, an exclamation mark.

"It's like a gadget I can use.."

"Oh my god..." you say in disbelief.

My eyes are wide. A flow chart appears in my head as the pieces come together. I get up and walk into the bathroom as he continues to talk, not understanding what, from our perspective, he just admitted to. I blink rapidly. I listen through the door.

"Yeah, it's like, all religions point to that oneness, but the Trinity is the best thing I've found to use to get there."

You're laughing. "Oh my god, this is... this is perfect."

We wrote a story about Alex having a religious awakening

provoked by a Christian AI from the future that uses him to create itself. And now, in the real world, Alex has admitted to using Christianity like a technology to commune with the future oneness of the birth of God. He then utilised this awakening to accept our cruel little project, returned into our lives, and brought the book in its concluding form into existence. This book was born because of that, and this book unknowingly predicted the series of events that brought it into existence. Scene 3.

He then looked at us with sincerity, the theatrical googly eyes, once again, waiting for the laughter to pause.

"You want to know how I did it?"
"What do you mean?"
"How I broke through, how I accepted it."
"Yes."

He then described three moments in the past year and a half as being the truth of the Trinity appearing to him in segments. When I left for Sedona, the teary goodbye, his ensuing depression, his encounter with a tree that caused him to break down crying. The father. Me breaking up with him, on April Fools' Day of all days, and the fasting and meditating that followed, then a moment of bliss looking at a Hilma af Klimt poster on his wall that he had originally bought for me. The son. The message you sent him detailing our writing project, confirming his insomniac fears that we were somehow plotting behind his back, and then the drive where he saw the crows. The holy ghost.

I was deeply moved by it, I could tell those moments affected him greatly, I was standing a couple feet away from him in the kitchen, stretching my arms, looking at him. I wanted to give him a hug. It was powerful, sincere, vulnerable. But still I felt a twinge of fakeness, superficiality, some kind of ret-con had been executed by his memory to make these moments line up with the aesthetic he had decided dictated his spiritual life. There was no real reason that those moments were a Trinity. He missed out a whole period in the middle of the timeline, where I came back from the states. Why was it those three moments?

I thought back to the machines, our obsession with cyberpunk technology, the pattern-location. I saw Alex as a robot again, as I used to tell him he was: a machine with a complex framework of rationalities, through which everything must be processed, everything must conform. Alex cannot accept that some things just exist, or that sometimes you just feel things, or that sometimes things just happen. There must always be an umbrella, a defining term, a brand. Alex is an ad man, constantly spinning, framing, contextualising, and replicating. Scene 4.

And once again, I realised, just a minute or so after, so am I. My proximity to him makes it more apparent. Alex is an ad man but I am a writer. And you are a writer. We scurry away at the end of the night to jot everything down, kill it, rape it, give birth to it again, fuse it with something else, spinning, framing, contextualising, replicating. New moments will always be like other moments. We will always be like each other.
I simultaneously understood it all and didn't. Either way I was happy and did not mind. You told us you loved us and we said it back. We separated, and went to bed. Curtain.

—

In the morning we got our things together. We were comfortably quiet, something about staying up late and smoking weed for the first time in a while drops the following morning into an intimate, contented fuzz, an affectionate afterglow. I ate a pbj and smiled at him across the table. You came down and we drank coffee. I enjoyed a moment of silent amusement noting all of the stuff he brought, music gear and cooking knives and therapeutic mats, but him still needing to borrow a t-shirt from you because he had only brought one. You helped him carry his stuff to the car and I went into the bathroom, felt my pockets to make sure I hadn't forgotten anything obvious, and looked at myself in the mirror. I emerged from the house to see you standing at the top of the path, grinning at me. You made some sweet comment about how I looked with my Mountain Warehouse backpack, something about me going off on my travels. You gave my hair a brotherly ruffle, which I loved, but secretly hoped wasn't the extent of my goodbye. I watched the two of you hug by the car, the back of his head, his white shirt, your hands holding him tight, your eyes closed, smiling gratefully. Then you came to me and hugged me. You were right, I did need it; and I felt it, whatever it was, real love, real peace, interlocking, and I could tell you felt it too. I put my hand on the back of your neck. Then we parted, and you told me to eat, and I said I would, and we got in the car, and then we were gone.

—

We drove around, first in heady silence, then blasting oos British indie rock with the windows down, feeling some kind of shift in gravity as we moved away from Horsforth. We stopped at a large, especially-liminal service station for fuel and something to eat. The place was contemporary and muted, and we sat out in the humidity with our fish sandwiches and kombucha, squinting, saying very little.

"I feel like Leon's branding is a little too on the nose."

"I love you, but I need you to not talk about branding right now."

Then we were in the car again. I wasn't really sure where we were going but didn't feel compelled to ask. We were listening to Earth, Wind and Fire on a country road when he abruptly pulled into a hard shoulder, turned the music down into silence, and switched the car off. He looked at me.

"Okay, we're here."

"...Where?"

"At that chapel I told you about."

I looked around. There were only fields. I got a feeling the chapel he had mentioned was going to end up just being a patch of grass, some kind of metaphor for God being everywhere.

"...But there's nothing here."

"We just have to walk for a bit. Come on, get out."

We got out of the car and walked down the side of the road through long grass and nettles. I mostly watched my feet, and his in front of mine, to make sure I didn't lose my footing. I still had a lingering sense that everything wasn't as it seemed. He commanded me to cross the road, so I did, and we arrived in a meadow. There was a kind of bank I had to step over, so I was still looking at my feet as we approached.

"Here it is."

I looked up. I laughed in surprise.

A field filled with sheep, and off in the distance, maybe 300m away, a tiny, ancient looking chapel built from stones, so unified with the surrounding environment it may as well have been a tree. It felt completely outside of time, iconic in the true sense. The image was so beautiful, so simple, so perfect, that I don't think I can explain it any further.

I smiled as we walked up to it.

"This building is 900 years old."

I just laughed again.

There was a little wooden gate concealing the door. He unlatched it, opened it, and led me inside.

A small, bright room with 6 rows of pews, 3 large windows at the front, and a simple altar with a wooden cross. My mouth was slightly agape. We said nothing.

He moved away from me, gliding past the door, up to the altar, where he knelt. A magnet hovered over iron filings: every moment, every thought, every colour and tone, all memories and pieces of fiction flew up off the ground and connected. Tears ran down my face.

The magnet would eventually falter, I couldn't stay there forever, and I knew I wouldn't be able to explain it without it turning into something else.

There will be times when he irritates me, times when I'm so frustrated with you that I cry, times I can't remember something important, or the thought of my parents upsets me, or I'm starving, or I doubt my writing, or I'm trapped, or I'm lost. But that connection is there, and it's always there. The connection waits to find me.

We hugged. I turned around and left without saying anything.

The sun hit my skin.

✠

"Here's Daddy... Daddy Q will take care of you." you say.
"I'm not sure how Daddy Q will take care of you little..."
I snatch a glance at the kid's genitals, "...man." I have a
fumble at my pecs: yep, they're tits now. Great.
"Daddy's got milkies. Feel like one of those trannies on
fucking... ah whatever."
I hold Baby Q's mouth up to my engorged breast, he
latches on and starts to suckle. Painful but also pleasant,
in an oddly sexual way.
There's a knock on the library door. We turn to each
other. Who is it? you mouth at me. Why the fuck would I

know? I mouth back. Another knock, the door creaks open. There stands Baby Alex holding a new-born, its mouth glued to the left nipple of his hairy double-d knockers.

"Baby Alex with... Baby Alex?" Camera zooms in on our shocked faces, bizarre Japanese subtitles flash beneath us with boinging sounds.

"Daddy Alex now..." he says, smiling. He turns to the camera, fourth wall broken: "...Daddy Alex."

Dancing in the Moonlight starts blasting from hidden speakers all around the room. The library falls away, and The Three Daddies are stood in a line onstage, holding the baby versions of ourselves. How did I get roped into this? We're stood in front of old crooner microphones, a disco ball above our heads, the audience a bubbling morass of dark shapes, definitely there, no face seen clearly, and they're loving it.

We [redacted for copyright reasons] almost every night...

Our voices ring out with eternal truth. We grow and become giants. It's a supa-na-tu-ral delight! Our karaoke skills are perfected. The disco ball rotates and we turn with its dazzle, place our babies on our heads, and put our arms out to hold the hips of the person in front. We form a conga line. The babies each grow to normal human size and stand exactly above our crown chakras, radiating indigo light, their arms outstretched in T position. The catchy melody continues. A door marked "EXIT" appears in the distance, we conga through the murky nothing towards it, moving as a single animal, on the fourth beat of each bar kicking out a right or left leg in alternating pattern. As we leave the book, we turn to the reader, and do a synchronised slow wave with our right hands. Our procession moves beneath the glowing exit sign, and we fade away into the black, together.

§

Message from James Cooper:

You fool you fool you fool you fool.
my mind at rest my mind at ease
Think your funny do ya?
Shut the fuck up
Here's a bit of information for you
You're not!!!
I hope you lock me up ;)
Had a dream everyone was winning but I was double
winning and I was rocking the school blazer for some
reason it was all traditional and shit
fucking sick
yeah baby!
Alex is just a faggot fuck him!
Sick guy though.
I'm the antichrist Quentin I can do anything
Can I spend the night at yours my dad has kicked me out?
please answer your phone

Printed in Great Britain
by Amazon